Middle Ground

MIDDLE GROUND

A FRAISIER CREEK NOVEL

BOBBI MACLAREN

Middle Ground

Copyright © 2024 by Bobbi Maclaren

All rights reserved.

No part of this book may be reproduced in any form or by any electronic or mechanical means, including information storage and retrieval systems, without written permission from the author, except for the use of brief quotations in a book review.

Paperback ISBN: 978-1-7383063-1-2

Cover by Summer Grove

AUTHOR'S NOTE

Please note that this book does contain: mentions of the death of a grandparent, fire, violence, stalking, a car accident, and sexually explicit material.

If you would like to avoid the explicit material, the chapters to skip are: 23, (part of) 27, 29, 33 and 34.

CHAPTER 1

"Now, we just have the matter of Dog Days Inn."

I simply blink at the lawyer sitting across from me. Turning to my parents, I find them equally as confused. Everything else in my grandmother's will has been pretty standard, self-explanatory stuff. This, however, is not.

"I'm sorry," I say, "but what is Dog Days Inn?"

The lawyer's brows furrow. He looks from the document in his hands, then up to my face. "It's in a place called Fraisier Creek," he supplies, as if that's supposed to tell me anything.

I don't even know where the hell Fraisier Creek *is*.

"And what does this have to do with my mother?" Dad asks from beside me.

"Well, she owned it," the lawyer replies. "Half of it, anyway."

Looking at the rest of my family, aunts and uncles and cousins, I can tell that no one has a clue what he's talking about. Surely someone would know about this place if it were true.

I shake my head. "I think there might have been some kind of mistake. She didn't own an inn."

"It's written here in her will," he replies. He turns the paper around and points at a section. "And you, Jackson, stand to inherit her shares."

"*Me?*"

I pull the paper across the desk. It isn't like I expected the lawyer to flat out lie to my face, but seeing the proof for myself hardly makes it feel real. But there it is, in writing. My grandmother owned half of an inn.

Cherie, what the hell were you thinking?

She didn't like being called Grandma or Nana or anything of the sort, but right now, thinking her name feels like a curse. Especially because I would have a few choice words for her if she were alive to hear them.

It's been a month since her funeral, but I can still hear her voice—can still picture the way she would smile as I scolded her and then crack jokes to make me laugh off my frustration. The ache in my chest deepens.

"Dog Days Inn is in a small town a few hours north of here," the lawyer continues. "I have the contact information for you."

I hear the words he's saying, but they hardly register.

Cherie Cheval did as she pleased and didn't give a shit what anyone thought about it. That's what I loved about her most—her insistence in defying expectations and living life on her terms. Still, just because I loved her and her roundabout way of life didn't mean that I approved of every decision she made. Buying into this random business, for instance, would not have been one of them.

It's not at all uncommon for people with the kind of wealth my grandmother had amassed to invest some of it elsewhere. But it seems a waste to bankroll a small-time business like this—not when she could have easily bought a hockey team or half of the goddamn city.

The meeting carries on, the lawyer going over the rest of the will and laying out what everyone else stands to inherit. I'm in a fog, though, which isn't unusual for me as of late. My mind keeps spinning, and I barely notice when they all stand to leave.

"Jackson?"

As my family shuffles out of the office, I hang back. The lawyer holds an envelope out to me.

"What's this?" I ask.

He offers me a sympathetic smile. I wonder how many of those an estate lawyer gives out in a day. "A letter from your grandmother. It was in the file with her will. She wanted me to give it to you."

Wary, I take the envelope and stuff it in the pocket of my suit jacket. I'm not even sure why I wore a suit today, but it felt weird leaving home in something more casual.

I nod, clearing my throat. "Thanks."

When I step outside, the sounds of the city greet me. I'm used to the rush of cars and the crush of bodies on sidewalks, but these days, it all sounds like white noise. These past few weeks, I've felt like I've been trapped underwater, moving in slow motion. Yet all around me, the world is still spinning.

Life goes on, even when you're at a standstill.

My mother is waiting for me on the sidewalk. "What did the lawyer want?" she asks.

For some reason, telling her about the letter feels wrong, like Cherie meant for only me to know about it. I have no idea what it says, but that seems like something my grandmother would do.

"He was just giving me those contact details for the inn," I lie. "How did no one know about this place?"

Mom places a comforting hand on my arm. Her smile is sad. "You know what your grandmother was like. But I agree, that was a lot to take in. Are you doing alright?"

Am I? Truthfully, I'm not sure what I'm feeling. But I know that if I stand here any longer, she'll start to pick me apart, looking for things she can fix.

I know my ending up in the hospital again dredged up a lot of memories for my parents. And I know it scared all of my family and friends.

More than anything, though, it was embarrassing. Collapsing at work in front of a conference room full of executives was not part of my five-year plan. That, or being forced to take six months off of work to get my stress levels and blood pressure under control. At twenty-seven, I shouldn't be having these types of issues.

I return her smile as best as I can. "I'm okay, Mom. Just tired. I'm gonna head home, so I'll see you later."

I don't give her a chance to reply before I'm walking down the street toward my car, the letter burning a hole in my pocket.

———

"Are you sure you don't want me to come with you?"

My mother wrings her hands in front of her as she follows me around my condo while I stuff clothes and toiletries into an overnight bag. Five days after the reading of the will, I'm on my way to check out this inn. I've been emailing with someone named Meyer, who seems to be managing the inn for my grandmother's business partner.

Zipping up the bag sitting on my bed, I say, "I'm sure."

When I meet her worried eyes, I have to look away. She sighs. "I just don't want you feeling like there's all this pressure on you. Taking something like this on is a big responsibility."

Giving in, I pull Mom into a hug and press a kiss to her cheek. "I know you're trying to help, and I appreciate it. But you're busy. You don't have to drop what you're doing to come follow me to the middle of nowhere."

"You're my son. I'd drop everything in a heartbeat."

I hold back my own sigh. While this behaviour isn't uncharacteristic for her, it has gotten increasingly more overbearing in the past two weeks. I know I'm partially to blame for that, but it doesn't make the feeling any less oppressive.

"I think this is something I need to do on my own," I admit. "It's what Cherie wanted."

She goes to say more, but her smartwatch chimes with a notification. She reads it, and then she turns apologetic eyes on me. "Your father wants me to meet him for brunch."

"Go," I say. When she hesitates, I start guiding her toward the front door. "Seriously, Mom. I'll be alright, I promise."

After another minute of back and forth, she finally gives in and says goodbye. When the door shuts behind her, I let out a breath, leaning against it for a minute. I've had to weather these waves of fatigue for weeks now.

Once I've caught my breath, I cross the condo and enter my office. The space is tidy, as it always is, but the letter on top of my desk feels out of place. Sitting in my chair, I take up the paper and read over it again.

Jackson,

If you're reading this, that means I've finally kicked the bucket. That also means my lawyer has read you my will, so by now you should know all about the inn.

I was a guest of this inn for many years. I became great friends with the owner, Beatrice Ellison. Dog Days and Bea both hold a special place in my heart. When she fell on hard times a number of years ago, I didn't hesitate to buy into the business so my friend could keep doing what she loves. Now that I'm gone, my half of the business belongs to you.

I know what you're thinking. Why did my beloved grandmother leave this small-town inn to me when I've got my fancy pants job in the city? Well, if I told you, that would make things too easy. Soon enough, you'll understand.

If I know my grandson (and I do), you will wish to be rid of this unwanted responsibility as soon as possible. To that, I say: give it six months. Stay in Fraisier Creek, work at the inn. After that, if you truly still want to wash your hands of it all, I won't blame you.

And for the love of all things holy, take care of yourself.

Love, Cherie

With no work to return to for the next few months, I suppose my grandmother will get her wish. Although I'm inclined to believe this inn isn't as great as she made it out to seem, going there beats staying cooped up in my condo, dodging my family's efforts to hover.

Resigned, I grab my overnight bag from my bedroom and then I head down to the parking garage to find my car.

Fraisier Creek, here I come.

CHAPTER 2

MEYER

HAVE you ever had that feeling? You know, the one that says you're exactly where you belong.

I hadn't known that feeling until I clocked in for my first shift at Dog Days Inn when I was fifteen. Long before that, I haunted the halls, following my mother around as she demonstrated what it meant to be a fair but firm business owner. But it wasn't until I started working at the inn myself that I really understood.

I thought the feeling would fade over time. Perhaps I would get tired of catering to the public. But if anything, it's only gotten stronger—the notion that this inn is my destiny.

Maybe that's a little dramatic, but what else do you call the thing that feels so inherently like home?

I won't pretend it doesn't feel like work. A job is a job after all, though it's one I take on each day with pride. The business ebbs and flows, but the one constant is my commitment to showing up for my guests and my employees.

I run my hand along the wall as I walk down the corridor

leading from the main entrance to the attached restaurant. The floral wallpaper is somewhat outdated. One day, I'll get around to upgrading it, but for now, it serves as a reminder of Mom and the mark she has left on this place.

Just outside the entrance to the restaurant, I straighten the picture frame hanging on the wall. It's a photo of my mom and her best friend the day she bought the inn. They met years before when my mom was just an employee here, and they were friends up until the day Cherie died.

I don't pretend to know why a woman like Cherie, who grew up in Toronto and travelled the world, ever gave our little inn the time of day. I don't think even Mom knows. But it's an indisputable truth that Cherie will be missed by us all.

Cherie is the reason that my mother even owns the inn in the first place. She encouraged Mom to buy it from the previous owners—the owners both my mother and her mother had worked for as housekeepers once upon a time.

Taking over this business was a full circle moment for my mother, and the fact that she is getting ready to hand it down to *me* is nothing short of nerve-wracking. Because failure is not an option, but right now, it's all I can see. Every night when I try to sleep, I'm bombarded with all the ways I could potentially let her down.

In the empty corridor, I let my stress swallow me like a storm cloud. But as I gear up to enter the restaurant, I steel my spine. I take a deep breath. I outwardly become the confident businesswoman that I pretend to be.

As they say, fake it 'til you make it.

"What's cookin', good lookin'?" I call.

Behind the bar, a harried Pippa scowls down at the worn

rag in her hand. I round the bar and grab my apron, tying it around my waist as I wait, well-adjusted to my best friend's mannerisms. Many think that Pip is shy, but really, she just chooses her words *very* carefully.

Her scowl turns to a frown as she meets my gaze. "Sorry I had to bring him again, Meyer," she says. "His regular sitter has the flu. I called Tommy's mom for a playdate, but they're out of town. And I tried to get Shawn to come over, but he's...busy, I guess."

Ignoring the anger I feel toward her shitty boyfriend, I set a hand on her arm. "It's fine, Pip. You know that. What's really bugging you?"

The restaurant is experiencing its typical Sunday morning lull before the after-church crowd starts to trickle in. I watch Pippa scan the room for anyone who is sticking their nose where it doesn't belong—par for the course in Fraisier Creek—but we're essentially alone.

"My parents have been sniffing around again," she finally says.

I suck in a breath. At the same time, we both cast sidelong glances at a nearby table. Pippa's son Atticus sits forlornly on a chair much too large for his five-year-old body, halfheartedly maneuvering a T-Rex across the tabletop.

"Assholes," I mutter, turning back to Pippa. "They don't know where you are, do they?"

She shakes her head. "No, not as far as I can tell."

"*Good*. They don't deserve you. Either of you."

Her frown deepens. "I don't know. Sometimes, I wonder if I'm doing the right thing, keeping him away from them."

"Pippa..."

She twists the rag in her hands. If I were her, I'd be pretending it was my parents' necks to practice wringing them. But that's just me. Pippa Rhodes doesn't have a violent bone in her body.

As quickly as her frustration manifests, it disappears. She sets her shoulders and tosses the rag back onto the counter.

"Whatever." She shakes her head, her russet tresses swishing with the movement. She tips her chin, standing tall, and her pretty green eyes hold a fire in them that I'm damn sure going to watch burn. "We don't need them. I'm more than enough for Atticus."

I grin, slapping the counter. "Hell yeah, you are!"

At my outburst, Atticus perks up, just now realizing I've arrived. He smiles. "Auntie M&M!"

I move toward his table, holding out my fist for Atticus to bump. He does, and then we both make explosion noises with our mouths.

"Attie, did you keep our pinky promise?" I ask.

He nods emphatically. "I was good all week. I brushed my teeth when Mommy asked *and* I didn't sneak out of bed once!"

I tug the package from the back pocket of my jeans. Atticus's eyes glitter when he spots the iconic M&M's branding.

"Knew I could count on you."

As soon as he could chew them, I've been sneaking him packages of the coated-chocolate candy. It's my go-to bribe and special treat. Atticus knows it, too, which is why I've been known as Auntie M&M ever since he could properly speak.

Pippa shakes her head, but a smile tugs at her lips. "Are

you planning to come hang out while he's bouncing off the walls later?"

I turn toward her with a winsome smile. "You see, I *would*, but I kind of have an inn to run."

Now she rolls her eyes. "The inn would still be standing if you took a day off, Meyer."

I shake my head. "I'm not in the business of tempting fate."

Pippa goes to reply, but her attention snaps to her son instead. "Atticus, one at a time! You might choke."

"S'okay, Mommy. I'm a *pofessional*," he insists, shoving another handful into his mouth.

She tips her head to the sky. "I'm going to go grey prematurely."

Although she gets exasperated with the best of them, there's no doubt she was meant to be a mother. The love she has for Atticus, and the love he has for her in return, is the most wholesome thing I've ever witnessed.

And I've been lucky enough to tag along for the ride. They came into my life when Pippa and I were both nineteen and a little lonely, so we became fast friends. The three of us have been a tight-knit trio ever since.

I make a face at Atticus. "Your mom is a drama queen."

"Don't I know it," he replies with an exaggerated huff.

Pippa chooses to ignore her son's dig. Instead, she asks me, "Any idea when it might happen?"

As my best friend, Pippa knows all about Mom handing the business down to me. And how bittersweet it is.

I shake my head. "Not sure, but I think soon. Mom's

arthritis is flaring up more often than not these days, so the inn isn't something she needs to worry about."

Pip offers me a soft smile. "I'm glad she has you. At least with you taking over, it won't feel like she's giving the place up completely."

"It's going to be strange, having no one to answer to but myself."

She nods, chewing on her lip. "Who's going to replace you as restaurant manager?"

I bite back my grin. My first order of business as owner of Dog Days Inn: promoting Pippa to restaurant manager. There is no one I would trust more with my former role. I know if I tell her now, she'll try to refuse it. So I'm taking the *ask for forgiveness, not permission* route.

"We'll see" is all I say.

As I wait out the lull, I spend the next ten minutes straightening the supplies that Pippa has already meticulously organized. I'm miraculously caught up on paperwork for once, so I need something to do with my hands.

"Hey, Dec!" Pippa calls.

I pause my unnecessary tidying to look up at the newcomer. Declan Rhodes looks, at all times, like he's just stepped off a cover shoot for *Working Man Monthly*. His strawberry blonde hair is shaggy, and his stubble makes him look rugged. He completes the look with work pants and a pair of Timberlands. And, just like always, he flashes me that megawatt grin that softens his face, giving him the countenance of a lovable golden retriever.

I only met the guy a couple months ago when he showed up on his sister's doorstep looking for a place to stay, but he's quickly wormed his way into my heart. In a totally platonic, younger brother sort of way. Much to his chagrin.

It's no secret that Declan has been harbouring a small crush on me. He knows nothing is ever going to happen between us, though that doesn't stop him from laying on the charm.

But the fact is, Meyer Ellison doesn't date. The only love I have is for the Dog Days Inn. I don't have time for picnics and candlelit dinners and whatever else nice guys like Declan do to woo a woman.

"Uncle Dec!" Atticus yells. "Look! Auntie M&M brought me M&M's!"

Declan plucks the bag of chocolate off the table and spins away from his nephew's grabby hands, stealing a couple candies for himself.

His gaze finds mine. "Thanks, *Auntie M&M*."

I roll my eyes. "Stealing candy from a child. Pretty sure that goes against your saintly ethics."

He shrugs. "Hey, we can't all be perfect."

I tip the backwards baseball cap off his head, covering his eyes. "What are you doing here?" I ask. "Shouldn't you be helping old ladies cross the street? Or getting someone's cat unstuck from a tree?"

In his short time in Fraisier Creek, Declan has become a legend of sorts. All over town you can hear whispers of *that nice young man*, and whether you like it or not, you'll soon know everything about his latest altruistic exploit. Just yesterday, he was spotted fishing a pair of sunglasses out of the gutter for a perfect stranger.

He gives me his charming grin again. "Do I need an

excuse to come see my favourite ladies?" He reaches out to ruffle Atticus's hair. "And my favourite nephew."

Atticus's brows furrow adorably. "I'm your *only* nephew."

"Which automatically makes you my *favourite*." Declan turns back to me. "I'm on my lunch break. I was hoping a generous inn owner would take pity on me and feed me."

I may not be the owner yet, but hearing it still sends a little thrill down my spine.

I smile despite myself. "Fine. What do you want?"

"Surprise me."

As Declan sits down at the table with Atticus, I put an order in to the kitchen for a burger and fries. When I return, the uncle and nephew duo are in the middle of an argument over which is better: M&M's or Smarties.

"Definitely M&M's," I interject. "The chocolate tastes *so* much better."

Atticus nods enthusiastically. "*See*, Uncle Dec? I told you!"

"Somehow I feel like this is an argument I'm not going to win," Declan says with a shake of his head.

I leave the two to their chocolate debate when my phone buzzes in my back pocket. The new front desk clerk needs help, so I spend fifteen minutes on the computer with him, troubleshooting a booking issue. By the time I return, Declan is eating his burger and playfully slapping Atticus's hand when he tries to steal a fry.

I smile as I survey the room. It's almost time for the lunch rush to kick in. Still, I'm surprised to find an extra customer seated at a table on the far side of the room.

"Who's the suit?" I ask Pippa.

Like many other women, I'm partial to a man in a suit. This suit, in particular. Although he's sitting, I can tell the material hugs his body in all the right places. The matching tie hanging from his neck adds to his air of composure.

The man's face is clean-shaven, and his dark hair is styled to look intentionally tousled. He looks like the type of guy whose appearance is carefully curated each day when he wakes. He's probably even a morning person.

Pippa shrugs. "Never seen him before. Can you bring him this water?"

I take the glass she extends toward me, put on my customer service smile, and then I head across the room.

CHAPTER 3
JACKSON

My Audi R8 looks extremely out of place in the pothole-infested parking lot of Dog Days Inn. The inn my grandmother conveniently forgot to mention that she owned.

Admittedly, I expected it to be a bit run-down. Looking at it now, I'm pleasantly surprised. The building was, at one time, some kind of estate house from the nineteenth century, but it has since been renovated and expanded. There is a modern addition at the back of the building as well as a glass-panelled atrium off to the right side. Based on my minimal research, the atrium holds the inn's restaurant.

An incoming call sounds over my car's speakers, pulling my attention away from the building. I accept with the press of a button on my steering wheel as I maneuver into a parking spot. At least, I think it's a spot—with no yellow lines to delineate, I'm just crossing my fingers that no one gets too close and scratches my paint.

"Hey," Wells says, "have you made it yet?"

I've known Wells McKenna for as long as I can remember. We grew up together in Toronto, attending the same private schools. My father is a bigwig in the music industry, while Wells's father is a movie producer and his mother is an actress. As a consequence of this, Wells and I share a healthy aversion to the spotlight.

"Just pulled in."

"I Googled the place. It's really in the middle of nowhere, huh?"

Fraisier Creek is three hours north of the city, but it might as well be on a totally different planet. As I drove, I traded in the skyscrapers and bumper-to-bumper traffic for sprawling farmland and the occasional gas station that reminds you civilization isn't *too* far out of reach.

"Just how Cherie liked it."

My grandmother had a knack for going off the grid. When she decided she'd had enough—attention, social interaction—she would simply pull out a map and choose a spot at random. She would lie low for a while, and then she would come home, starting the cycle all over again.

"How's the heart?" Wells asks.

My lip curls at his question. "You sound like my mother."

"Hey, I choose to see that as a compliment. Your mother is a gem."

"Try being on the receiving end of her incessant phone calls and then tell me how much of a *gem* she is."

"She's just worried, man. It was scary for her." He clears his throat. "It was scary for all of us."

My grandmother's request for me to take care of myself flashes in my mind. One way or another, Cherie always gets what she wants. Because now I'm here in Fraisier Creek to pay my dues.

I sigh. "My heart is fine."

Maybe fine-adjacent is a better descriptor. But he doesn't need to know that.

"Glad to hear it," he says. "I've gotta run, but I'll talk to you later. Let me know how your meeting goes."

I say a quick goodbye before exiting the car. Then I tug my suit jacket from the passenger seat and shrug it over my shoulders, adjusting the cuffs before buttoning it at my front.

After wearing a suit nearly every day for five straight years, it would be a hard habit to break. I'm not sure I even want to—putting on a suit feels like donning armour and gearing up for battle. Something I have a feeling I'm going to need today if I don't want the cracks in my façade to show.

I don't pay much attention to the main lobby of the inn as I enter. After all, I have six months to thoroughly inspect the place—and I plan to do just that. Instead, I make my way toward the restaurant that juts off the side of the main building.

On my walk, a framed photograph catches my eye. I recognize Cherie—though she's about thirty years younger than she was when she died—standing next to an unfamiliar woman. They're both smiling as they embrace in front of the inn. I touch a hand to the frame, and then I carry on.

The atrium appears bigger inside than it does on the outside. Square-panelled glass stretches the perimeter and over the roof, allowing the spring sunshine to filter in through translucent panes. It's only April, but the weather is mild and the sun is blazing, warming the space.

"Take your pick," a willowy redhead calls from behind the bar, gesturing to the slew of tables. "As you can see, we've got a full house."

I glance around the decidedly *not* full house. Other than two people at a booth in the far corner, and a man and little boy at a square table in the centre, the place is empty. This lack of customers doesn't seem to bode well for the business's bottom line.

Yet another sign that Cherie shouldn't have been involved in this place. It's probably a money pit.

I make my way to a table across the room, away from the few other patrons. Unbuttoning my jacket, I take a seat as I let my gaze roam the restaurant.

"Can I get you a drink?" the redhead asks, still standing at the bar.

"Please. Water's fine," I reply. "Thank you."

My perusal continues. The interior, much like the outside, is charming. It's certainly nothing like the hotels and restaurants I generally frequent. They're all modern finishings and sleek lines. Although the atrium is clearly an addendum, the bones of this place have stood the test of time, and features like the wallpaper in the hallway suggest a string of renovations over the decades.

"Here you go."

A glass of water slides across the tabletop. It's in one of those cutesy glasses that's made to look like a Mason jar. My gaze trails up a slender arm and to the face that belongs to that pretty voice.

The first thing I notice is startling blue eyes. They're clear and bright like water from a melting glacier. She has a heart-shaped face, and a prominent Cupid's bow on pink lips. A gem glints from where her nose is pierced.

My eyes involuntarily follow the curves of her body. I note the way her black v-neck shirt dips to reveal ample cleavage. In her jeans, her hips flare in the most delicious way, and I itch to settle my hands there.

When she brings her right hand up to tease out a tangle in her long blonde hair, I notice a small tattoo on the side of her wrist. Her movements are quick, but I think I catch it—a strawberry.

My tongue flits out, wetting my bottom lip. It's not often I indulge my attractions. Work keeps me plenty busy, so there isn't much time for eating or sleeping. Much less socializing in the hopes of finding someone to spend the night with.

But for once in my adult life, I don't have work to think about. And something tells me this woman would be the sweetest kind of indulgence.

"Anything else I can get you?" she asks.

"No, I think that's all." She turns, ready to walk away, but then I change my mind. "Actually, wait."

Before I can think better of it, my fingers are closing around her wrist. *Shit.* We both look down at my offence at the same time. I'm not the guy that manhandles waitresses.

"Sorry," I apologize, retracting my hand. "I just meant to ask you a question."

Her lips quirk. She rests back on the edge of a nearby table, bracing her beverage tray on her thighs. It's inexplicable, but I find the action to be sexy as hell.

"Ask away."

"What's your favourite thing about working here?"

I can't help myself—it's the analyst in me. My career may be on pause for the time being while my body gets its shit together, but I can't turn off the part of my brain that thrives on data.

At my question, something ignites in her gaze. She juts her chin in the direction of outside. "We're right off the highway," she says, "so we see a lot of people passing through. Mostly truckers during the winter, and a slew of tourists during the holidays and in the summer. I like hearing their stories. How much alimony they pay their ex wives; that time they stole an overpriced pair of jeans; how they're still in love with the one that got away."

"People truly offer up personal information to you like that?"

"Nothing beats confiding in a stranger you'll never see again." She shrugs. "Sometimes, I'm the most human interaction these people see all week. Makes them feel good to connect with me. And I like to connect with them, too."

I take a sip of my water. My nose twitches. It tastes kind of...*fishy*. Nothing like the sparkling water I usually get at restaurants in the city.

"A regular extrovert," I say.

At this, she grins. "Or I'm just really nosy," she counters. "Like this. What brings you to town?"

I chuckle. "Business."

"My God, *please* spare me the details. My delicate sensibilities can't handle all this talking."

The smile I wear stretches my lips impossibly wide. "Fine. Maybe you can put your connections to good use and help me out. Give me an inside scoop," I say. "I have a meeting with a lawyer and someone named Meyer Ellison tomorrow morning."

At this, her demeanour changes completely. Gone is her smile. Instead, her eyes narrow on me. "No, you don't."

Her tone takes me aback. "Uh... Yes, I do. I've been emailing him for a couple weeks now."

She hums. "I think it's time I introduce myself," she says. She sets her tray on the empty table behind her and unties her apron. Then she sticks out her hand. "Meyer Ellison, soon-to-be owner of Dog Days Inn. And the woman you absolutely do *not* have a meeting with tomorrow morning. Or any morning, for that matter."

Fuck. Two epic blunders in the span of one goddamn conversation. *You've lost your touch, Vaughan.*

I stand from my seat and tuck my hand into hers. Her grip is firmer than I expect, but I suppose at this point, I should throw all my preconceived notions out the window. "Jackson Vaughan," I say.

Meyer settles into the chair opposite me. I retake my seat, eyes still on her.

"I'd say sorry that I disappointed you by not having a dick, but I'm actually not sorry about that at all."

I clear my throat. "I apologize. The name threw me off. I—"

"Have a habit of making assumptions," she finishes. "You're not the first big shot to underestimate me, and you won't be the last. It's your stupid mistake to make."

"Okay. First impression, total shit on my part," I admit. "Any chance we can start over?"

She cocks her head, assessing me. "Depends."

"On?"

"Why you think you have a meeting with me. And what this supposed meeting is about."

My brows furrow. "I'm here to talk about the future of the inn."

"Well, I don't really see how that's any of your business."

"Okay," I say slowly, "I feel like there's some kind of knowledge disconnect here. So I'm just going to go ahead and lay everything out on the table."

Her nod is condescending. "That would be a good idea."

"My grandmother was Cherie Cheval. For God knows what reason, she owned half of this inn. Now that she has passed, her shares have been left to me."

Meyer blinks. "Is that supposed to be funny? Because your standup routine needs some work."

I shake my head. "I'm not trying to be funny."

She crosses her arms. "I have never emailed with you. I've never even heard of you before."

I pull out my phone and open my thread with Meyer. Or, apparently, whoever was pretending to be Meyer. "Here," I say, nudging the device across the table. "Believe me now?"

Her eyes rove over the words. After a moment, I hear her curse under her breath. "That was not me."

Taking my phone back, I tuck it into my pocket. "Well, you've obviously got a cyber security issue on your hands, but the fact still remains. As stated in the terms of Cherie's will, I own half of this place."

She shakes her head. "This inn belongs to my mother, and soon it will belong to me. *You* are not part of the equation. As much as I loved her, neither was Cherie."

"Maybe you should have a talk with your mother, then, because it seems she's fed you false information."

Meyer glares. "I think I'm inclined to believe my own mother over some *stranger*."

I pinch the bridge of my nose. "Look, Meyer—"

"*Ms. Ellison*." Those bright blue eyes I was admiring earlier are frosty now. "It's Ms. Ellison, Mr. Vaughan."

"*Ms. Ellison*," I amend, "if it was up to me, my grandmother would've had no part in your business. But the reality is that she *did*. And now *I* do."

"Don't worry. I'll do you the courtesy of waiting until after you leave to have a good laugh at your expense." She fakes a grimace. "I bet it'll be *really* embarrassing when you find out you're wrong."

I smirk. "I believe that's what they call projection."

She huffs as she stands from her chair. "If you're not going to order food, get out of my restaurant, Vaughan!" she calls over her shoulder. "We need the table for *paying* customers, not stingy rich guys who take advantage of free water."

I raise my glass in mock toast. "Lovely to meet you, Ms. Ellison. I'm looking forward to tomorrow!"

CHAPTER 4

JACKSON

ALTHOUGH I'M loath to admit it, the three-hour drive from Toronto and the ensuing back-and-forth with Meyer totally wiped me out. Ever since I woke up in the hospital a few weeks ago, I haven't been feeling in tip-top physical shape.

I do my best to hide it, though. Everyone in my life is already watching me a little too closely after Cherie's death. I don't need to give them more of a reason to worry over me.

As I sit behind the wheel of my car, the urge to drive back to the city is strong. But I'm beyond tired, and the meeting I scheduled for tomorrow morning, whether Meyer acknowledges it or not, is important.

Not for the first time, I'm tempted to say I don't want this place and all the trouble it will inevitably bring. But I also don't want to let my grandmother down.

I've always been the odd one out in my family. They were all cut from the same creative cloth. My analytical brain, on the other hand, has rendered me rather useless in that department. Although Cherie didn't share my obsession with numbers or concrete facts, she made it a point to connect with me. To understand just a little bit.

Maybe that's why it hurts so much that she's gone.

I haven't let myself dwell much on my feelings since her funeral. For a time, I could safely say it was because I was focusing on my physical health. Now, I don't have the luxury of that excuse. So instead, I'm going to do what she asked and kid myself into believing it'll make up for her glaring absence.

I survey the inn's parking lot. It really is atrocious, the amount of potholes. The sign out front has also seen better days. A coat of paint would help, but a total rebrand would be better.

Despite the small part of me that says I should run—away from this inn, from dealing with Meyer—I'm not going to. For Cherie, I'm going to do my best to help it thrive. For some reason, my grandmother was fond of this place, so letting it flounder is not an option.

Not that it seems to be floundering. Come lunchtime, cars packed into the lot, and families and couples of all sorts entered the building. Perhaps it isn't the money pit I first painted it out to be.

It's this thought that reminds me how very little I know of this place. How blindsided I felt when this piece of my grandmother's life was revealed because I thought I knew about all her out-of-the-box endeavours. I truly could be shackling myself to a dying business, one steady lunch rush aside, for the foreseeable future. Maybe Cherie hoped I could work a miracle with the books.

Or maybe I am, as Meyer put it, just a big shot who likes to make assumptions.

I know one thing for certain—if I so much as suggested having lunch at a place like this, my colleagues back in Toronto would've laughed me right out of the city.

A year ago, I would've laughed right along with them. Now, knowing how much a place like this meant to my grandmother, I feel like a grade-A asshole. Even if it's hemorrhaging money, the least I can do is try to fix it.

And in six months, I'll be back in the city—back to my life.

It's this thought that spurs me into action. The sooner I get situated here and start turning things around, the sooner I can go home.

As I round my car to grab my overnight bag from the trunk, a pair of voices coming from the back of the building captures my attention.

"Reggie!" She sounds young, maybe high school age. "Meyer told you that you couldn't smoke back here anymore."

"Beatrice didn't care," he snaps. "Not my fault she's trying to throw her weight around and change the rules."

"The rules have always been there. Beatrice just didn't *catch* you. Come on, the smoke is getting inside and making the kitchen smell."

"Fuck off, Ashley."

A door slams, followed by a handful of muttered curses. My eyes narrow. I wait to see if this Reggie kid will round the side of the building, and I'm not disappointed. He does a moment later, cigarette held between his fingers.

He's wearing some bastardized attempt at the inn's uniform, with ripped jeans and combat boots, but it's the scowl on his face that makes him look like a punk. My eyes narrow further.

He leans back against the wall, kicking a foot up to rest on the white siding behind him. He raises the cigarette to his lips and takes a slow drag.

With a shake of my head, I find my bag and close my trunk, then make my way across the parking lot.

Although it feels a lot like admitting defeat, I reenter the inn's lobby, and I let my eyes rove over the details I skipped earlier. There's entirely too much floral, like a greenhouse threw up all over the wallpaper and upholstery. It's undoubtedly dated, but there's also something surprisingly endearing about the space.

The front desk is small. It hosts a rundown computer monitor and a phone. A young woman with dark braided hair sits behind it, mindlessly spinning in her chair. Big, colourfully beaded earrings dangle from her ears. A hardcover book is open in her hand, and a bag of chips rests in her lap.

"Hi," I say. "I'd like to book a room."

The woman blushes as she jumps up from her chair. She tosses both the book and the chip bag onto the counter. She then brushes her hands over her thighs to decrumb them.

"Sorry. Yes, sir, of course—"

"Winona," a familiar voice interjects. "Can I have a word?"

I turn, finding Meyer with her head poking out of an office door behind the counter. She ignores me and looks expectantly at the employee. Winona glances between the two of us, unsure.

"Sorry," she squeaks before turning away from me.

I sigh. I can't tell what they're talking about, but I have a feeling it has to do with me. Winona is somewhat taller than Meyer, so she completely blocks my new business partner from sight. I can't even attempt to read her lips.

When Winona returns to the desk, she looks nervous. "We have one room left, sir. Just one," she says. Her eyes shift to the side as she speaks. "It's our best suite."

In other words, it's the most expensive suite. I chance a glance at Meyer. She offers me a razor-sharp grin in response.

I return my gaze to Winona. "You're telling me you're booked solid on a random Sunday in April?" I prod.

Winona looks to Meyer and then back at me. "Uh...yes?"

Yeah, not fucking likely.

My eyes cut back to Meyer. She's pretending to examine her nails as she leans against the doorframe, but her faux relaxed stance doesn't fool me. Winona is clearly lying right to my face, on the instruction of her boss.

"It's not a room at the Four Seasons," Meyer says, "but I'm sure it's closer to your *usual* standards."

It seems I'm not the only one making assumptions. Although, in this case, Meyer would be right. My go-to accommodations are not tiny inns like this. But I resent the implication that I can't—or *won't*—hack it here.

"I'll take it," I say.

I should be annoyed—miffed by Meyer's pettiness. I should call their bluff, not because I can't afford the room but on principle alone. However, I'm too bone-weary to argue right now.

I offer Winona my Amex. I can feel Meyer's eyes on us again as the clerk inputs the reservation and then hands over my room key.

"Thanks for choosing Dog Days Inn," Winona says. "We hope you have a relaxing stay!"

I almost snort. Relaxing, my ass.

CHAPTER 5

JACKSON

THE NEXT MORNING rolls around entirely too quickly.

This sleepy town is almost too peaceful. The room Meyer forced me into is nice, with its four-poster bed and its en suite bathroom complete with a claw-foot bathtub, but as I settled beneath the sheets, I couldn't shake the weird feeling. Because it was *too* quiet.

I wouldn't say Toronto is a city that never sleeps, but there's always something interrupting the silence of the night. Whether it's raucous shouting after a hockey game or the whir of an air conditioner, motion is a constant. But Fraisier Creek is disconcertingly still.

When I didn't immediately nod off, my brain took that as permission to wander. It first settled on the inn's parking lot and how much money it would require to repair the crater-sized holes in the asphalt. A handsome sum, no doubt.

Then, predictably, my thoughts drifted to my business partner.

It's easy to claim plain curiosity. Anyone would have an

interest in the new person they were supposed to work alongside. But I would be lying to myself if I didn't admit that it's more than that. In the simplest terms, Meyer Ellison intrigues me.

Especially when I walk downstairs and catch her mid-argument.

"You *stole my identity*," Meyer hisses from inside the back office.

The door is open, giving anyone passing by the freedom to observe. To his credit, the man—Trystan, according to his name tag—standing behind the front desk pretends not to listen. I have no such qualms as I lean against the desk.

"Meyer," an unfamiliar woman says, "I can explain."

I imagine Meyer crossing her arms and levelling her opponent with that icy gaze of hers.

"I don't want to hear it right now. What I *want* is for you to tell me he's wrong. That there's been a big mistake and this is all a nightmare."

There's a beat of heavy silence. "You know I can't do that."

I straighten when Meyer comes rushing out of the office. Her head is down, but it snaps up when she nears me, and she stops short.

Gone are her jeans and t-shirt from yesterday. In their place is a poufy-sleeved blouse tucked into a pencil skirt that hugs her hips even better than the denim. She's mesmerizing.

It doesn't matter what she wears, though—she's still my off-limits business partner. And consequently, the woman who hates my guts.

"What are you doing here?" she bites out.

I grin, knowing it will infuriate her. Because feeling her wrath is better than seeing the pain in her expression.

"Like I told you yesterday, we have a meeting."

She sneers. "If you think I'm going to sit in a confined space with you, you are sorely mistaken. I'd rather chew on glass."

This pulls a laugh from me. "You have a rather creative imagination, Ms. Ellison."

Meyer nods, crossing her arms. "You wouldn't even want to know what I've imagined doing to you."

To this, I can't help my smirk. "Oh, but I think I would."

I can see the moment the double meaning of her words hits her because she goes stiff, jaw clenching. Fire ignites in her gaze, and fuck, if that isn't enticing. These thoughts are dangerous, but I can't help myself. I want to—

A throat clears behind us.

We both turn to the older woman standing in the office doorway. She looks to be in her sixties, with silver hair chopped just above her shoulders. The woman in that photo with Cherie, I realize. This must be my grandmother's friend and business partner.

I step forward, hand outstretched toward her. "Jackson Vaughan. Nice to meet you," I say.

She returns my handshake with a smile. "Beatrice Ellison," she replies. "You look a lot like Cherie, you know."

The comment tugs painfully on my heart, but I push the feeling aside. It's something I don't have time for today.

"I presume you are the one I've been speaking with over email?"

Beatrice's gaze flits to her daughter, then returns to me. "I am. I apologize for the subterfuge, but I'm glad that we could all be here today to sort everything out."

Meyer lets out a snort of derision behind me.

The front door opens then, cutting our conversation short. A man in a tan suit comes striding in, briefcase in hand. The inn's lawyer is here.

Beatrice offers me a strained smile. "Let's get started."

———

"So I think that about sums it all up," Louis says, leaning back in his chair. "Any questions?"

The business lawyer, whose name I barely caught because I was focused on the way Meyer was glaring holes into my chest, is an older man both short and stout. He talks faster than the speed of light and sports a fedora that he, as far as I can tell, wears unironically.

I shake my head, and then I chance a glance at Meyer. If she clenches her jaw any harder, she's liable to turn her teeth to dust from the sheer pressure.

She opens her mouth, readying to say something, but her mother places a hand on her arm. A silent reprimand.

"That'll be all, Louis," Beatrice says. "Thank you very much."

Louis replaces his fedora on his head and tips it in her direction. "My pleasure," he replies. He then addresses me and Meyer. "Once I wade through all the paperwork on my end, I'll just need your autographs, and then you'll both be the proud new owners of Dog Days Inn!"

Suffice to say, the lawyer's enthusiasm is leaps and

bounds ahead of ours. And he seems totally oblivious to the pure ire radiating off of Meyer.

I stand from my seat and stick a hand out. "It was nice to meet you, Louis," I say. "I look forward to working with you."

A slight exaggeration, but that's the name of the game.

Louis turns to Meyer, looking like he's gearing up to go in for a hug. As he moves closer, Meyer's hand shoots out between them, almost jabbing the lawyer in the belly from the force. She clears her throat.

"Man, I remember when you were just a tyke," he says as he takes her hand, unperturbed. His tone then takes on a teasing quality. "Are you sure you're grown up enough for this?"

"Thank you for your time, Mr. Montaigne," Meyer says, tipping her chin up with a smile. It's polite, but I can detect the frustration simmering below the surface. "I look forward to hearing from you."

Louis squeezes her elbow. "Talk soon, little lady."

Meyer's jaw hardens ever so slightly. Her annoyance with him isn't as outright as with me, but I detect it all the same. Hell, *I* feel annoyed on her behalf. Still, she doesn't say anything. But letting that belittling remark hang in the air doesn't sit right with me.

"Ms. Ellison has a name," I say firmly. "I suggest you use it."

When the lawyer leaves, looking chastised, Meyer whirls on me. "I do *not* need you fighting my battles," she seethes.

I cross my arms. "Well, someone had to set him straight, seeing as you weren't doing it."

Her cheeks heat as her eyes blaze. "And who the hell decided that you were that person? Don't kid yourself into thinking you're my knight in shining armour, Vaughan."

"Hey—"

A throat clears. Both of us turn to see a very stern Beatrice staring us down. I wonder how often Meyer was on the receiving end of this look growing up.

Beatrice's brow is arched. "Are you two just about finished?"

I nod, now feeling chastised myself. Meyer opens her mouth again, but she wisely decides to shut it before she utters another word.

Beatrice sighs. "Why don't we all sit back down and have a proper conversation?"

I settle back into the mismatched chair opposite Beatrice at the office desk. Begrudgingly, Meyer slides into her own chair beside me. It feels a lot like sitting in the principal's office after being pulled out of class, some kind of punishment imminent.

"It can be an uphill battle trying to make something of yourself in a town that's seen you in diapers. But it's a battle Meyer knows well, and one she is equipped to handle how she sees fit," Beatrice says to me. Then she turns to her daughter. "And Meyer, Jackson was trying to help you. Don't forget that."

"The road to hell is paved with good intentions," she mumbles.

Then silence stretches for a moment too long. I can tell that Beatrice is waiting for one of us to make the first move.

Judging by Meyer's sour expression, that won't be her, so I resolve to be the bigger person.

"My grandmother thought very highly of you, and this inn," I tell Beatrice.

This coaxes a sad smile from her. "I thought the world of her as well. Both in a professional and a personal capacity."

I look down at my hands clasped in my lap, turning my thoughts over in my head. I want to know why my grandmother kept this place from me. I have the strong urge to ask, but I'm fairly certain neither one of them will have the answer.

That's just how Cherie was—she kept a lot of stuff to herself. But I always thought there were no secrets between us. Obviously, I was wrong.

"Well," Beatrice says, "I would offer you a tour, but these old knees don't work like they used to."

Some of Meyer's anger shifts. In its place is unbridled concern. "Are you okay?"

Beatrice smiles at her daughter. It's reassuring and apologetic all at once. "Same old, same old." She wiggles the cane in her grip. "Just meant I would be no fun hobbling through the halls with this."

"That's alright," I say. "I can figure it out."

"Nonsense. Meyer will show you around."

Meyer, at this very moment, looks like she would rather be on the receiving end of a lobotomy gone wrong. Or, more likely, she's imagining what it would be like to perform said operation on *me*.

"I'll stay here," Beatrice continues, addressing her daughter. "After your walkabout, you can treat me to lunch and then drive me home."

Beatrice's words drip with finality. And despite how angry Meyer may be with her, she doesn't plan to go against her mother. She stands from her chair and strides into the hall without so much as a backwards glance.

I say my farewell to Beatrice and then I follow Meyer out of the office. When I spot her standing with her arms crossed, I sigh. "Listen, you don't have to—"

She holds up a hand. "Don't take pity on me, Vaughan. We're not going to be friends. You don't want to be here, and I don't want you here. So," she says, "I'm going to give you this tour and then we're going to stay out of each other's way as much as possible. Got it?"

No, I want to say. As much as these initial interactions have been one clusterfuck after another, I don't want to be at odds with her. Working together would make the process much smoother.

But Meyer is stubborn. I can tell she's in no mood to hear me out, so I simply nod. "Got it."

Fuck, it's going to be a long six months.

CHAPTER 6
MEYER

Jackson fucking Vaughan.

At first, I admittedly found him charming. His easy grin and his nice-to-look-at face drew me in. And when he asked me to tell him my favourite thing about working at the inn, my heart felt a little fuzzy. Because no one had ever asked me that question before, let alone cared about the answer. Then he had to go and ruin it by stomping on my dreams.

During our disaster of a meeting this morning, he managed to charm both my mother and our lawyer. Neither one of them seemed put off by the unfairness of my new reality.

Then, to top it off, Louis Montaigne had to go and try to hug me when Jackson got a handshake. What's more, he *little lady*'d me. It was cute when I was five, but two decades later, I'm over it.

All in all, it hasn't been a good day.

What I should be doing is finding a way to distract myself. Instead, I'm ruminating. I stare disappointedly at the documents in front of me—the original ones that spell out Cherie's involvement with the inn. Up until yesterday, I truly thought she was simply a guest.

When Mom arrived earlier, I pulled her straight into the office. Because someone had sent those emails to Jackson, enabling him and his outlandish insinuations about ownership, and I knew there was only one person it could be.

The conversation devolved from there, and now I'm pissed as hell that she didn't tell me about all of this sooner.

Pippa has been trying to get ahold of me for the past few hours, but her texts and calls have gone unanswered. She was the first person I told about my encounter with Jackson, and we both laughed at the absurdity. I don't have the guts to tell her we've been made fools. Or, more specifically, that *I* have been made a fool.

I take another swig of wine, straight from the bottle. The sweet taste slides smoothly down my throat.

"Meyer?"

I slump in my makeshift seat—an old crate I found in the corner of the storage room. "You found my secret hiding spot."

Declan looks down at me, hands tucked in his pockets, a concerned frown on his face. "Pip's been trying to call you," he says. "She asked me to stop in on my way home from work. Winona told me you were back here."

Damn. I guess my secret hiding spot isn't so secret after all.

"You can tell Pip I'm okay." I wave him toward the door. "Now, begone. You're interrupting my wallowing."

Instead of listening, he drags another crate across the

floor until it's in front of me. Then he plops down, bracketing my feet with his. He holds a hand out for my bottle. I relinquish it, watching as he takes a drink.

"What the hell is that?" he asks in disgust, wiping a hand over his mouth.

I snatch the bottle back and hug it defensively. "Strawberry wine."

"Christ, Meyer. That's *sweet*."

"You say that like it's a bad thing."

He shakes his head. His blonde hair, usually held back under a baseball cap, is flying free tonight. A longer piece falls onto his forehead. It distracts me so much, I almost miss his next question.

"Care to share why you're getting drunk in a storage room?" he asks.

"Because all my hopes and dreams have been shot to hell."

"That's a little dramatic for a Monday evening."

I glare. "Do you want me to spill or not?"

He holds up his hands. "Sorry. Shutting up now."

I sigh. "Apparently, my mother's friend owned half of the inn. She has for the past fifteen years. Now that she's gone, her shares have been left to her grandson."

Declan's brows raise in disbelief. "You're shitting me."

"'Fraid not, bud." I take another mournful drink of wine. "She's been coming around all my life, but to me, she was always just a guest." I let out a bitter laugh. "And I thought I knew everything there was to know about this place."

"Okay," he says, rubbing his jaw in thought. "Super

unexpected. But her grandson owning part of the inn, that's a bad thing...why?"

I throw my hands in the air, nearly losing my hold on the wine. A few drops slosh out of the bottle, coating my hand. I lick the escaped alcohol from my skin before answering.

"Because I have to share, Declan!"

"Again, that's a problem...why?"

I scowl. "My five-year plan centred around me showing the world what an accomplished businesswoman I can be. Look, world! Meyer Ellison did *that*. Now I have to *share* with some business guy from Toronto who probably eats Rolexes for breakfast and doesn't know a thing about physical labour. He's probably going to want to sell and— *Oh my God*."

"What?"

"He's gonna want to sell!" I wail. "They *always* want to sell!"

The night I learned that I am a weepy drunk was the night of my senior prom. I'd only had alcohol a handful of times before then, and it was never in excess. Prom night, however, my friends dragged me to a party.

Pippa didn't get to town until the following year, so I had a different group of friends back then. Friends who left me and Fraisier Creek firmly in their rear view when they set out for university.

As I watched my friends having the time of their lives with our graduating class, I was hit with a *this is the end* kind of feeling. It was an odd melancholy that seeped into my bones and left me feeling exposed. So I did what any rational eighteen-year-old would do: I resolved to get blackout drunk.

I didn't quite make it there because I can still vividly recall my friends finding me on my back in a hayfield, crying up at the stars. The pitying looks they shot me as they carried me home almost exactly match the look that Declan is giving me right now.

"It'll be okay, Meyer," he says, placing a comforting hand on my arm. "This isn't goodbye."

"Sure feels like it."

That melancholy is back, and this time, she's here to stay.

"Maybe we could take up a collection?" he suggests. "I know I haven't been in Fraisier Creek long, but I get the feeling you folks protect your own. I'm sure everyone would be more than willing to help you buy him out."

I smile at Declan's naivety. He's not stupid by any means, but at twenty-two, he somehow hasn't been jaded enough by the world to see it the way I do. Even with shitty parents like his, he's still good to his core.

I can't resist telling him as much. "You're one of the good ones, Declan Rhodes."

He rolls his eyes, though he's smiling, too. "I'm never going to escape that label, am I?"

I shake my head. "Probably not, but that's okay. You just be you. A good man. A good friend."

He slaps his thighs and then stands. "Well, as your friend, I think I should get you home."

"I'm not ready to go home," I admit.

The thought of going back to my dark, empty cottage makes the melancholy grow. Sure, my cat is there, but he definitely won't have patience for my drunkenness.

"Come home with me, then. We can order pizza to soak

up some of that disgusting wine and then you can crash in Pip's bed."

I smile, but it slowly loses its shine until it drops altogether. "You go. I'll be okay. I pinky promise I won't drink any more wine."

———

I drank more wine.

Never before have I broken a pinky promise. But after Declan finally left, the melancholy sprouted teeth and took a chunk out of my heart. So I decided more wine was in my best interest.

This is so *not a good idea.*

I should really listen to myself. I'm pretty smart. Usually. But my brain is kind of fuzzy, and I think I've fallen right off the weepy scale and into an even more unfamiliar territory. I feel...angry?

"Vaughan!" I shout. *Oops.* My fist pounds on the door to the room Jackson is staying in tonight. "I know you're"— hiccup—"in there!"

In hindsight, I should've taken Declan up on his gentlemanly offer to walk me home. Instead, I'm standing outside the best room at the inn, waiting for my new sworn enemy to open the door.

Thankfully, this side of the building is otherwise empty. Not that Jackson knows that. Like hell was I going to comp his stay, so he's paying for our most expensive room while he's here. Might as well milk that fancy credit card while I can.

I ready my fist to knock again when the door swings inward. Jackson leans against the doorframe, one ankle crossed over the other. The picture of smug relaxation. A lazy, amused grin stretches his lips.

I take this moment to drag my eyes down his form. Drunk Meyer is nothing if not an opportunist. I half pictured him to sleep upside down in his suit like some kind of well-dressed vampire bat, but I'm pleasantly surprised to note the sweatpants slung low on his hips. His white t-shirt certainly doesn't leave anything to the imagination. His muscles are not of the beefy bodybuilder variety, but they subtly define his stomach and chest. He's also got *marvellous* biceps.

His attire and musculature, coupled with his angular jaw and warm honey-coloured eyes, leave me weak in the knees. He's even got dark brown hair that's short on the sides and a bit longer on top. Perfect to run your fingers through. Perfect to grab during—

"*Ugh.*"

Why does hotness always come with a heaping side of *asshole*?

"Did you just come here to check me out, Ellison? Or is there another point to your visit?"

My eyes snap up to his. "I'm not *checking you out*! You're the anemone. *My* anemone."

Jackson steps away from the doorframe and into my space. I tip my chin up, unwilling to break eye contact. This, however, puts my lips entirely too close to his. Too close—because we're *enemies*.

Kissing your enemy is bad...right?

Even if maybe his lips look like they would be good at kissing. Even if maybe his hands look like they would fit perfectly against my waist. Even if maybe I would love to know what it would be like to feel his weight settle on top of me—between my thighs.

"Are you drunk?"

I squint as I pinch my thumb and pointer finger together in front of his pretty eyeballs. "Just a *little* bit. But drunk words are sober thoughts, buddy, so you best believe that what I'm saying is the *truth*."

"And what *are* you saying? So far all you've done is undress me with your eyes and call me your *anemone*."

Shit. That's not the right word.

"I'm saying that this inn is literally all I have going for me, so if you want to get your grubby little mitts on *my* shares, you're gonna have to pry them from my cold, dead hands. Even then, you'll lose because my ghost *will* fight you."

He regards me like I'm cheap evening entertainment. "Is that all?"

"No, that's *not* all, Mr. Interrupter," I say. I stab his chest with my finger. It's nice and sturdy—hurts my finger a little. "I also wanted to say that I'm sorry for your loss. Your grandmother was a hell of a woman and I'm going to miss her a lot."

For a moment, I think I spot a flicker of something in his eyes. Sorrow? But then it's gone and his lips quirk upwards. "Most people wouldn't give their enemy condolences."

I set my shoulders. "Lucky for you, I'm a *nice* enemy."

Now his grin is crooked as it stretches across his lips. "Lucky me."

My lungs stutter as he continues to look at me. I've met my fair share of attractive people. I've slept with a few of them. But none have made my breath *falter* from a single look in my direction.

It's the wine. It has to be the wine.

"Don't smile at me," I scold. "You're not allowed to smile."

His grin deepens. Honest to God dimples appear on his cheeks. Fucking *cheek dimples*. It's official: the universe is out to get me.

"Why not?"

"Just because."

This only elicits a chuckle. Jackson steps farther into the hall and shuts his door behind him. Then he tucks his hands into his pockets and starts off down the corridor.

"Let's go, Ellison," he calls. "Time for bed."

"What are you doing?"

"Walking you home."

"I don't need you to walk me home," I protest.

He stops and turns to me, sighing. "Can you please just humour me?"

"Why?"

"Because lucky for you, I'm a nice enemy, too. And despite what you may think, I don't want anything bad to happen to you, especially while you're not yourself."

My heart does a funny little skip. *Traitor.*

I try really hard, but it's difficult to be indignant when he says something like that. I don't even point out that Fraisier

Creek's crime rate is practically in the negatives. Instead, I follow him down the hall, and then I lead him out the front door of the inn.

My home is off to the edge of the property, shielded by trees to give the illusion of privacy. All along the gravel path from the inn to the front door of my tiny cottage, Jackson keeps pace with my slightly unsteady wobble.

Now that the adrenaline of confronting him has worn off, I'm dead on my feet. Trying to unlock the door requires herculean effort, but I swat Jackson's hands away when he tries to assist. I certainly don't need *his* help.

"Son of a bitch," I curse as I drop my keys for the umpteenth time.

Before I can bend down again, Jackson swipes them off the ground and nudges me out of the way. Within seconds, my door is swinging open.

Do I enter? No, I linger like the stupid drunk woman I am.

The nighttime air smells of spring. It kisses my skin, sending goosebumps scattering across my exposed flesh. It's now that I realize I left my jacket in my office at the inn.

Standing here in the moonlight, my keys clutched in my palm, the teeth biting into my flesh, a wave of embarrassment washes over me. Not only am I a sloppy drunk, but I fully leaned into that sloppiness and made a *complete* fool of myself in front of Jackson.

And I'm somehow supposed to run an inn with this man.

Nausea does a gold medal-winning somersault in my gut. Why did I ever think I could do this? I haven't even signed the paperwork to officially become the owner and I'm already fumbling, big time.

Abruptly, I turn away from Jackson and step into my house. I throw a small *thank you* over my shoulder—because my mama raised a woman with manners—and then I move to slam the door. I want to shut out this night, both metaphorically and physically.

Jackson still stands on my stoop, hands in his pockets. "Ellison?" he calls.

I reluctantly meet his eyes. "Mhm?"

I was fairly certain I couldn't dislike this man more, but then he decides to drive the knife of humiliation even deeper.

His smirk is taunting. "I really hope you remember this in the morning."

CHAPTER 7
MEYER

IT WASN'T until I was five years old that it occurred to me that my mother and I look different. While my friends and classmates all had similar features to their parents, I had none.

My mother likes to think that the reason she found me was an act of God. I think it was the strings of fate being manipulated by the universe. Whatever the case, we both agree that it was some kind of divine intervention, God or otherwise, that led her to me.

Back in 1998, the Fraisier Creek Fire Department was made up of volunteers—mostly still is—which meant there was only one person in the building at the time. The chief was preoccupied listening to his Discman, so he didn't notice newborn me wailing outside the front door where I had been left.

Mom is the gentlest woman I think I'll ever have the privilege of knowing. But that day, when she happened to be walking by after her car broke down, she cradled me to her chest and then marched into the fire station to give the chief a piece of her mind.

Children's Aid wanted to take me to a nearby city to a foster home. Mom reportedly said, "She was left in Fraisier Creek, so Fraisier Creek is where she'll stay." And then she did everything in her power to keep me.

Growing up, I didn't always make things easy. I definitely put her through her paces, but she's never looked at me with anything short of love.

When her arthritis started flaring up really bad five years ago, I made a promise to myself that I would take care of her like she's taken care of me. And a few months ago, when it became apparent that she needed more care than Fraisier Creek had to offer, I got her set up in a retirement condo just thirty minutes down the highway.

Now, whenever I'm not at the inn, I'm travelling to Calderville to visit her.

My head throbs as I push through my mother's front door. I don't make it a habit to get drunk—especially not off of wine in the loneliness of my own company—but when I do, the hangover is brutal. However, just like Jackson hoped, I remember everything about last night.

Stupidity, thy name is Meyer.

"Honey, I'm home!" I call.

I toe off my shoes and enter the open-concept kitchen. I place the takeout bags on the counter and then I move into the attached living room. It reminds me of the inn a little bit, with all the floral patterns. I know my mother has contributed to some of the inn's decor over the years.

In the corner, Mom is snuggled in her recliner, a mass market paperback romance in her hand.

"Beatrice Ellison, is that a *dirty* book you're reading?"

She nudges her glasses further up her nose. "Mind your own business," she says. "Besides, they're not called dirty anymore. They're *open-door romances*."

I laugh, and then I point toward the kitchen. "I brought Chinese food."

"With egg rolls?"

I give her an offended look. "Of course. Who do you take me for?"

She grins, placing her book on the side table after dog-earring her page. She sets her folded glasses on top. "The best daughter I've ever had," she replies. "Does this mean you're done giving me the cold shoulder so we can talk?"

Well, damn. I've been so focused on the pounding in my skull, I forgot that I haven't exactly been on speaking terms with my mother since yesterday.

"Hacking my email, Mother?" I opt to dive right in, picking up our argument from before the meeting. "*Really?*"

She shrugs. "You need a better password."

"Well, I do *now*." I settle onto the couch opposite her chair. "What exactly was the purpose of that?"

Her sigh is full of weariness. Although she has assured me this is what she wants, I know this transition of power hasn't been easy on her. I worry she's having regrets.

"After Cherie's passing, I knew it would only be a matter of time before Jackson would be looking to get in contact. Since you've been running things, those messages would have gone to you. I wanted to get in front of it, find a way to tell you myself."

"And then you still didn't tell me. I had to find out from...*him*." It's hard to keep the contempt from my voice, but I manage. I think. "Why?"

"I'm not sure," she admits. Mom has always been brutally honest about her feelings with me, and this conversation is no different. I can see the shame in her expression. "Pride, mostly. I didn't want you to know about my struggles. Especially not when you were a child."

"But I'm not a child anymore."

"No." She shakes her head, a wistful smile curling her lips. "No, you most certainly aren't, my darling girl. I'm sorry I wasn't honest with you. I should have been a long time ago."

It's weird to think of your parent as someone who is capable of making a mistake. Adults always seemed like they had their shit together when I was a kid. Now, though, I realize we're all just a little too human for that.

Still, I have been known to hold a mean grudge from time to time. But I've never quite been able to manage that with her. My anger has already fizzled into a steady stream of frustration.

I nod. "I get it. It just...really sucked being blindsided."

Not to mention, it was humiliating. And that doesn't even touch on my behaviour from last night. Suffice to say, if I never see Jackson Vaughan again, it'll be too soon.

The smile she offers me is sad. "I promise there are no more secrets. That was my one and only."

"One too many to keep from the likes of me," I declare. "How did Cherie get mixed up in this anyway?"

"She found Dog Days by accident one summer, and she fell in love. You know that part already. What you don't know is a few decades later, when the recession hit, she offered to buy part of the business so I could stay afloat."

I sigh. "And now Jackson Vaughan, the bane of my existence, has stakes in *my* inn."

"Come now, he can't be that bad. He was perfectly nice when I met him yesterday!"

"He assumed I was a man before he met me, he wears pretentious suits, and he wants to *sell*." Sure, he didn't actually *say* that, but I just know it. I cross my arms defensively. "He's the devil come to be a pain in my ass."

I spent a great deal of time scrolling through his LinkedIn profile—because he's *totally* the type of guy who uses LinkedIn—last night, confirming most of my suspicions about him. He lives in Toronto, works at some fancy office there, and he's the son of some music producer guy.

Mom frowns. "Cherie wouldn't like the sound of that."

"I *know*, right? Like, tone down the Tom Ford. Even if it does look really goo—"

"I meant the fact that he wants to sell," she interrupts. "Did he say why? He didn't mention that during our meeting with Louis."

I grimace. "Well, he didn't *exactly* say, in so many words, that he wants to sell..."

She sends me a look that she has perfected over the years. It's the look she has given me every time she wants me to fess up about something.

"You just made an assumption," she supplies when I don't say anything.

Touché, Mama.

"Why did Cherie have to leave it to Jackson?" I lament. "Doesn't she have a more pleasant grandchild?"

A sparkle of amusement enters my mother's eyes. "Cherie had her reasons. She always thought you two would make good partners. Business and otherwise."

I cough as the notion of me and Jackson becoming a *couple* chokes me.

"As if. And you were in on it!" I scoff, and Mom simply shrugs. "What happened to setting your daughter up on a blind date like a normal mother?"

She laughs. "I know you better than that."

I glower. "Apparently not. Because your guy is *horrible.* I'm officially sinking your ship."

She pats my hand. "Cut him some slack. He just might surprise you."

"Highly doubt it."

Now, she raises a brow. "You're being awfully judgmental for a woman who was raised better than that." Then she smiles that patented soft smile. "I know you don't like change, my prickly pear, but it's not always a bad thing."

"It's not always a good thing either," I counter.

No one seems to recognize the real possibility that Jackson is *bad* at business. Having a fancy degree does not preclude you from sucking. But, like always, my concerns aren't being taken seriously.

Mom just shakes her head. "Serve me up some of that food. I'm starving."

When I make it back to Fraisier Creek after my dinner with my mom, I stop at home to feed my cat, then trek across the path to the main building to make my rounds of the inn.

Trystan, the manager in charge of the hotel aspect of the business, mans the front desk again this evening. I compliment him on the new pin tacked to his lanyard—a heart the colours of the bi flag.

I then swing by the restaurant. Even though it's only been a day, Pippa has already transitioned gracefully into her role as manager here, just as I knew she would. She's not working tonight, but the staff are keeping things running smoothly.

I always feel a bit uneasy leaving this place, like as soon as I drive out of the parking lot, a sinkhole will open and swallow the inn whole. I wonder if this is how parents feel when they start letting their children have bits of independence. It's not a pleasant feeling, which is why I barely leave.

As I'm just about to head inside my office, a thought occurs to me. I catch myself on the doorframe and stick my head back out. When Trystan finishes up with a guest, I call his name.

"Have you seen Mr. Vaughan?"

We haven't said anything official to the employees yet, but Pippa has been in the loop since the beginning, so it only seemed fair to bring Trystan in, too.

It doesn't take long for news to spread in Fraisier Creek, especially when you have an argument as loud as ours on Sunday. By now, I'm sure everyone and their mother has heard some version of the latest development, but only Pippa and Trystan know the full truth.

Trystan shakes his head. "Not since he was down for breakfast this morning." He glances at the computer and clicks a few buttons. "Looks like he checked out."

Huh.

I nod, my thoughts whirring. "Thanks."

When I fall into the chair behind the desk, I try to focus on the paperwork crowding the surface in front of me. Instead, all I can think about is Jackson.

Why did he leave? He seemed very intent on making my life miserable by inserting himself into the inn's operations, so where did he go?

Not having to face him today means that my pride has undoubtedly been spared a blow. I remember everything about our interaction last night, and there is no doubt that he does, too. The last thing I need is his smug reminder. Yet I still find myself oddly disappointed by his absence.

"Stupid Jackson Vaughan," I mutter.

Even when he's not here, he's messing with my life. With my head. I've been wanting nothing more than for him to leave, and now that he has, I question it?

My office door clicks open, and then Trystan pokes his head in. "Sorry, did you say something, Meyer?"

I wave a hand. "Just talking to myself. Don't worry about it."

He holds up a piece of paper and approaches my desk with it. "After you walked away, I remembered this was left out front for you earlier."

"Thanks, Trys."

When he leaves, I unfold the paper.

Ellison,

Sorry to disappoint, but I had to briefly head back to the city. Looking forward to our future endeavours as business partners.

—your anemone, Jackson Vaughan

My cheeks heat. For one, because I find the slight messiness of his scrawl kind of endearing. But mostly because he has a penchant for figuring out exactly how to burrow his way under my skin. To press on the bruise that is just beginning to fade.

I crumple the note and toss it toward the wastebasket. It circles the rim and promptly falls to the floor. A fitting metaphor for my life. I slump in my seat, utterly defeated.

Stupid Jackson Vaughan.

CHAPTER 8

MEYER

Five days.

Jackson hasn't shown his face in *five* days. I keep telling myself that's a good thing—I don't need said stupid face distracting me from my work—but I can't shake the anxious feeling. Like I'm just waiting for the other shoe to drop.

Mom was right when she said I'm not a fan of change. Especially when it comes to the inn. What we have going right now is working—it *has* been working for as long as my mother was in charge.

Letting Jackson come in and disrupt that flow, potentially to the detriment of the business I love with everything I have, is nerve-wracking, to say the least.

"*Fish.* Not the clean laundry!"

The fat orange tabby cat peers up at me with an unbothered expression from his spot inside my basket of laundry. Granted, it has been sitting on my bedroom floor for two weeks, so it's understandable why Fish would think it now belongs to him. But I wasn't really counting on cat hair being an accessory to my outfit today.

I found Fish in one of the inn's dumpsters a couple years ago. He was hungry and in need of a good bath, so I brought him home and nursed him back to health. As a thanks, he eats me out of house and home, and he steals my underwear.

If I'm ever running low on clean panties, I just have to look under the couch. He usually has a decent stash under there.

I nudge Fish out of the basket. He lets out a meow of discontent as he disembarks, and I can feel his glare. "Don't look at me like that," I say. "I need to find a shirt to wear to work."

Then my phone buzzes in the back pocket of my jeans, distracting me.

TRYSTAN

Jeanine called in. No one available. Can you cover?

I sigh. Of all the jobs to be done at the inn and restaurant, I don't mind most of them. Housekeeping, on the other hand, is a different story. I can barely stand doing my own laundry, let alone someone else's.

Not a problem! See you soon!

TRYSTAN

The exclamation points aren't fooling anyone, Meyer.

Fine. Housekeeping sucks!!! But I'll do it anyway.

TRYSTAN

> I know you will and that's why you're the
> best. See you soon, boss!!!

With a grin, I tuck my phone back in my pocket and rifle through the stack of folded t-shirts. I toss the one from the top of the pile onto the floor—it's predictably covered in a million orange hairs. I find one that's acceptable and begin to tug it over my head.

My arms are just about through the holes when a knock at my front door startles me. I bump into my nightstand, my knee smashing against the side.

"*Son of a bitch.*"

Fish lets out a meow that sounds strangely like a laugh. Once I have the shirt over my head, I throw a glare in his direction where he sits across the room, cleaning his paws.

"I'm beginning to regret saving your ass," I mutter. Fish only flicks his tail and saunters out of my bedroom.

Another knock sounds, so with a sigh, I follow the cat's lead. A quick glance in the bathroom mirror on my way by reveals my hair is a dishevelled mess, which adds another few seconds to the delay while I tame the strands.

In the living room, I peel back the curtain on the front window to see who is out there.

A scowl paints my lips as I throw the door open, rubbing my smarting knee in the process. "What?" I snap.

Fish takes the opportunity to dart out between my legs, bright pink panties flapping in the wind as they hang from his mouth.

Jackson watches the cat go. "I take it those are yours?" he asks.

I abandon my knee and stand up straight, crossing my arms. "No," I reply, tone sarcastic. "Fish likes to accessorize."

He gaze swings back to me. "You named your cat *Fish*?"

"Yes. It's *ironic*."

I take this moment to assess him. The last time he stood outside my front door, he was dressed in sweatpants, and I was very drunk. Today, he is wearing a navy suit, and I am, unfortunately, very sober.

Though I suppose drinking was part of my problem the other night.

"What are you doing here?" I ask.

For one, shining moment, I think he's not going to bring it up and a little of my dignity will remain intact. But apparently, I'm not that lucky.

He smirks. "I thought I'd come to you this time," he says. "Though I'm a little too sober. Have any good alcohol on hand?"

I glower, taking a step backwards. The door is just about closed when a foot is wedged in the gap.

"Wait," Jackson says.

I swing the door back open. "*What*?"

"Give me six months."

"For what? Your timely demise? That's a lot to ask of me."

Jackson looks like he's trying to cling very hard to whatever is left of his patience. "Give me six months to show you that I'm an asset."

"I don't need six months to know that you're a pain in my *ass*," I counter.

He sighs. "Ellison."

"Vaughan."

Another long-suffering sigh. "Alright, fine, you can play it your way. But I'm not going anywhere. I'll be here in Fraisier Creek, so whether you like it or not, I'll be around."

Make no mistake, I would never *like* having Jackson Vaughan in my space. In my town. His very presence is a reminder that the inn, and everything I've worked so hard for, isn't truly mine. Not fully.

And that makes me hate him just a little bit more.

I go to reply, but my eye catches on a small gift bag sitting on my front step, right beside Jackson's feet. It looks so out of place, just like the man in the fancy suit.

I point to it. "Did you bring me a gift to butter me up? Not so sorry to be the bearer of bad news, but that's not going to work."

His brows furrow as he glances down. "I have no idea what that is. It was already sitting there when I arrived."

Not entirely believing him, I take another step outside and snatch the bag up. It's bright pink and decorated in balloons, like something you would give someone for their birthday. But my birthday isn't for another few months, and neither Pippa nor Declan would leave my gift outside. They'd force me to have dinner with them and then watch as I opened my presents.

I ignore Jackson completely as I dip a hand inside the bag. When I pull the solitary object out, my confusion grows. A small teddy bear, not dissimilar to ones I had as a kid, sits in my hand. I peer inside the bag now, looking for a card or a note of some kind, but it's empty.

"Is this some kind of joke?" I ask, thrusting the bear toward Jackson.

He shakes his head, hands up in placating surrender. "I have no reason to ply you with a child's toy. It wasn't me."

My eyes narrow as I scrutinize him. After I showed up at his door, drunk, I wouldn't blame him for wanting to get back at me in some way. Maybe giving me a toy insinuates he sees me as a child, just like everyone else seems to. But, more than that, if he's telling the truth, that means there is some merit to the uneasy feeling in my gut, and I *so* do not have time for that right now.

After a moment, I decide, begrudgingly, that I believe him. "Alright," I say as I shove the bear back into the bag. Then I toss it to the floor just inside my front door, ready to forget it exists. "You're serious about the whole six months thing?"

He nods. "I am. Cherie asked it of me, and I don't intend to disappoint her."

For a fraction of a second, something like sympathy dips low in my belly, but it's gone before I can fully analyze it. That's another thing I don't have time for—feeling sorry for Jackson Vaughan. Luckily, an idea begins to form, pushing those feelings aside.

I cross my arms, cocking a hip. "Fine. You want to help, Hotshot? I'll give you something to do."

Rich boy, meet toilet brush.

———

When I show up to the inn, Jackson on my heels, and tell Trystan we are on our way to clean, he simply shakes his head, trying to contain his smile. He's no stranger to the scheming gleam in my eye.

If there's one thing I can safely assume about Jackson, it's that any kind of physical labour is foreign to him. Anyone wearing shoes as nice as his has never had to get their hands dirty. Not on his own behalf, and certainly not on behalf of anyone else. That ends today.

While I don't particularly enjoy housekeeping, I can respect how much hard work goes into it, and I'm appreciative of every person we have on our cleaning staff. It's far from an easy task.

With any luck, it will only take one shift to break Jackson. To have him running for the hills, back to his fancy condo in the city that probably gets cleaned weekly by an equally fancy team.

After a brief tutorial, I send him off to start on one room while I go to another. Because I don't do this job often, it takes me a while to get into it, but then I'm on a roll and I don't look up for an hour. When I pause to take a break, I remember that I'm meant to be coaching Jackson, so I go to check on him.

But when I get to the room he's in, I stop short in the doorway.

The sight of him with the sleeves of his white dress shirt rolled to his elbows is something out of a Harlequin romance. Or a porno. There's just something about a well-dressed man in a state of slight dishevelment that does something to a woman. And sadly, I am no exception.

Upon closer inspection, I see the sheen of sweat gathered on his brow. Usually, perspiration doesn't do it for me, but again, there's something utterly lewd about this scenario.

I hate it.

I step into the room, pretending I didn't just spend the past thirty seconds ogling him while he leaned against the dresser. I wouldn't hear the end of it if he knew. "How's it going, Molly Maid?" I ask.

"I don't know," he replies, turning to face me fully. "You tell me."

I cross my arms as I take in the space. I expect to find it worse off than when the occupants checked out earlier this morning. But as my eyes roam over the room, I'm begrudgingly surprised. My annoyance only grows when I take in his satisfied expression.

He wasn't supposed to be good at this task, but he most definitely wasn't meant to *enjoy* it. He was supposed to be broken, goddamn it. He was supposed to regret ever setting foot in Fraisier Creek.

I walk over to the dresser and run a finger over the top, right beside where he's standing. It comes back spotless, free of dust. So does the top of the TV and the ring of the lampshade.

Well, shit.

"It's...alright," I admit.

His expression is one of mild shock. "Alright? *Just* alright? Do you know how hard it was to get those condensation rings off that nightstand?"

The way he looks right now, so passionate about condensation rings, I have the strong urge to laugh. *Damn it.* He's not supposed to be *funny* either. My mouth twitches as I fight my chuckle.

Jackson notices—because *of course* he notices—and smirks. "You can laugh, Ellison," he says. "Rest assured, I won't start thinking that you like me if you do."

I shrug, unbothered. "If you need a stroke to your ego that desperately, Vaughan, just say so."

"Only if it's you who will be doing the stroking."

A warning flashes in my mind. *Danger, abort—do not travel down this road, you idiot.* I shake my head with a huff, brushing him off, as a flush creeps up my neck. Embarrassment over letting him see that I'm flustered.

I pretend to inspect the way he's made the bed, knowing it will be frustratingly perfect but needing to put my focus on something other than him. When my flaming cheeks have calmed, I turn back to him.

"So." He rocks back on his heels, looking all too pleased with himself. "Did I pass the test?"

"I don't know what you're talking about."

He nods. "Sure. We'll pretend this wasn't some kind of hoop I had to jump through in a vain effort to prove myself to you."

Double shit. Am I that transparent?

I turn on my heel and march out of the suite. "Back to work, Vaughan!" I call over my shoulder. "These rooms aren't going to clean themselves."

CHAPTER 9

MEYER

I am officially late.

On Monday mornings, the doors to the restaurant stay shuttered until eleven. Not only does this give the staff ample time to unload and put away the weekly food delivery, but it also creates a window for all the staff, not just those that work in the restaurant, to gather for meetings.

It's not unheard of for me to bring baked treats to these meetings—usually from some new recipe I wanted to try out, or when I feel particularly stressed—so when I woke up at four and couldn't get back to sleep, I decided this particular Monday called for blueberry muffins.

As I gathered the ingredients in the small kitchen of my cottage, moonlight bleeding in through the window above the sink, my eyes kept catching on the stack of papers sitting on the island.

The cause of my fitful rest is not something that would require a professional to deduce. The presence of those papers—the ones the lawyer had personally delivered the evening before, with another grating remark about how young I am—signify that my life is about to significantly change.

All that's left is two signatures—mine and Jackson's.

Driven to distraction by my worries, I didn't notice that Fish had hopped up onto the counter. In typical Fish fashion, my cat couldn't care less that he's not allowed up there. In fact, I'm certain he does it for the attention. But when I didn't scold him right away, he took to rubbing up against the big bag of flour that still sat open.

That was how I wound up cleaning the infernal white powder off of almost every surface in my kitchen.

By the time my mess was clean and the muffins were cooling, I was running late, though a punctual arrival was still salvageable. Until I saw myself in the bathroom mirror and realized the kitchen wasn't the only thing affected by Fish's troublemaking.

I jumped in the shower when it was still freezing cold, the cottage's water heater not as quick to heat as it used to be. From there, things only got worse. When I lathered my hair, I got shampoo in my eye. Then I realized my legs needed to be shaved, and in the process, I nicked myself—not once, but twice.

And the cherry on top of my saga of bad luck: the shower mat decided to come loose as I was stepping out of the tub, causing me to perform a haphazard version of the splits while I caught myself on the shower curtain.

So not only am I officially late to work, but my hair is still damp, wetting my shirt, and my shin is starting to bruise from my near-slip, causing my fast walk across the gravel path to look more like a hobble.

As I near the entrance to the restaurant, I force a steadying breath.

My mom introduced me to baking when I was a kid. It had been a favourite pastime of hers, something she did with her own mother, and she wanted to share that with me. I've never been one to get caught up in the particulars of life, but the precision of baking has always fascinated me. One wrong move, one mismeasurement, and your whole recipe is ruined.

I once tried to bake a cake for Mom's birthday. It was the first time I had endeavoured to make something on my own. Instead of arriving home from work to the sight of a perfectly iced birthday cake, she found me crying over the collapsed blob I had somehow created. Turns out, I had added too much of one ingredient and not enough of another.

Sometimes, I feel like that cake. Or, more accurately, I fear turning into that cake. As if I'll make one wrong decision and my life will deflate around me like a recipe gone wrong.

Baking—the careful control I have over the measurements —grounds me. It also doesn't hurt that everyone in town heaps on the praise whenever they get a taste of one of my desserts. Even the owner of the local bakery has joked that she's glad I have the inn to keep me busy or else I'd run her out of business.

Even though this day has started out as a colossal disaster —and all too soon, I'll be faced with Jackson yet again, who has aggravatingly stuck to his word and not left me alone the past few days—nothing will take the joy out of getting to share my muffins with my staff.

And honestly, I'm not above a little bribery.

During today's staff meeting, Jackson and I are going to officially announce our new positions as co-owners of the inn. I'm certain everyone has already heard, but I don't want to take that for granted. I trust my employees, and in return, I want them to trust me.

To say I'm a little worried about their reactions is an understatement. With my mother officially retiring, things have been a little up in the air, which is why I've tried to keep things around the inn from changing. I don't want to scare them off.

Chatter greets me as I step into the restaurant, letting a small smile grace my lips. Then I ready myself to announce that I come bearing gifts when all of a sudden, I see—

What the fuck?

Cookies. Giant cookies.

I've heard about the new shop that just opened in Calderville. Their claim to fame is giant cookies baked in a variety of flavours, including some that are filled inside. Pippa took Atticus there the other day after school and she said his eyes almost fell out of his head at the sight of the sweet treats.

The fact that a whole box of these cookies is being passed around to all the staff rankles me. It's clear from his showboaty expression that Jackson was the one to bring them. Something a lot like inferiority slithers in my gut.

Who needs a stupid homemade muffin when you can have a stuffed cookie half the size of your face?

As everyone around me raves about the cookies, I silently ponder my next move. Do I barge in with my muffins anyway? Or do I dump them in the office and pretend they never existed? Neither option sounds appealing enough to get me to make my move.

Then Jackson turns from a conversation with Winona, spotting me immediately. He sidles up to me, and in his hands, a box half-full of those cookies stares back up at me.

"Want one?" he asks.

The offering, coupled with the amused tilt of his lips, is too much. Tears sting the backs of my eyes. No one is looking at me—no one but Jackson—so I turn abruptly on my heel, decision made for a hasty escape.

I truly thought my horrible morning couldn't get any worse. I thought all my bad luck was spent. How foolish.

Maybe it's childish, running off. *They're just cookies, Meyer, get it together.* But I need to leave before I say something I'll regret. Sharp, bitter words lace my tongue.

A hand catches my elbow as I reach the lip of the corridor. Shaking Jackson off, I make a beeline for the office. He's still hot on my heels, so I don't even bother attempting to close the door behind me.

Though I would love nothing more than to slam it in his face.

The tray of muffins clatters to the desk. My back to Jackson, I brace myself against the sturdy piece of furniture. I bite my lip, hard, as I blink furiously to will away the unwanted tears.

"Are you okay?"

He's a lot closer than I want him to be. He hasn't touched me again, but I can feel his presence hovering just over my shoulder. Watching. Analyzing.

I clear my throat. "I'm fine," I say. With one final hard

blink, I turn around. Jackson's honey eyes roam over me. I ignore this, searching through the purse on my shoulder until I find the stack of papers. Those goddamn papers. I wish I could set them on fire. "Mr. Montaigne dropped these off last night."

He doesn't ask what they are. He knows. He *knew*. He knew about Cherie's hand in all this. Maybe not always, but he certainly knew before me, and that leaves me feeling at a disadvantage. Yet again.

Jackson barely grasps the pages before I retract my hand, like he's a live wire and I'm in danger of electrocution. I watch as he scribbles an initial here and there. Then my intake of breath is sharp when he signs the last page.

He offers me the pen, and *fuck*, it's like he's holding out that stupid box of cookies all over again.

What's worse is that in his gaze is the absolute last thing I want to see. Understanding.

"We can wait," he says. "We don't have to do this right now."

Well, he can try, but Jackson Vaughan *doesn't* understand me. He doesn't understand me at all.

I pluck the pen from his fingers. Quickly, so I don't think on it too hard, I flip through the pages, initialing and signing. Then I drop the pen.

"There." I shove the papers toward him.

"I'll get them to the lawyer after the meeting."

I nod stiffly. "Fine."

His gaze is still probing. "Ready to head back?" he asks.

I nod again, making my way out the door. I hear Jackson

follow me out, but I don't slow my pace. When we enter the restaurant, all eyes turn to us.

"That cookie was bloody delicious," Marsaili, one of the housekeepers, says. Her Scottish lilt has never fully gone away, even though she's lived in Canada for over thirty years. "Between that and my breakfast, I've got no room left."

"I hope you have a bit of room," Jackson says, "or else I'll have to keep all of Ms. Ellison's muffins for myself."

Turning to him, I find he's holding the muffin tray I purposefully left on the desk.

Marsaili perks up. "Blueberry?" she asks me.

I clear my throat. "Yeah. I know it's a fan favourite."

"Give 'er here, lad. Perhaps I'll just have a wee taste."

Her *wee* taste turns into her devouring the whole thing. Everyone else follows suit, and as I watch the baked goods quickly disappear, I'm reminded that I do have people in my corner.

Jackson passes the tray around and eventually takes his own.

His intention is clear, and begrudgingly, I appreciate him a little for it. Even feel a bit sorry for intending to bribe the staff. Then I remember that he did the same thing and the guilt melts away.

Well played, Vaughan.

When everyone seems to be satisfied, well on their way to a sugar high from the sweet treats, I settle into my place at the front of the room. Jackson stands beside me.

From the crowd, Pippa's eyes find mine. She mouths, *Everything okay?*

I offer her a small nod. I had my moment of weakness, of

breaking down, but now I'm here to do what I have to do. And that is surviving the next six months.

"Alright," I say, and the group of employees grows quiet. "I have an announcement to make. I'm sure most of you have probably already heard, but I wanted to do this anyway."

I take a deep breath as I let my gaze settle over my employees. Some of them are newer, but a lot of them, I grew up following around as they worked. They were loyal to my mother, and I hope they'll remain loyal to me.

"I'd like to formally introduce you all to Jackson Vaughan, my...business partner," I continue. "His grand-mother, Cherie Cheval, was a silent partner when my mother ran Dog Days. Jackson has inherited her half of the business, and I have taken over my mother's."

My spine stiffens when I hear someone mutter under their breath, "And now we're all doomed."

Doomed.

I struggle to find words. I can feel Jackson looking at me, wondering why I stopped, but I can't speak. He quickly takes a step forward, addressing the group in that smooth voice of his.

And I try to be present, to smile at the right moments, but all the while I keep wondering when my cake is going to deflate.

CHAPTER 10

JACKSON

AFTER SIGNING the papers and informing the staff of our official status as business partners, Meyer and I have fallen into something of a routine.

Since going home to pack enough clothes for my extended stay in Fraisier Creek and then arriving back in town, I've done little but gain my bearings. The first day, I moved into my room at the inn—the same one Meyer came to that night, banging on my door in her drunken passion. Then I took to acquainting myself with the rest of the building and the grounds.

The first couple days, every time I saw her, Meyer's shoulders would crowd her ears. She tensed whenever we were in the vicinity of one another, like she thought I might do something to force a fight or flight reaction out of her.

When I didn't do anything to overtly offend her, she almost got more suspicious. For the next few days, I could feel her eyes trailing me everywhere I went.

After that, she finally relaxed. I'm not sure what she

thought I was doing, but whatever it was, she seemed happy I was steering clear of her and all inn business.

But that stops today.

Observation is my specialty, and while Meyer has been worried about my inaction where she's concerned, I've been doing reconnaissance. Meyer has made me her enemy, and everyone knows you don't walk into the territory of your foe without first making a plan.

The office door—the one I'd just shut when I heard Meyer making the first of her typical hourly rounds—bangs into the wall. Just as I predicted it would. The *Do Not Disturb* sign I hastily put together earlier is crumpled in her fist.

"What the hell are you doing?"

There's a spark of rage in her blue eyes, and seeing it pleases me. Is it messed up that I find joy in annoying the shit out of her? Yeah, probably. Is it even more messed up that I find the angry flush on her face incredibly attractive? Definitely.

"Ellison," I say, tipping back in the wonky desk chair. It's definitely going on my list of things that will need to be replaced. "Lovely morning, isn't it?"

"It *was*," she says through gritted teeth. She holds a to-go cup from the same café I was patron to a few hours ago, and she brandishes it like a sword, ready to cut me down. "I repeat. What the hell are you doing in *my* office?"

Trying to ignore the bags under my eyes from my restless night. That, and the tightness in my chest. The band of anxiety that held me captive as I tried to sleep. When all else fails, I turn to work.

So after a fitful night, I rose at five and got ready for the day. I drove to the café on Main and was this morning's first customer. I was so early, I had to wait for the coffee machines to wake up. Not that I should be having much caffeine, especially with how I'm feeling, but I'd need to inject it intravenously if I wanted to be able to function properly.

By six o'clock, I had my ass in this lumpy chair, poring over paperwork. Whatever I could get my hands on, really—financial reports, supply orders, employee files. My hunger for data was insatiable. Looking at me then, you would think I was right back at my office in Toronto. Like I hadn't even left, prioritizing work over my health.

I guess some things really don't change.

"Hate to break it to you, but all *this*," I say, twirling a finger in the air, "belongs to me as much as it belongs to you."

Catching Meyer's glare with my own eyes is pointless when I can *feel* it singeing my skin. Especially when her gaze rakes down my body. She takes in my suit jacket draped over the back of the chair, the sleeves of my shirt rolled to my forearms, the loosened knot of my tie. I look like a man who's had a long day—not a man whose day is only just beginning.

Her eyes snap back to mine. "You look like shit."

I place a hand on my chest. "*Ouch*," I say. "Nice deflection, though."

But beneath my palm, my heart pounds a bit harder than it should. Back home, my haggard appearance would be a badge of honour. Here, under Meyer's scrutiny, I've never felt more insecure in my life. I've known this woman for about two weeks collectively and already she's seeing right through me.

She doesn't know *what* she's seeing—and she won't, if I can help it—but she recognizes it all the same. It's rather unnerving. I'm here to complete a task, not be picked apart by my business partner's shrewd gaze.

She reminds me of Cherie, in a way. My grandmother, with her take-no-prisoners attitude and her blunt way of speaking, wouldn't hesitate to tell me if I looked terrible. If I looked like I was on the verge of collapsing again. Meyer's brutal honesty is somewhat refreshing. It's something I've missed since Cherie has been gone.

"*Vaughan.*"

I sit forward in my chair, startled back to reality. "What?"

Based on the strange look she's giving me, I definitely spaced out. That IV full of coffee is looking more and more appealing by the minute.

She cocks her head, scrutinizing me again. Then she shakes it. "I asked you—for the *third time*, might I add—what the hell you're doing."

"Compiling data."

She mutters something under her breath that sounds vaguely like the word *nerd*. I hide a smile behind my fist, not prepared for her to see how amusing I find her. That would only make her resistance stronger.

"Has anyone ever told you that you share too much?" she asks dryly. "Compiling data on *what*?"

"Everything," I reply. "I need to know this place inside out in order to create an optimization strategy."

"And why would you do that?"

"To ensure all of the processes we employ are running efficiently. Recognizing changes to be made to smooth them out further if necessary."

"Absolutely not."

I continue, as if she hasn't spoken. "First optimization strategy: we need to fire Reggie Gaines."

I officially render her slack-jawed for all of two seconds before she clamps her lips together tightly. And then she begins to protest, as I suspected she would.

"We're not firing anyone," she declares.

I sigh, leaning back in the chair again. It groans beneath me. "We're wasting money on his salary, Ellison. He doesn't do his job. The other kitchen staff have to pick up his slack, which wastes their time."

"He's worked here for *five years*!"

"That may be the case, but that doesn't preclude him from being lazy. In the individual interviews I conducted—"

"You *interviewed my staff*?" Meyer's voice has grown shrill.

"*Our* staff, Ellison. I talked to our staff."

She shakes her head. "We can't fire Reggie."

A noise of frustration leaks out of me, unbidden. "This laissez-faire leadership style you've got going on isn't working for me."

She scoffs. "Yeah? Well, you being a smug asshole isn't working for *me*."

I brace my hands on the desk and stand. "I'm trying to work with you, but you keep shutting me down."

Meyer looks up at me, hate in her cool gaze. "Because I don't want you here!"

"Above all else, we're running a business," I try to explain. Try to return to my rational brain. Getting into a shouting match with her won't help matters. "It's nothing personal."

"*Everything* is personal in a small town."

I shake my head. "Your mother gave him more than his fair share of warnings, Meyer. It's all documented in his file. He's lucky he's been given this long."

"We're *not* firing Reggie." She slams her cup down on the desk. Some of the coffee escapes the opening and lands on the back of her hand, and by the way she flinches, I assume it's still scorching. "Son of a bitch!"

I sigh. "Are you alright?"

She doesn't answer. She just glares. I retake my seat, running a hand over my face as my bone-deep exhaustion hits me once again.

I have to look away when Meyer laves her skin with her tongue, clearing away the coffee and simultaneously nursing the burn. It shouldn't be enticing at all, yet it has my mind wandering to places it shouldn't.

"You cleaned."

It's not a statement but an accusation. I deem it safe to return my gaze to her and find Meyer now glaring at the newly organized files.

"What? Do you have something against tidiness, too?" I ask.

My office in Toronto is pristine. Scratch that, my whole life in the city is pristine. I stepped one foot into this office and instantly had the desire to spend a small fortune at the office supply store. The space wasn't dirty by any means, but it was messy. How Meyer ever managed to find anything was nothing short of a miracle.

She crosses her arms. "I had a system."

"Well, now you have a *new* system. One that doesn't make my eye twitch."

She reaches both hands in front of her and mimes strangulation. I try, honestly, but I can't hold back the laugh that escapes me. Her ire, though meant to be formidable, only draws me into her orbit more.

With a grin, I say, "Now there's no need for violence, Ellison."

"You're a prick," she spits.

"And *you* are the most stubborn woman I've ever met," I reply. "I take it we won't be seeing eye to eye on this Reggie business."

Her lip curls into a smirk. "At least you've got something right."

Resigned, I sigh again. A headache has been edging into my brain all morning, and now it's finally making its full appearance. I rub at my temple, trying to soothe the flair of pain.

Coffee and an ibuprofen. That's what I need.

I stand again, reaching for my jacket from the back of the chair. Instead, I have to brace against it when a wave of dizziness clouds my vision.

My head swims, and I'm sure I'm seeing things, but Meyer's expression seems to soften. Fractionally. Try as she might to keep it concealed, my business partner has a heart. I'm sure it eats her up inside that she can't feel completely indifferent toward me.

But I would take her chilling hatred over indifference any day. It sets something off inside me, this inherent need to get under her skin.

"You puke, you clean it" is all she says. But I think I see worry behind that uncaring façade, and I'm fucking sick of all the worry. So I straighten, pulling on my jacket, and I will myself to stay steady.

"I'm going to get some air," I say. "Try not to miss me too much while I'm gone."

She tosses the balled up paper at my retreating back. It falls short, hitting the floor behind me. "Trust me, there's no risk of that."

My laugh follows me out the door.

CHAPTER 11

MEYER

With a sigh, I flop against the back of Pippa's couch.

Beside me, my best friend quirks a brow. "Alright," she says, "that's the tenth dramatic sigh in as many minutes. What's wrong?"

My lips curl into a sneer. "Jackson Vaughan is what's wrong. His presence in my life. His existence, period."

What little money I've managed to save for retirement is officially being earmarked for bail. Because I'm one self-righteous remark away from wrapping my hands around his pretty boy neck, and not in the fun way.

I knew trying to be business partners with Jackson would be hard, but I didn't expect to feel so out of control. He's only been back for a week, but I'm already wishing the six months had passed and Jackson would be returning to the city, tail tucked between his legs.

A futile wish, though, since the powers that be seem hell-bent on ignoring me.

Instead, I'm left to suffer. The man rearranged my office.

My sanctuary. My mother hadn't spent much time keeping things orderly when she was in charge, too busy being present with the staff. I followed her lead. Everything had a place, even if that place didn't make sense to him.

Now, I spend half my days searching for the things I need and letting out a curse of frustration when Jackson tries to explain his theory of organization. I usually tune him out.

Pippa doesn't react to my outburst. Even wearing mismatched pajamas with her long red hair trapped in a messy bun, she still exudes poise. She may get flustered and blush something fierce from time to time, but she's self-assured. I envy that.

I pick up another slice of pizza and shove it into my mouth. Even the greasy comfort food from the pie shop downtown can't erase my bad mood.

Pippa sighs. "What happened this time?"

"He keeps trying to change things," I reply. I frown as I pick at a piece of pepperoni. "Just because he's got a fancy MBA and I don't doesn't mean he's better than me."

All of my insecurities—about failing my mom and running the inn into the ground—gain strength when Jackson talks about optimization strategies and efficient processes.

Well, screw optimization and efficiency. The Ellison Way works just fine, and it will *continue* to work just fine.

Pippa dropped out of university when she came to Fraisier Creek with Atticus, so she knows all too well what it's like living in a world that overvalues post-secondary education.

"That's true." She nods. "It's not a matter of one of you being better than the other. You both have your strengths."

I snort. "Yeah, and his is being a pain in my ass."

An amused smile crosses Pippa's lips. "You know, for hating the guy so much, you sure do spend a *lot* of time discussing him," she muses. "He's really all you seem capable of talking about these days."

"Are you for real?" I say, my voice muffled through my mouthful of food. I swallow. "Pip, he's *everywhere*. In my office, at the restaurant. No matter what I do, he's just *there*. So I think I have a right to complain."

She takes a bite of her own slice—smaller, much more graceful than me. As she chews, she contemplates. Unlike me, she doesn't talk at all until she has swallowed.

"What he's suggesting... Is it really so bad?"

I cringe, hating the flicker of betrayal I feel. "Not you, too..."

Tears prick my eyes. I will them away, gaze focused on the pizza I suddenly no longer have an appetite for. I toss my half-eaten slice back in the box and wipe my fingers on my pants. They're black, so at least the grease won't show.

"Meyer," Pippa says softly, "don't shut down on me."

I sniffle. "Change makes me itchy."

Pippa's lips quirk slightly. She places a hand on my knee and gives me the loving mom look she's perfected for Atticus. And me, I guess. She may only be two months older, but she's taken to parenting me from time to time.

"I know, babe. But like it or not, you're not in this alone."

"I choose *not*."

At this, she laughs. "*Clearly*. However, since neither one of you seems keen on walking away, you're going to have to figure something out. You can't just veto everything he suggests. Just like he can't bulldoze his way in and change everything you love about the place."

I huff, crossing my arms. "Quit saying such reasonable things."

Deep down, I know Pippa is probably right. Seeing as there isn't anything I can do—*legally*, that is—to get rid of Jackson, I'm going to have to learn to live with him for now.

Pippa sets a hand on my arm. "I know it's hard, but maybe *try* to meet him halfway. Some kind of middle ground. If he's the type of guy I suspect he is, he'll follow you there."

I raise a suspicious brow. "How would you know what type of guy he is?"

"Because I've *talked* with him. Genuine conversations. Something you should maybe think about doing."

"You really should be saving all this motherly wisdom for your son, you know," I say.

She gives my arm a squeeze and then returns to her slice of pizza. "Don't worry. There is plenty of my smarts to go around."

I pick up my slice of pizza again. "Alright, enough of my depressing shit. What's going on in the world of Pippa Rhodes?"

She shrugs. "Nothing new."

Despite what she says, I know that tone. My eyes narrow. While I tend to overshare between the two of us, Pippa does the opposite. Luckily for her, I'm here to make sure she doesn't bottle everything up and hurt herself in the process.

Now it's her turn to deposit a half-eaten slice back into the box. Her shoulders slump. "I got another email from my mom," she explains. "They want me to come back home."

It took many months of Pippa living in one of the rooms at the inn when she first arrived for me to coax her story out of her. Even then, I'm sure I don't know all of it. What I do know is that Pippa and Declan's parents are pieces of work who don't deserve their children or their grandson.

"Fuck that! You and Atticus belong in Fraisier Creek. You're not going anywhere."

She looks down at her hands. "They blame me for Declan leaving."

I scoff. "They need to look in the goddamn mirror. Besides, he's a grown man who can make his own decisions."

I know Pippa has never regretted leaving home, despite how much her parents try to guilt her into believing it. But when her brother followed in her footsteps and showed up in town with nothing but the clothes on his back, I knew she felt bad. Like it was her fault for showing him a different life was possible when it was really the best gift she could've ever given him.

She shivers. "Alright, let's not talk about them anymore. They're ruining my appetite for perfectly good pizza."

For her sake and mine, I change the subject entirely, and we forget about Jackson and her parents for the rest of the night.

———

I regret eating so much pizza.

Usually, I can put away a good three slices no problem, but tonight, the food sloshes in my stomach with unease. I thought just going to bed would help, but that has only made it worse.

I lie on my back, staring up at my bedroom ceiling. I used to have some of those glow-in-the-dark stars stuck up there, but over the years, they've fallen down. All but one. That lonely star sits in the corner, mocking me.

A loud meow shatters the quiet, and then Fish jumps onto my bed. He prowls across the mattress until he climbs on top of me. Despite my protests, he kneads his paws into my boobs, and then he plops all his weight onto my sternum. I let out an *oomph*.

"I saw you with those lace panties earlier. Did you at least return them?"

It's dark, but I can just picture his unbothered expression. The simple *no* to my question.

I begin to stroke his back. Sometimes, he deigns to purr for me. Tonight is not one of those times. Still, he doesn't leave. He just lets his weight soothe me, little by little.

"Am I a failure, Fish?" I ask. He chirps in response, as if to say *yes*. "That's it. No more catnip for you, buddy."

With a resigned sigh, I close my eyes, and I try again to fall asleep. Instead, my mind continues to race. It's in the dark, when I'm completely alone, that I contemplate everything.

All I've ever wanted is to make my mother proud. To channel all this love I have for the business into something beautiful. When I was a kid, I conjured up grandiose plans of what I would do once the inn was mine one day. Now that that day is here, I'm paralyzed by fear.

How did my mother ever think I would be good enough for this?

After another futile attempt at sleep, I nudge Fish off my chest and then sit up. I grab my phone off my nightstand, the brightness illuminating my face in the otherwise dark room. Good thing I picked it up—it's nearly dead, and without an alarm clock, it's my only defence against sleeping in.

I plug my phone into the charger, and then I fire up my trusty search engine. My latest trivial questions feel like a bad omen as I type my new search terms. *College business programs.*

I spend some time reading about online courses, and an in-person one at the college in Calderville. The forward momentum feels good at first. Exciting.

When I was in my last year of high school, I didn't spend hours researching universities and colleges like the other students. I knew exactly what I wanted, and what I wanted was the inn.

I stop in my tracks, thumb hovering over my phone screen. Am I really about to change myself because some guy is trying to flex his business prowess? I never saw anything past high school in my future. Not because I thought I couldn't do it, but because I didn't *want* to.

I think it's really rare to find your place in this world so young. My place, undoubtedly, is the inn. I didn't want to waste a second of my time with it by going to school. I still don't.

I slam my phone down on my nightstand harder than

necessary. I should care that I've maybe cracked the screen, but I'm too keyed up to care about much of anything other than my raging dislike of Jackson Vaughan.

He's been here for two seconds and he's already come in swinging, like one of those cranes with a big wrecking ball attached. The only thing standing between him and the impending wreckage is *me*. My mother trusted me to do right by her. I'm not taking that lightly.

Meet in the middle? Sorry, Pippa. It's high time I really dig my heels in.

Meyer Ellison is not going down without a fight.

CHAPTER 12

JACKSON

Despite the wary looks I receive from the townsfolk now that news of my involvement with the inn has spread, my day started out relatively good.

After a short, doctor-approved workout at the gym in town to work on getting my strength back up, I hit the café for some breakfast. And coffee. Can't forget the coffee. Even strolling into the inn, I was looking forward to what greeted me.

Any contentment falls out the window as soon as I step into the office.

Meyer sits behind the desk, holding herself in that janky chair as if she's resting on a throne, presiding over her kingdom. All around her are bankers boxes. An excessive amount of bankers boxes.

"What is all this?" I ask, slowly perusing the room.

Meyer's eyes hold a thread of mischief I haven't seen before. So far, I've been met with nothing short of contempt.

This almost feels...playful. I'm not entirely sure what to do with that.

She sits straight in the chair, a sly smile curving her lips. "*This* is Fraisier Creek history, Vaughan."

I eye a particularly large stack of boxes to my left. "What did you do? Rob the archives?"

I'm not sure a town the size of Fraisier Creek even *has* archives, but clearly Meyer managed to get all this from somewhere. She must've been up half the night hauling all of this in here since she also managed to beat me into the office.

"You wanted data," she reminds me. "So I brought you data."

I'd be annoyed if I wasn't half in awe of her.

"I did say that, but I didn't mean every town record dating back to its inception. I was talking about the inn."

Meyer wags her finger. "See, I think that's *exactly* what you need. To understand the inn is to understand the town."

She pulls the lid off the box closest to her and reaches inside. Then with a thud, she lets the various books and piles of paper hit the surface of the desk. A cloud of dust shoots into the air, indicating these materials haven't been touched in a good long while.

"Seriously, where did you get these?" I ask again.

"It's like I told you. Everything is personal in Fraisier Creek, and it's all about who you know. I would think someone like you would be all too familiar with that concept."

I sigh. "Meyer—"

"As a bonus," she continues, as if I hadn't spoken, "I even

brought my old diaries so you can read all about the crush I had on my math teacher in grade eleven."

"As much as reading your teenage ramblings appeals to me," I say, "don't you think this is a waste of my time?"

She shakes her head. "Nope."

"Why?"

She stands from the chair and rounds the desk. When she's in my space, I can clearly see her eyes—always so startling blue. Now, they have a spark of retribution in them.

"Because, Vaughan, I want you to know exactly what you're trying to destroy."

I pinch the bridge of my nose as another sigh falls out of me. "I'm not *destroying* anything."

"That's a matter of opinion."

It seems no matter what I do, Meyer is always going to have this idea of me in her head. This role I'm meant to play. As long as she keeps this wall between us, we aren't going to get very far, and I only have a limited amount of time here.

"Ashley called in sick, so if you need me, I'll be covering in the restaurant," she says. She does a little condescending finger wave. "Happy reading."

She leaves the room with a flourish, and then it's just me and all the boxes.

When I settle into the chair she just vacated, it makes a slow descent to the lowest setting, as if it, too, is mad at me. Instead of sitting comfortably at the desk, all I can manage is to rest my chin on the surface.

I huff out a frustrated breath as I stand again, pushing the broken chair to the side. Then I drag one of the other chairs around to sit behind the desk.

Number one on my to-do list: order a new fucking chair.

As I sit and contemplate all the boxes surrounding me, I realize something. The key to getting her to cooperate is understanding why she's so reluctant in the first place.

It's not the town I have to study—it's Meyer. And I happen to be a very good student.

———

Hours pass, and I make them count. I don't touch the town history like she wanted me to, but I do succumb to my curiosity and flip through her old diary. I normally wouldn't, but the temptation was too great, and she left it right there on the desk.

Teenage Meyer was exactly as I expected. The perfect blend of angst and rage at the world, mixed with a certain kind of vulnerability that comes with trying to find your place in it. If I had to guess, the adult version of her isn't as different as she wants everyone to believe.

When Meyer enters the office, I don't even have to look up. Partially because I can smell her intoxicating floral perfume, but also because I have begrudgingly developed a sixth sense for her. Since that first day, my body has become finely attuned to her presence.

"You're kind of a workaholic, Vaughan."

For the first time in my life, that sounds like a bad thing.

I set aside the book I was holding and lean back in my chair. "You're one to talk."

She crosses her arm, cocking a hip. "What's that supposed to mean?"

"You haven't taken a single day off since I got here."

"How would you know?"

I hesitate. The real answer is something I'm not sure I should divulge. *I've been watching you* admittedly sounds a bit creepy. But I can't help it. She intrigues me.

"All my staff interviews have one thing in common," I say instead. "They literally all mentioned your inability to relax."

This makes her tense. "You talked about me?"

I study her. Her posture is rigid, but something a lot like worry flashes in her gaze. She's quick to mask it, but it's too late—I've already seen.

I want to set her mind at ease. I don't want her to think that I'm trying to go behind her back to dig up information on her. She already doesn't trust me. That would push her over the edge.

"I'm pleased to report that everyone loves you. So much so that they were all very unsure about talking to me. I essentially had to beg for information."

A bit of hyperbole on my part, but what the staff think of Meyer is nothing short of the truth. They essentially all told me that Beatrice had been an excellent employer. Since Meyer took over the day-to-day operations, it's been no different. This town sure loves its Ellisons.

"What else did you talk about?"

There's still a wariness about her, but her tone now borders on curious. I'm counting that as a win, small as it may be.

"I asked them the same question I asked you," I say. "What their favourite thing is about working here. If they had any suggestions of ways we could make their jobs easier to do."

"Asking for their input isn't a revolutionary concept around here. We have a suggestion box," she says. "And I make a point to check in with them all the time."

I nod. "They told me that, too. But sometimes that makes it harder."

Now, she truly can't hide her curiosity. I have to stop myself from smiling. "How so?" she asks.

"As I said, they all loved your mom. They love you. So it's understandable that they would be a little apprehensive about suggesting any changes." When she still looks confused, I elaborate. "They don't want to hurt you."

This catches her by surprise. She looks like she wants to say more, but she doesn't. She just studies me, like maybe she's seeing something different than she has all the times before.

I stand from the desk, ready to call it a night. My stomach is seconds away from eating itself, but my body also craves sleep. Sleep I haven't been able to give it.

"You know, we're not all that different, you and I."

At this, Meyer scoffs. "We're not even remotely the same. The things we want couldn't be more different."

"How do you know what I want?" I counter. "You've never asked."

"I just do."

I nod. "Right. Very sound reasoning you've got there."

With a roll of her eyes, she says, "*Fine*. What do you want out of all this?"

For as long as I can remember, I've been goal-oriented. I lock onto something and sprint in its direction—damn anyone or anything that gets in my way. But in the face of Meyer's question, I'm more lost than I've ever been before.

I sigh. "Truthfully, Ellison, I don't know. I just know that I don't want to be the villain in your story, but I don't know how to do that."

She's quiet for a beat, following me as I exit the office and start down the hallway. "I don't know either," she admits.

We let the silence settle between us as we head for the stairs. We ascend, and then we start toward my room.

I glance sidelong at her. "Is there a reason you're walking me to my room?"

She doesn't look my way when she replies, just keeps her gaze trained on the patterned carpet under our feet. "Because you look like death, and I can't have you keeling over in my inn."

In danger of seeming like she cares too much—scratch that, cares *at all*—she opens her mouth to add a sarcastic remark, like she often does. I seem to have the same idea.

"Too much paperwork," we both say at the same time.

It's a stupid, unoriginal joke. Lame, even. But in my tired state, it sounds *hilarious*. Meyer seems to think so, too, given the slight upward curve of her lips that she tries to hide.

"Get out of my brain," she huffs.

I grin. "See? Not so different."

She reaches out and shoves at my shoulder. I can almost feel her touch through my sleeve. "All that proves is your boringness is rubbing off on me."

When we make it to my room, I unlock the door and push inside. Turning, I lean against the doorframe as I look down at her, ready to bid her goodnight.

Meanwhile, Meyer not-so-subtly tries to peer around me into my room. I open the door wider and take a step back, sweeping an arm out. "Since you seem so interested, you might as well come in."

She accepts the invitation, gaze searching the room. "You haven't let housekeeping in since you've been here. I was just curious as to why."

I shrug. "I'm going to be staying here for a while. They don't need to constantly be cleaning up after me."

"Hmm," she hums as she continues to walk the room.

I turn to hang my jacket in the wardrobe, and then I spin back around. She's standing by the bed now.

I eye her warily. "Are *you* feeling alright? This sudden concern for my wellbeing is concerning in itself."

She rolls her eyes. "Excuse me for trying to be nice. I won't make that mistake again."

I laugh as she heads for the exit. "Goodnight, Ellison."

She waves over her shoulder and then shuts the door behind her.

I should go find something to have for dinner, but my body is calling for my bed, so I flop onto the mattress and settle against the pillows. I inhale deeply and then let it out slowly, trying to convince my body to relax.

It isn't until the next morning that I wake, actually feeling rested for once. When I turn toward the window, I notice the sun is high in the sky. It's long after I should've been roused by the beep of my alarm. I turn to the bedside table, and a scowl tugs at my lips.

Last night while she was in my room, Meyer unplugged my fucking alarm clock.

CHAPTER 13
MEYER

I flinch at the tone of his voice. Naively, I thought this conversation would go a lot smoother. We both know he messed up—the proverbial final nail in his coffin.

"Reggie," I say, trying to inject some remorse into my voice. Even though I'm the farthest from remorseful. "It's unfortunate, but we need someone we can rely on to get the job done. And...someone who doesn't steal."

I *hate* to admit it, but Jackson was right about this. About Reggie. I should have listened and cut him loose before he decided to try his hand at lifting money from the register.

After Jackson spilled the beans about his interviews with the rest of the kitchen staff, I went and spoke to them myself. They admitted the same thing to me—that Reggie makes their jobs harder by not doing his fair share. Then I went and spoke to him. I *told* him what would happen if he didn't clean up his act. Yet here we are.

We're sitting in the office, me in the chair behind the desk and him directly across from me. I called him in here a few minutes ago, despite the nerves that plagued me. But I got us into this mess, so I'll be the one to get us out.

My phone buzzes on the desk beside my elbow, an irritated text from Jackson flashing on the screen, but I ignore it and focus on the task at hand.

"That's a bullshit accusation," he replies. His fingers are wrapped around the arms of his chair, his knuckles white.

I sigh. "I checked the cameras. I saw you." Not to mention, Ashley had brought it to my attention as soon as she noticed the float was short.

"*Bullshit.*"

"Reggie, I know this is hard, but—"

The door to the office swings open then, and Jackson enters looking none too pleased. I figured he probably wouldn't be happy when he realized I sabotaged his wakeup time. It only takes him a second to register what's going on, though, and then he rounds the desk to stand beside me, crossing his arms.

Reggie glares. "Oh, so now you need backup so you can gang up on me?"

I shake my head. "No. Jackson is my business partner, he has every right to be here. But this meeting is between you and me."

Because this Reggie is not the Reggie that I know. I'm firing him, yes, but I also want to help him. If something is going on in his personal life, I want to be there for him. Up until this year, he was a model employee.

"I can no longer have you working here," I reiterate. "But

if something is going on with you, Reggie, I want to help. I—"

"You're a fucking bitch, Meyer Ellison," he spits, cutting me off. "A certified, ice cold bitch."

The words slam into me as if he physically threw out his palm and let it connect with my cheek in a reverberating *smack*. My ears ring with his words.

Jackson tenses beside me. "What did you just say?"

Reggie is stupid enough to meet his eyes. "You heard me."

This meeting is devolving, quickly turning into something it was never meant to be. The urge to cry hits me then, but I can't. I won't. I *refuse*.

"You need to leave. Get out," Jackson says. Pure ire coats his words, leaving no room for argument. "You are no longer welcome on the premises."

Normally, I'd be telling him to shove it—I can handle myself, thank you very much—but this uncharacteristic reaction from Reggie has admittedly frayed my nerves. *A certified, ice cold bitch.* Is that true? Is that really how people see me?

I try to be a good person. A kind person. I know I'm not the most open and inviting all the time, but am I truly that bad? Reggie apparently thinks so. Do the rest of my employees feel that way, too?

"You know what? I'm sick of this shit anyway. It's only a matter of time before this place runs itself into the ground now that Beatrice is gone," Reggie says, shoving out of his chair.

Calling me a bitch, although a bit jarring, I can handle.

Kind of. But sticking a hot fireplace poker right into the heart of my biggest fear? That has me second-guessing every decision I've made in all of my twenty-five years. I suddenly feel very, very small.

"*Out*," Jackson barks. "Now."

I hold my head high, staring at Reggie. Or rather, Jackson's back. He shifts slightly, shielding me from the disgruntled employee. *Ex* employee. Admittedly, I'm grateful.

When Reggie finally decides to heed Jackson's command, the sound of the door slamming in his wake is enough to reanimate the dead. A framed picture, formerly on the wall, plummets to its death from the force. My chin wobbles.

"Well, that sucked," I say. My nose stings as I blink back the tears. "But c'est la vie and all that."

"Ellison..."

I grab the computer mouse and start to mindlessly click around on the monitor, unseeing. "He stole money from the restaurant. I had to do it."

Jackson nods. "You did the right thing, but—"

"Okay. Good." My shoulders lift in a shrug. "Then I'm just gonna get back to work now."

"Meyer," he says. His voice takes on a softness I haven't heard from him before. "Are you alright?"

I sniffle, working to clear my throat and stop my nose from running. My eyes are also still threatening to leak, a fact I find very annoying.

For fuck's sake, Meyer. No crying in front of your business partner! You can't show weakness.

My palm clenches around the mouse. "I'm fine," I manage to get out. "Just...something in my eye."

Silence settles over us, though I can still hear the sound of that door slamming. Then Jackson takes a step closer to me and I brace for what he's going to say.

Reggie's right. You've been nothing but a bitch to me since I got here. Maybe you should let me buy you out and be done with it. The inn will be better off without you.

"You're allowed to find that difficult," he says instead. "Anyone would."

He says that, but I have a feeling he would have had no issue coming in here and telling Reggie to pack his things. He wouldn't have even thought twice about it. Partially because he hasn't known Reggie for years like I have, but also because he's frustratingly composed when it comes to work.

"Don't patronize me, Vaughan," I snap. And then I turn away from him, staring down at the desk in front of me to keep the tears at bay.

I sense Jackson approaching me slowly, but I don't look in his direction. Don't bother to lash out and demand he stay away. And when he kneels beside my chair and turns my head toward him, hand on my chin, I don't stop him. I don't think I could, even if I wanted to.

"I'm not trying to patronize you, I promise." His gaze searches mine. "I'm not *judging* you, Ellison. I haven't yet, and I'm not about to start now."

For some reason, I think I believe him.

"I'm okay," I finally get out. "Thank you for...kicking him out."

Jackson nods, releasing my chin and then standing, putting space between us. "Of course. I won't tolerate anyone speaking to you like that. It was uncalled for."

But what if he was right?

I bite my tongue. Maybe he hasn't been judging me, but other people certainly are. Reggie has proven that. Still, I don't need to get into all of it with Jackson. I can stew about it tonight in the comfort of my bed.

"Why didn't you tell me you were planning to do this?" Jackson asks. "I would've been here."

The unspoken words hang between us. If I hadn't been so petty as to unplug his alarm clock, he would have been here. He truly did look like death last night, so I thought I'd kill two birds with one stone—I'd get him out of my way for a while *and* force him to catch up on the sleep he so desperately needs but seems to be resisting.

I shake my head. "This is my mess. I was cleaning it up."

"That's the thing, Ellison. None of this is yours—it's *ours*. We have to both make these types of decisions."

My eyes narrow on him as I glare. "So you're mad that I fired him on my own?"

Jackson pinches the bridge of his nose. "I'm not mad that you fired him on your own. I'm *frustrated* that you insist on feeling like you had to. We could have done it together."

"Together isn't part of my vocabulary."

"Well, maybe it's time you add it."

The room grows quiet again, only this time, I can feel the pulsing tension from our disagreement hanging in the air. I should be the bigger person here—break the silence and move on. But I can't bring myself to do it.

And then Jackson beats me to it.

"Go out to dinner with me."

I almost choke on my own saliva. Because *what*? One

minute, we're arguing, and the next, he's asking me out? Did I somehow wind up in the twilight zone? After the morning I've had, I wouldn't be at all surprised.

Turning a critical eye toward him, I make a show of inspecting his face. "Did you hit your head on your way down here?"

"No," he says. "Why?"

I lean back in my chair, still unsure. "Because last I checked, we don't like each other. The only explanation for you asking me on a date is a head injury."

Jackson laughs. The sound makes something in the pit of my stomach curl. In a pleasant way. Weird.

"It's not a *date*, Meyer. I just think we could both benefit from getting to know one another better."

"Like a *date*." I cross my arms. "I'm not going."

He crosses his own arms, not afraid to square off with me. He even stands with his feet shoulder-width apart. "Like two strangers who have been thrust into business partnership. *Not* a date."

I narrow my eyes. "Fine. We can have dinner in the restaurant."

If I asked, the cook would make our food a priority, and then we'd be able to get out of there faster. I wouldn't normally take special treatment like that, but anything to keep from spending too long in Jackson's company.

He shakes his head. "I think we need to be on neutral territory for this to work."

I'm not sure why he's so insistent on this. Things have been going fine thus far. But I can tell by the determined gleam in his eye that he isn't going to back down, and after everything that just happened with Reggie, I'm too tired to fight him. So I sigh.

"Alright, neutral territory," I agree. "What did you have in mind?"

Jackson blinks, almost like he's surprised I gave in so easily, and then his expression turns to one of satisfaction. "I heard about this new Italian restaurant in Calderville. Tomorrow night?"

I want to lie and tell him that I'm busy tomorrow, just to be a little difficult. But I know he'll call me on my bluff. He has an uncanny ability to see right through me. Besides, if I show him how unpleasant it will be having a meal together, he won't be so eager to try it again.

I smile. "Sounds perfect."

He arches a brow. "It does?"

"Yes, Jackson. It does."

This time, his skeptical look is directed at me. But I pretend not to see it, turning back to the computer. And I try not to think about Reggie and what he said or about Jackson and this not-a-date of ours.

I'm not entirely successful.

CHAPTER 14
JACKSON

FROM THE MINUTE Meyer met me in the parking lot of the inn so I could drive us to the restaurant, I knew it was a stupid fucking idea to invite her to dinner.

We're a stark contrast—her in ripped jeans, a plain white t-shirt and polka dot flip flops; me in my usual suit and dress shoes. She knew I would wear a suit because I always do. She, on the other hand, made it a point to dress as casually as possible to sabotage our non-date. I could tell by the smug gleam in her eye as I scanned her outfit.

Little does she know, my perusal was in appreciation, not annoyance.

It's a well-established fact that Meyer Ellison's jeans cling to her ass and hips like they were crafted just for her. And her t-shirt is snug around the bust, leaving nothing of her full tits to the imagination. The flip flops, with their multicoloured polka dots, just make me want to smile.

So, like I said, horrible fucking idea.

I can handle, though barely, the wayward thoughts I have

about Meyer when we're in a work setting. But at dinner? That's going to require herculean effort to stop my mind from wandering.

I planned to take her to Calderville, but at the last second, I veer off the highway and onto a street that will take us into town.

"What the fuck, Vaughan?" Meyer grips the handle of the door. "I agreed to dinner, not to end up in a ditch."

I wince. "Sorry."

Sitting across from Meyer in the romantic low lighting of a fancy Italian restaurant? I think I'd rather eat gravel for breakfast. The pizza place on Main will have to do.

There's nothing sexy about Papa's Pizza Emporium.

"How'd you even manage to get your licence?" she continues.

"Never underestimate the power of a good bribe."

"*Seriously?*"

I let out a chuckle. "No, Meyer. I earned my licence just like everyone else, shitting my pants beside the scary driving examiner."

She glares at me from her seat, and I smile. We ride the rest of the way in silence. There's luckily a spot right outside the pizza place, so I park and we head in.

"Meyer!" a guy calls from behind the counter. He looks to be about Meyer's age, and he's wearing a grin that could only be described as shit-eating. "How's it going? How's Mama Ellison? I haven't seen her in a while."

Meyer smiles. "Hey, Rudy. I'm good. So is my mom. She's apparently got a hot new instructor for her water exercise class, so she's rather smitten at the moment."

When Rudy's eyes land on me, he scowls. "This him?" he asks Meyer, jerking a thumb in my direction.

Meyer sighs. "This is him."

Never in my life have I been referred to with such disdain.

The cool glare that settles on his face leads me to believe that a handshake would be unwelcome, so I settle for a nod. "Jackson Vaughan. Nice to meet you."

"Rudy Ciccarelli," he replies.

I notice that he makes it a point *not* to say it's nice to meet me.

The thing I've noticed most about Fraisier Creek is that its residents are loyal to a fault. On the one hand, it's endearing to be witness to such a tight-knit community rallying around my business partner. But on the other, it's been making my life a hell of a lot more difficult than it needs to be.

Like Meyer, everyone in Fraisier Creek seems to think I'm out to destroy their precious inn. I'm not sure what I can do to convince them otherwise. I'm just hoping that after some time, they'll begin to see reason.

Cherie saw something special in this place. For the first time, I'm beginning to think that maybe she's right. When I first got here, I was only in this to kill time and fulfill my grandmother's wish, but now? Now, I'm invested.

"What am I making you? Your usual?" Rudy asks.

"Yes, please," Meyer replies sweetly.

He turns to me. "And for you?"

Apparently his dislike of me isn't going to stop him from taking my business.

"I'll do a Hawaiian, but add green olives."

With a wry twist of his lips, Rudy goes about making our pizzas.

"You have *got* to be shitting me," Meyer says with a scoff.

"What?" I turn to her, eyes narrowed. "Are you one of those people who hates pineapple for no good reason?"

"No," she says. "You stole my order!"

I chuckle. "I wasn't aware someone could hold ownership over a pizza topping preference."

She crosses her arms and turns away, pretending to inspect the photographs and artwork on the walls. I take her lead, sidling up beside her, hands in my pockets. More than once, I can sense her turn in my direction to shoot me a glare, but I keep facing forward.

I point toward a photo just above her eye level. "Nice shiner," I say.

It's a picture of a local children's soccer team that Papa's Pizza Emporium sponsored years ago. Right there, in the centre of the front row, is a little Meyer. She's probably no more than eight, but she carries herself the same way present day Meyer does. And she's sporting a gnarly black eye.

Meyer can't hide the proud grin that stretches across her lips. It's not directed at me, but I feel a strange sense of accomplishment because I did that. I made her smile. It's a welcome departure from her typical scowl when I'm around.

"One of the boys in my class was making fun of my friend," she explains. "She needed braces, but she couldn't get them yet. He made one too many comments about her crooked teeth, so I gave him something else to talk about instead."

Another well-established fact about Meyer Ellison is that her protective streak is a mile long. I see it in the way she cares for the employees at the inn—the way she cares about the inn itself.

It's an innocuous anecdote from well over a decade ago, but I relish this new information. And I crave more. My fascination has been apparent from the moment I laid eyes on her, but it was purely physical then. Having been in her presence these past few weeks, I find myself wanting to know how her mind works.

"Are you still friends?" I ask, just to hear her talk a little more.

She shakes her head. "We were until the end of high school. Then she moved to Kingston for university. She comes back home sometimes, but if anything, we just wave at each other from across the street."

"I have friends like that. Acquaintances, really." I rub a hand along my jaw. "If I'm honest, I've only ever had the one friend."

By the time high school hit, besides Wells, no one was willing to put up with my near constant studying. And when I started working, the long hours left me too exhausted to contemplate more than a casual drink with colleagues every now and then.

"Pizza's up!" Rudy calls, shutting down our conversation.

When I pull out my wallet, I send a teasing glance to Meyer. "Aren't you going to offer to pay for yours?"

She smirks. "No. I'm pretty sure you can afford it," she

replies. "Besides, you're the one who asked me to dinner, Hotshot."

Rudy rings the pizzas up and I pay. Then I drop a hefty tip into the tip jar before grabbing my pizza box. Meyer already has hers in hand.

"Thanks, Rudy!" She smiles. "Another month and it'll be prime picking season. Then I'll whip up a pie just for you."

Rudy points a green bell pepper in her direction. "I'll hold you to that. Best fucking pie I've ever had."

She places a hand to her chest with a grin. "Oh, how you flatter me."

"Yet you still won't give me a second chance." He winks. "Say hello to your mama for me."

She waves, and then *finally* we're heading out the door. Once outside, I jut my chin in the direction of the park across the street. There's a small playground farther down with a couple swings, a modest slide and a set of monkey bars. A gazebo with chipping white paint stands sentry in the middle of the green space. We find a picnic table sitting under the shade of an oak tree, perfect protection against the setting sun.

Well, almost. The tree does nothing to shield me from the mesmerizing way the orange and red hues play in the reflection of Meyer's crystalline eyes.

Apparently even eating a greasy pizza in the middle of a public park isn't enough of a deterrent to keep my mind from drifting.

In an effort to make the most of this time I have, I ask, "What kind of pies do you bake?"

"Any kind, really, but my specialty is strawberry."

I lift up my wrist and point to the spot where I saw the tattoo on hers. "Is that why you have one on your wrist?"

She looks surprised, as if maybe I'm the first person to notice it. Maybe it's new.

Slowly, she nods. She rests her elbow on the wooden table and twists her arm so the strawberry is on display for me. I only noticed the vague outline and the colours the first time, but now I can see the intricate details.

"I used to bake a lot with my mom. She doesn't really do it anymore, but I still do. When I have the time."

I itch to trace the design of her tattoo with my finger, but I refrain. Instead, I trace it with my eyes, roving over each delicate seed and crease of a leaf on the stem.

"It suits you," I say.

Then Meyer does something incredible—she blushes. It's not the same flush that crept up her face that night she came to my room, drunk and adorable, ready to brawl. This blush is a pretty pink that dusts the apples of her cheeks and brings warmth to her otherwise cool appearance—the light blue of her eyes, the icy glares she offers me.

In an instant, the moment is gone. She snatches her wrist back and tucks in to her pizza. I let her retreat, picking up a slice of my own.

Being away from the inn, I sense that some of the fight has left Meyer. She's still guarded, but the walls she has erected aren't nearly as tall. Perhaps, with time, I could scale them entirely.

"Tell me something," she says, tossing a piece of crust back into her box.

"What do you want to know?"

She laces her fingers together and rests her elbows on the table. Her chin drops on top of her clasped hands as she regards me. "How many suits do you own?"

"Eight," I reply easily.

"Huh."

I chuckle. "You sound surprised."

She shrugs. "I figured a guy like you would have at least twenty."

"It's not about the suit. It's all about the tie," I explain.

She cocks her head, scrutinizing my tie. I arch a brow.

"Sorry," she says with a crooked grin, "but I think that's just about the nerdiest thing you've ever said to me."

I laugh.

After that, Meyer really starts to relax. We talk more about her baking and I tell her about all of my non-existent hobbies. Eventually, we finish our pizzas and throw the boxes in the garbage by the sidewalk.

An older man passes us, and he tips his chin in our direction. "Lovely evening," he says.

Meyer offers him a polite smile. "It is. Have a good one."

"Do you know him?" I ask as we cross the street to my car.

"No." She shrugs. "He's probably a tourist."

Unlike earlier, the drive back to the inn isn't fraught with Meyer's unease. Instead, it's full of a different kind of tension. The kind that tempts me to make a stupid decision when I park and turn to face her in the passenger seat.

"I, um—" Meyer's tongue darts out, smoothing along her bottom lip. My eyes track its movement. "I didn't have a terrible time."

I grin. Coming from her, that's the closest to a compliment I'm probably going to get. "Finally see that I'm not so bad?" I tease.

Her lips quirk. "I haven't fully made up my mind yet."

She gets out of the car first. I linger for a moment, sighing when I realize the scent of her perfume still floats in the air. Meyer has already made it to the side of the building by the time I catch up.

This is the moment where we say goodnight. She'll retreat across the parking lot and down that path toward her little cottage. I'll watch her leave until I can't see her anymore, and then I'll make my way to my room.

But none of that happens.

Meyer shifts backwards, turning toward me, and her foot gets caught in one of the many craters littering the parking lot. To save her from a sprained ankle, I spring forward with a curse, catching her around the waist.

Her hands find purchase on my shoulders. Her eyes, big and wide and so *fucking* blue, latch on to mine. I like the way her hands feel on me almost as much as I like the way my fingers dig into her soft curves. When she swallows, I itch to trace the delicate skin of her throat—with my fingers, with my lips.

Her lashes—which I would gamble are naturally a pale blonde that rivals her hair but are generally covered in a layer of brown mascara—flutter.

Then Meyer's eyes slide to the right and her whole body tenses.

"Oh my God," she whispers, a hand coming up to cover her mouth as tears well in her eyes.

I whip around, an arm still anchored to her waist. I'm not sure what I expected to find, but it wasn't the angry red lettering splashed across the side of the inn. It looks like blood marring the white exterior, but it's more feasible that it's paint.

Still, that isn't what makes the blood in my veins run cold. It's what the message says that has me tightening my grasp on Meyer. For her sake...or maybe for mine.

You will regret this.

CHAPTER 15
MEYER

You will regret this.

Despite the fact that the letters are indistinguishable now, the message is burned into my brain. Stamped behind my eyelids. I turn the words over and over in my mind, trying to make sense of them.

A hand touches my arm. "Meyer."

I jump. I've been on edge since Jackson and I got back and found the paint. But my body relaxes marginally when I realize it's only Pippa standing beside me.

Despite this, I don't cease my angry scrubbing. I've been at it for hours. As soon as the police wrapped up their report, I took to the supply closet to find a bucket and some sponges.

We'll have to have the white siding repainted. There's no way around that. Even if I scrub until my fingers bleed, there will be no erasing this completely.

"Meyer," she says more forcefully, grabbing the sponge I'm holding. "Stop."

"I already tried that," Jackson says. He pushes away from where he was leaning farther down the wall, looking as weary as I feel. "It didn't end well."

We all look at the patch of red slashed across the front of his white shirt from where I pressed a hand against him. He abandoned his jacket some time ago, so at least I don't have to feel bad about possibly ruining one of his suits.

Pippa sighs. She retracts her hand and folds her arms against her chest, hugging herself. "Who would do this?" she asks. "*Why?*"

I let the sponge fall to the ground with a splat. Then I stare at my hands, tinged red from the water and paint mixture I created. It looks a lot like blood.

Wordlessly, Jackson passes me a dry cloth, and I wipe my palms clean.

"You should go home, Pip," I say. My voice is scratchy, my throat impossibly dry. "It's late."

She shakes her head. "I'm fine. Declan's home with Atticus. My priority right now is *you*."

I offer her a reassuring smile. At least, I try to. Her frown indicates that perhaps it turns out more like a grimace.

"Really, it's okay. I promise I'm done with the scrubbing. I just want to go to bed."

She chews on her bottom lip, thinking. "Maybe you should stay in one of the rooms tonight. Or you could stay with me."

I shake my head. "Sorry, but I need my sleep. I need my own bed, and I can't be kept up by your snoring."

Her mouth pops open in shock. "I do not *snore!*"

"You *so* do." This time, my smile is genuine. "Seriously. Please go home. I'm alright."

After carefully assessing my face for signs of a lie, Pippa nods. She wraps her arms around me in a gentle hug as she reminds me how much she loves me. Then she sets across the parking lot toward her car.

"C'mon, Ellison," Jackson says, nudging my arm. "I'll walk you home."

On a normal day, I would protest. But there's nothing normal about today.

After checking in with the staff working the night shift to make sure they have everything they need, Jackson and I make the trek to my cottage.

When I step inside, Jackson follows. I whirl around. "What do you think you're doing?"

He frowns, crossing his arms over his broad chest. "If you're insisting on staying here alone, then I'm making sure the house is clear first. And that all your windows are locked."

"My house wasn't broken into," I insist.

Jackson sighs. "Anything else, Ellison, I'll let you fight me until you run out of breath. But your safety is not something I'm willing to argue about."

That strangely sounds like he *cares*. And that makes the words dry up in my throat. All I can do now is nod, and then I let him into my house.

True to his word, Jackson inspects every nook and cranny of my tiny cottage. As his search proves fruitless, my muscles begin to relax, and I decide that maybe we're all a bit paranoid. The spray paint was probably just some dumb high school kids with nothing better to do. Wouldn't be the first time a building in town got graffitied.

But it wasn't just graffiti, a part of me says.

Like it or not, this was intentional—a way to get under my skin. My mind drifts to Reggie. He's the only person I know of that would be mad enough to want to hurt me like this. But he wouldn't do that. Or would he?

I thought I knew him, but I had never expected him to act the way he did the other day when I fired him. That was a side to him I hadn't ever seen before.

When the last window is unlocked, opened, slammed shut and then locked again, I feel more at ease. Everything is right in my tiny corner of Fraisier Creek. Even Fish comes out from his hiding spot, sans panties, to swish against my shins.

When he spots Jackson, he hisses. This causes a small giggle to burst from my lips. Then I take note of Jackson's offended expression, and the laughter turns hysterical, verging on unhinged.

"Like mother, like son," Jackson muses.

"He takes a while to warm up to people," I admit.

Also not unlike his mother.

I think of my mom's nickname for me—prickly pear. *Sharp on the outside, but all around sweet on the inside*, she would say.

It's natural to me to distance myself, but over the years, I've honed my skills. Other than with my select inner circle, closeness breeds vulnerability, and I can't afford to be vulnerable when I want to be taken seriously by my employees. By this town.

I was raised by this town, and I know they love me. But

it's also not lost on me that to most, I'm still that little girl who would play make believe in the corridors of the inn. As a woman—and a young one, no less—I'm already at a disadvantage. Giving off the impression that I can't handle whatever comes my way is not an option.

So I'm a prickly pear, and I'll be damned if I let Jackson Vaughan crack me open.

I clear my throat. "Thanks," I say quietly. "I'd, uh, really like to go to sleep now."

He almost looks hesitant to leave, but he nods. "Okay," he says, heading for the door, "we can talk about this tomorrow. Make sure you lock up behind me."

"Believe it or not, I know how to operate a lock," I fire back, holding the door open for him. "It's this little flippy thing back here, right?"

His lips quirk when he turns to look at me over his shoulder. "There she is."

Here I am, prickly and closed off. While any other man would've already written me off as too difficult, Jackson doesn't look deterred. He looks amused. Glad, even, that my public persona has slipped back into place.

But it doesn't matter what he thinks of me.

I sigh as I shut the door, lock it, and then flip Jackson the bird for having the utter audacity.

Tonight, my bedtime routine feels like a gruelling workout. By the time I'm done, I'm even more exhausted than I was before, with none of the benefits of exercising.

I settle into bed, a lamp illuminated on the table beside me, Fish curled at my feet. And I don't sleep a wink.

The next two weeks trudge by slowly. The police get nowhere with tying the spray paint to anyone, much less Reggie, who seems to have skipped town. In the absence of answers, Jackson has taken it upon himself to distract us.

The morning following the vandalism, Jackson brought me a coffee. Whether he thought I needed it or he was trying to butter me up, I'm still not sure. After clarifying it wasn't poisoned—to which I received an eye roll—I took one sip. And promptly gagged.

"*Black*?" I sputtered, incredulous.

He hummed, ignoring my question. "Not black, then," he muttered to himself.

The next day, another coffee awaited me. This one had a splash of cream. It was better than the bitterness from the day before, but again, I gagged.

It didn't dawn on me until the third day what he was up to. By trial and error, he was figuring out my coffee order. Instead of asking me—though if I'm honest, I wouldn't tell him—he decided to conduct an experiment. Collect that data he loves so much.

Jackson could easily ask Prachi, the regular barista at the café. Flash her his easy grin and she'd be a puddle of knowledge in no time. He doesn't do that, though.

I'd be annoyed if it weren't so nerdy and endearing.

No, I tell myself firmly. *Nothing about Jackson Vaughan is endearing. He's still enemy number one.*

"Morning." A to-go cup, complete with biodegradable

sleeve, is placed on top of the report I'm staring at with unseeing eyes. "Your caffeine fix."

I look up. *Damn it.* Jackson looks exceptionally good today in a navy suit. He's ditched the tie, and I'm tempted to ask what that means in his philosophy of suits, but I refrain.

Enemy, Meyer. E-N-E-M-Y.

He brings his own cup to his mouth, takes a sip, and then licks his lips. Over the last two weeks, I've managed to forget about our almost moment in the parking lot. At least, I forget about it until he does something like lick his kissable lips. Then, well, my mind wanders to places it shouldn't.

"Meyer." My eyes snap up, away from his lips. Jackson's gaze brims with amusement. "Drink your coffee."

"I will," I reply, "but not because you told me to. I'm drinking it because I'm thirsty."

I take a tentative sip. Jackson eyes me as I let the coffee settle on my tastebuds. *Shit.* It only took him two weeks to figure it out. I force a look of dissatisfaction so he doesn't know that he has hit the mark—medium roast with one sugar and a generous dash of hazelnut creamer.

I set my cup back on the desk and clear my throat. Jackson grins, and I internally curse my expressive face.

"That's it, right?" he asks. "I got it right?"

"Yes," I grumble.

His own cup can't hide the self-satisfied smile he wears as he brings it to his lips again. I hate it. Hate that he *sees* me, even if it's just something stupid like my coffee order.

Thankfully, I'm saved from Jackson's gloating when the office door swings open. It reveals an elderly man with greying hair and a practiced scowl.

"Where's my bench, Meyer?"

I sigh. "I don't know what you're talking about, Eddie."

He crosses his arms. "My bench," he says gruffly. "It's gone."

"I didn't touch your bench. You know I wouldn't," I reply, hand placed over my heart in earnest. I turn and raise my brows at Jackson. "Perhaps Mr. Vaughan knows something about it?"

Eddie wastes no time. He marches up to Jackson and shoves a finger into his chest. "You got rid of my bench."

"The one out front that was falling apart?" Jackson asks. "That bench?"

I nod. "Yes, that's it. The one that holds a lot of *sentimental value* for Eddie."

"My wife was sitting on that bench when I met her," Eddie adds. "That was *our* bench."

Jackson's gaze flits to me, unsure. I shrug, but inside, I'm grinning. "I can appreciate that, sir, but it really was in poor condition. Someone could've gotten hurt if they sat in it."

Eddie's voice takes on a choked up quality as he says, "It was all I had left of her." Now Jackson looks downright stricken. "This is what happens when you city folk come in and try to change everything. You wreck things!"

I almost feel bad about the guilt written on Jackson's face. *Almost.*

"I'm sorry, sir," he says. "I'll get your bench back."

"I've been visiting that bench for the last sixty years," Eddie continues. He truly is a good actor. "Don't fix what ain't broke."

He takes a step back, like he's preparing to leave, and

then he looks at me. Eddie and I stare at each other for a beat, and then we both start to laugh. He leans against the door-frame, tipping sideways from the force of his guffaws.

"Alright, I'm...confused," Jackson admits.

This only makes us laugh harder.

"That never gets old," Eddie declares, slapping his thigh.

Jackson crosses his arms. "What is going on?"

"Rite of passage to work here," I explain. "Try being fifteen and only officially on the job for an hour. Eddie almost made me shit my pants, thinking I had done some-thing to ruin his connection to his late wife."

"Then your mama had to go and cut my fun short," Eddie adds with a pout.

We dissolve into laughter again, but Jackson just shakes his head. Before he leaves, Eddie pats me on the back, and then he offers Jackson a handshake.

I'm still smiling as the door closes behind the old man.

"He is wrong, you know," Jackson says. "I know it was a joke, but I really am trying to help."

A sliver of guilt settles in my gut. Slowly, I nod. "I know," I say quietly, meeting his gaze. "I'm...starting to see that."

CHAPTER 16
JACKSON

THE POLICE HAVE OFFICIALLY GIVEN up. With nothing new to go on, our vandalism case has hit a dead end. I wasn't hopeful to begin with, especially with it being such a low priority offence.

Meyer has all but brushed it off, acting like it didn't even happen. I can't forget that easily, though. I've tried, but every time I see that siding, now repainted a fresh coat of white, it all comes back up again.

I knew Reggie was a problem. I should've fired him myself the minute I realized what a screwup he was, Meyer's protests be damned. If I had taken care of it, he wouldn't have had the opportunity to yell at her. To call her a bitch.

Despite all our ribbing and volleying of sarcastic remarks, I've never seen any words land for Meyer quite like Reggie's. The fact that he was able to rattle her to the point of tears has a renewed sense of anger washing over me as I enter the farmer's market in town.

Almost the entirety of Main Street has been closed off

and a plethora of tents have been erected to shade the attendees. A lot of businesses with storefronts have taken to the street to get out in the May sunshine, but there are a lot of smaller entrepreneurs taking their chance in the spotlight, too.

Almost as soon as I get pulled into the crowd, I spot a familiar head of blonde hair in front of me. Meyer had mentioned she had errands to run this morning, but she hadn't told me what. Like a moth drawn to a flame, I close in, sidling up beside her.

"Ditching work to go shopping?"

Her cool gaze slides in my direction. "I'm supporting the local economy. You should be all about that, Mr. Business."

I nod. "I am, thank you. That sounds perfect. I'll join you."

"Great," she mumbles under her breath, but the fact that she doesn't argue is a win in my book.

Hands in my pockets, I scan the stalls full of fruits and vegetables and various kinds of jam as we walk. She doesn't talk, and neither do I, my mind too caught up in thinking about that damn spray paint.

Out of the corner of my eye, I can feel Meyer looking at me. It takes another minute before she steps in my path, stopping me in my tracks.

"Okay, Hotshot," she says, "if you're going to insist on following me around, you need to lose the murderous look. You're scaring the children."

I turn my unintentional scowl on Meyer. "I don't look murderous."

She crosses her arms. "Could have fooled me."

I sigh, making a point to loosen my jaw and roll my shoulders. "Aren't you angry?"

"About what? The artisanal soaps? Hardly something to get your panties in a twist over."

"The spray paint," I reply, as if it should be obvious. "Doesn't it bug you?"

The siding has already been fixed. If you didn't know what had happened, you wouldn't guess that there had been an issue. But we know. *I* know, and that knowledge has tainted everything, even weeks later.

"Of course it bugs me." Meyer shrugs. "I'll never forgive Reggie for doing that. But dwelling on it won't get me anywhere."

My brows jump in mild shock. "That's a surprising response from a woman who seems predisposed to holding grudges."

"You know what they say about making assumptions," she counters. "Maybe I'm just predisposed to holding grudges against *you*."

I let a smirk cross my lips. "So you admit that you think I'm special."

She rolls her eyes, and a spark of something like desire shoots through my chest. "What are you doing here anyway?" she asks, redirecting the conversation. "Don't you have someone else to annoy?"

My smirk turns into a grin. "Doing what you said." I gesture to the market. "Furthering my quest to get to know the town you think I'm out to destroy."

Meyer's nose turns up as she saunters away. "If the shoe fits, Hotshot."

"Or maybe you're just making the shoe fit," I argue as I match her pace. "But I'm not wearing it."

"Okay, we can drop the shoe analogy. It's getting old."

"You started it."

"And now you sound like a child."

I laugh, which elicits another eye roll from her. I haven't gone a day without receiving one of those. I think I'd miss them if I did.

I let the conversation drop, and we walk in silence through the market. Despite what Meyer thinks, I do appreciate the town and what it has to offer. I've come to enjoy my early morning trips to the café and the quirky town gossip I hear while I wait for my order. It's a far cry from the fast-paced life I used to live in the city.

As we walk, random people stop and say hello to Meyer. Which means I've had to introduce myself no less than a dozen times. I don't mind it, though. It's nice to put names to some of the faces I've seen in town or at the restaurant. Even if they all grow wary as soon as they find out who I am.

If the glares from before weren't an indication, this only solidifies the fact that Meyer's dislike of me has spread through Fraisier Creek like a wildfire.

So far, neither one of us has bought anything, but I slow when Meyer does. She pauses at a table full of handmade jewellery. There are necklaces, bracelets and earrings, and all the charms are made of clay.

"These are so cute," Meyer says, almost to herself. She points to a pair of earrings in the shape of strawberries. They look similar to her tattoo. "I'll take them."

The woman behind the table smiles and begins to tuck the earrings into a box. Meyer fishes in her wallet for the cash.

"Thank you," the woman says as she hands over the box.

Meyer tucks it into her bag, and we keep going.

"I know you said your tattoo is for your baking, but I'm sensing an overall theme here," I say.

She fiddles with the hem of her shirt, trying to appear unaffected. "They're my favourite fruit."

But I don't buy it.

"Strawberries, Fraisier..." I've had the dessert before, and I spent my elementary school years in French immersion. "Is that why you got it?"

"Of course you understand French, too," she mutters. A light blush rises to her cheeks, and this only piques my curiosity more. "Yes, okay? The strawberries remind me of home."

She doesn't look at me. I can tell that offering up that piece of information about herself was hard for her. But I'm selfishly glad she told me. I file it away in the place where I keep every bit of precious information I know about my business partner.

Knocking her shoulder with mine, I say, "I like it. You look good in red."

I swear her blush deepens, but she increases her pace, putting distance between us, so I can't be sure.

Next, we come to a stop in front of a table full of flowers. There are some premade bouquets, but the rest are single-stemmed blooms that can be arranged to your liking.

"Good morning, Meyer," the woman behind the table says.

She looks to be in her early forties. She has striking blue eyes and white-blonde hair braided down her back. And she has a warm smile on her face, putting me immediately at ease.

"Morning, Ilsa," Meyer says, eyeing the flowers. "These are gorgeous."

When it becomes apparent that Meyer isn't going to, I decide to introduce myself. "Hi," I say, hand outstretched. "I'm Jackson Vaughan. I own Dog Days Inn with Meyer."

The woman smiles brighter. "Ilsa Veidt. I own the flower shop on Main."

"What are these?" Meyer asks as she brings a fresh bouquet to her nose.

"Chrysanthemum," Ilsa replies. "The birth flower for November. Yours, right?"

Ilsa looks almost nervous for Meyer's response. But Meyer only smiles. "That's right. How'd you know?"

Ilsa fidgets with the garden shears in her hand. "Oh, good memory, I guess. Pippa Rhodes ordered flowers for your birthday last year."

My companion's brows jump. "You *do* have a good memory." She holds the bouquet up. "I'll take these, please."

Before Meyer can unzip her wallet, I hold a twenty out to Ilsa.

"What are you doing?" Meyer demands.

I grin. "Buying you flowers, Ellison. What does it look like?"

"But— You can't—"

Ilsa bites her smile, and I wink. She works on making my change as Meyer short circuits.

"Thank you, Ilsa," I say. "We'll see you around."

I place a hand on the small of Meyer's back and guide her out of the way of the florist's other customers. When she doesn't immediately protest, I keep my hand there. I can feel her warmth through the thin fabric of her dress. All too soon, she spins away from my touch.

"You can't do that!"

"Do what?" I'm sure my grin is downright goofy at this point.

"Buy me flowers," she replies. "It's disconcerting."

This amuses me further, and I let out a laugh. "Disconcerting, huh?"

"Yes." She frowns. "You're not supposed to be nice to me."

"What? Why not?"

"Are you not listening? Because it's *disconcerting*!"

I take a step closer, almost daring her to take another step back. "You want to know what I think?"

She glowers. "When have I ever given you the impression I want to know what you're thinking?"

I lean in. "I think my buying you flowers contradicts the narrative you've constructed about me in that pretty head of yours, and you find that disconcerting because it means you might be *wrong*."

Based on the annoyance in her eyes, I've hit my mark. Slowly but surely, I'm beginning to understand my business partner. Try as she might to box me out, she can't—not fully. Because something about me gets under her skin. I won't lie and say that I mind it.

"Wrong about you?" She scoffs. "Never."

I grin. "We'll see."

"Meyer!"

We both turn and find a blond-haired man waving as he weaves through the crowd. Meyer smiles at his approach, and I wonder for a moment what he had to do to earn that.

"Hey, man," he says, holding out his hand. "We haven't had the chance to meet yet. I'm Declan, Pippa's brother."

"Jackson," I reply, shaking his hand. Then I throw an arm over Meyer's shoulder. "This one's new business partner."

Meyer sidesteps out of my hold. "Don't touch me."

The amusement in Declan's eyes is hard to deny, but I also see a softness there. I'm not sure why that causes a burning feeling to erupt behind my ribcage. Now *that* is disconcerting.

The affection gives way to concern as Declan studies Meyer. "Have there been any more issues with Reggie? Pippa said there hasn't, but she likes to hide things she thinks I need protection from."

Judging by his facial features, Declan is maybe in his early twenties. From what little I know of Pippa, I can see her taking on the role of protective older sister.

Meyer shakes her head. "Nothing new. Which is a good thing, even if that means he gets away with it. I'd rather that than have him do something worse."

I have no interest in thinking about what *something worse* could be.

Declan doesn't seem to either because he clears his throat. Then he changes the subject entirely after checking his watch. "I'm supposed to be meeting someone in a few minutes. I'll see you later."

At this, Meyer grins. "Who's the lucky girl this time?"

A blush coats his cheeks. "Alicia. She works down at the hardware store."

Meyer pats his arm. "Bye, Dec. I hope the date goes well. Tell Alicia I say hi."

"Thanks, will do," he says. Then he nods to me. "Nice to meet you, Jackson."

Declan waves, and we turn away from him, heading the opposite way.

"I'm going to get some food," Meyer says. "Keep up, Hotshot. I'm not waiting."

With a shake of my head, I start to follow after her, but goosebumps rise on my arms as a shiver runs down my spine. The hair at the back of my neck stands on end. When I turn around, I can't find anyone that seems to be looking in my direction, but I could have sworn I felt a pair of eyes on me.

"Jackson?"

I shake myself from my stupor and jog to catch up. "Thought you said you weren't waiting for me?"

She glances quickly up at me. "I was feeling generous, but I'll think twice next time."

I grin. "You're too good to me, Ellison."

CHAPTER 17
MEYER

"I did it, Auntie M&M! Look!"

I grin down at the little boy proudly holding up his basket, three strawberries rolling around in the bottom. "Awesome, Attie. Keep going! I need *lots* of berries for my pies."

Atticus nods and returns to his plant, carefully examining the fruit for ripeness. The furrow of his brows is downright adorable.

There are a few farms around Fraisier Creek that grow strawberry patches, and every summer, I spend some time at all of them, hand-picking the strawberries to use for my pies. The past couple years, Pippa and her son have joined me, and now it has become tradition for us.

"I knew it was going to be hot today, but I didn't expect it to be this hot," Pippa says with a groan. She adjusts the baseball cap on her head as she scrutinizes me. "Are you wearing sunscreen?"

I laugh as I toss another couple berries into my own basket. "*Yes, Mom*, I'm wearing sunscreen."

My best friend glowers. "Hey, you'll thank me in thirty years when you don't have as many wrinkles."

I throw an arm around her shoulders and tug her against my side, grinning. "Whatever would I do without you?"

Pippa tries to glare, but it quickly morphs into a smile and a laugh. I release her, and we continue plucking the berries from their plants in silence. Atticus chatters to himself farther down the row.

Then Pippa breaks the silence. "Have you heard anything more from the police about the vandalism?" she asks, voice low. For the sake of Atticus not hearing, but also the family in the next row over.

Sighing, I meet her eyes. "No, but I don't expect to. It isn't exactly high on their priority list, and who knows where Reggie is now. If he's even the one who did it."

She clutches the handle of her basket tighter. "If it wasn't him, then who would it be? It's not like you have a long list of enemies."

That was the part that scared me. But Reggie is the most likely culprit. I made him angry when I fired him, so it wouldn't come as a surprise if he wanted me to pay for that. Whatever part of him that made him steal from the inn could just as likely have made him take spray paint to the side of the building in an act of revenge.

But there is a small voice in the back of my brain saying *what if* it wasn't him? I still find it hard to believe the man I've known for years would commit theft, let alone vandalism.

"I don't know, Pip. No one else makes sense, but..."

The smile she gives me is sympathetic. "But you don't want it to be him."

I don't. Because that means I didn't *see* it. There had to have been signs, right? I was the one that pushed my mom to hire Reggie in the first place. She had started letting me observe more of the managerial side of things, and let me give my opinion on some potential hires. Reggie had been one of them. Did I blow past his red flags all those years ago?

"No, I don't." I sigh. "But it doesn't matter what I want. Whether he did or didn't do it, it's over now. I'm moving on, and I hope everyone else does, too."

Thankfully, the gossip mill is always churning, so I'm sure some small-town scandal will occur soon and steal everyone's attention. Then they won't have reason to dwell on me and the mess I've made.

Pippa looks like she wants to say more, but she bites her lip. I let out a relieved sigh and turn back to my work. It isn't that I don't want to confide in her. She's the one person who knows just about everything about me. But sharing my insecurities is never easy, even with her.

"Jackson!" Atticus yells.

My head snaps up, conversation with Pippa forgotten, and watch as Jackson picks his way through the rows of strawberry plants to get to us. Although he isn't dressed as casually as everyone else, I am surprised to see that he's ditched his suit jacket today. And again, no tie. Just slacks and a button-down shirt.

Atticus drops his basket and makes a run for it, dodging another family as he beelines for Jackson. His new favourite person. Apparently. They've only met a handful of times, but that was evidently enough to sway the six-year-old's opinion.

Jackson catches him when Atticus launches himself into his arms. They're both grinning as Atticus excitedly tells him all about his berry-picking adventures thus far. I'll admit, the sight is a little cute.

When I look away, I catch Pippa's knowing grin. I roll my eyes. She thinks I'm warming up to the idea of Jackson hanging around, but I'm not. My resolve is firm. The day he heads back to the city is a day I will gladly celebrate. Preferably with balloons and a cake.

Jackson places Atticus back on the ground and then saunters up to me, as if he's supposed to be here and he isn't sticking his nose where it doesn't belong. Which is a bad habit of his.

My eyes narrow on him. "How did you find me?"

He grins at the annoyance in my tone. "I asked Pippa where you were."

I shoot my best friend a look. She offers me a not-so-guilty smile in return. We're going to have to talk about this later because that is *so* not cool. She knows exactly how I feel about Jackson constantly being in my space, yet here she is, encouraging it.

I've begun to open up to the idea of working with him, but being out here in the strawberry patch is *my* time. Away from the inn and the constant pressure I feel to succeed, I can just *be* out here.

I turn back to Jackson, crossing my arms. "You're interrupting girls' day. What do you want?"

He arches a brow. "Atticus is here."

"Honorary nephews don't count," I reply. "So?"

"*So*," Jackson says, "I thought I'd come help. Pippa said something about receiving a pie as payment for my services."

I cut her a glare this time. Pippa, to her credit, looks slightly apologetic now. Good. She should be. Baking is my love language, and Jackson hasn't earned that.

"Come on, Ellison." His eyes are full of amusement. *Of course* he's enjoying my displeasure. "Put me to work."

"Ugh, fine." I thrust an empty basket at his chest. "Fill this."

Thankfully, he takes the basket without a word and follows Atticus over to his plant of choice. While they're occupied, I grab Pippa's arm and haul her away so my voice doesn't carry.

"Why would you invite him?" I hiss.

"It's hard being new in town," she replies, raising her brows at me. She would know—it had taken her a while to feel settled when she first moved to Fraisier Creek. "Even harder when the people aren't totally welcoming." Another pointed look. "I didn't want him to be alone this weekend."

My irritation slips and in its place is begrudging empathy. *Fucking shit.* Leave it to Pippa to make me feel sorry for Jackson Vaughan.

"Alright, you win. I'll play nice. For this afternoon." I point a finger at her. "After this, I make no promises."

She smiles, eyes twinkling in amusement. "Thank you. That's all I ask."

My eyes search the row ahead of us, landing on Jackson.

His back is to me as he crouches low, helping Atticus pluck a particularly troublesome berry from the plant.

The last thing I want to do is ruin my day with Pippa and Atticus, so if that means including Jackson, I'll do it. But I certainly won't be happy about it.

———

After a long afternoon full of strawberry picking, we head inside the barn-turned-market for food and drinks. Along with baked goods, they sell a lot of local produce and they have a deli counter that sells fresh sandwiches. It's one of my favourite places to come in the summer.

Despite the fact that Jackson has never gone to pick his own fruit before, he was annoyingly good at it. He always managed to fill his baskets faster than me. And by the end of it all, I was actually smiling. At him.

I think it's safe to say the heat has gotten to my head.

Atticus drags Pippa across the building to look at some candy he's eyeing, and Jackson goes to save us a table while I head up to the food counter. Just as I'm about to step up to place our order, a familiar voice stops me.

"Hey, Meyer."

Rudy sidles up to my side. As far as ex boyfriends go, Rudy is a good one. We weren't together long—hell, we weren't even really *together*—but it was fun while it lasted.

"Hey," I say. "Not working today?"

He shakes his head. "Damn pizza oven malfunctioned and screwed up some electrical shit. My dad had to close the shop for the next couple days while it gets sorted."

I bump his shoulder. "Looks like it's a blessing in disguise. You never take a break."

Rudy laughs, bumping me right back. "You're adorable when you're being a hypocrite."

"Whatever. I'll just keep your pie for myself, then."

He holds up his hands in surrender. "I take it back. I said nothing." Then he glances over his shoulder before leaning in closer. "You know, I am getting majorly burnt right now."

This causes me to laugh. "What are you talking about? You're inside."

"Not from the sun, Meyer." He hooks a thumb over his shoulder, in the direction of the table Jackson is sitting at. "From *him*. I can feel his eyes burning holes in my back."

I scoff. "Don't be ridiculous."

"I'm not!" He arches a brow. "I saw the way he was looking at you the other week."

"He wasn't looking at me like anything," I say. "And you know what, just because we were each other's firsts doesn't mean you should be privy to my sex life forever."

Not that Jackson and I are having sex. Because we most definitely are not. Pigs would fly and hell would freeze over before *that* happened. Even then, I'd have to be seriously hard up to even think about it.

"I'm afraid that is a bond that can never be broken," Rudy replies, hand placed on his chest.

I roll my eyes. "You're a worse gossip than the old ladies at the seniors' centre. Nothing is going on between me and Jackson. Now can we please talk about something else?"

"I did want to say that I was sorry to hear about the

vandalism." His expression has shifted from playful to serious in the blink of an eye.

I grimace. I've been getting condolences all over town lately. The news, as it often does in Fraisier Creek, travelled quickly. And while I want nothing more than to run and hide from all my problems—from the probing questions and sympathetic gazes—the well-meaning residents of this town don't deserve that.

"Thank you," I reply. "It was a shock, but I'm just trying to put it past me now."

"Let me know if you need any help getting it all fixed up."

This time, my smile is genuine. "I really appreciate that. I think we have it covered, but it means a lot that you would offer."

He slings an arm over my shoulder, pulling me into a side hug. "Hey, we take care of our own here, Meyer." He squeezes me once and then lets go. "I should probably get going before Lover Boy over there has an aneurism."

"You are severely overestimating how much he cares about me. I'm pretty sure I make his life a hundred times more difficult."

Rudy laughs. "Whatever you say. I'll see you later."

"Goodbye, Nosy Nellie."

As he heads for the exit, I turn back to the counter and finally place our order. Then I step to the side and wait while the employees get started on our lemonades and sandwiches. It takes them a few minutes, but soon, everything is set on the counter for me.

I bite my lip as I contemplate how I'm going to carry everything, then I feel someone come up beside me.

"What are you doing?" I ask.

Jackson picks up a plate. "I'm helping."

"What if I don't want your help?"

"Then I'd say you're too stubborn for your own good, and that's too bad because you're getting my help anyway."

I huff, but I don't argue. While Jackson takes care of our food, I grab our drinks. Turning away from the counter, tray in hand, I nearly collide with someone.

"I'm so sorry!" I say to the man. He's the same one we saw at the park a few weeks ago. He must be new to town, or maybe he's a tourist spending the summer here. "I wasn't looking."

The man looks down at Jackson's hand, which now rests on the small of my back, steadying me. Then his gaze meets mine and he lets a smile spread across his mouth.

"It's fine," he says. "You have a good day."

He walks away, but I stay rooted to my spot. The interaction was normal enough, but a weird feeling has washed over me. I can't explain why.

"You okay?" Jackson asks, brows knitted together in concern.

I nod, forcing myself to let go of these thoughts. "Yeah, I'm good. Let's go eat."

As we head back to the table, I can't help looking over my shoulder, but the man is already gone.

CHAPTER 18

JACKSON

WHEN I MAKE it downstairs to start working this morning, I find a small Tupperware container on the desk. On top of it, there's a hot pink sticky note and Meyer's familiar scrawl.

Thanks for your help. Here's your pie.

I open the lid, and I laugh when I see the strawberry tart sitting inside. She fulfilled Pippa's promise—technically.

I would like to say that things between me and Meyer have improved, but it's hard to read her a lot of the time. Though I suppose she never would have made a tart for me when I showed up in April.

I know whatever progress I make with her will be slow. She's stubborn by nature, especially when she feels like she needs to protect herself. I just wish she would see that she doesn't need protection from me.

Leaning back in my chair, I devour the tart. The sugary flavour melts on my tongue, made even sweeter by the knowledge that Meyer was the one to make it. After I'm done, I pull out my phone.

> I think Pippa was envisioning a larger pie when she made me that promise.

MEYER

A loophole is a loophole, hotshot.

That bubble appears, indicating she's typing, and then:

MEYER

Did you like it?

I tried a new recipe and I needed to test it out before I gave food poisoning to someone I actually like.

A laugh escapes me. Meyer shows up to every conversation armed with sharp words and biting remarks. She always seem to be on the offensive, never letting anyone close enough to take a shot at her. But that doesn't deter me.

> It was perfect. Feel free to test out recipes on me more often.

MEYER

Flattery won't get you free baked goods, Mr. Vaughan.

> Fine. Name your price.

MEYER

Anything?

> Anything.

MEYER

That's rather dangerous. And a little
foolish.

I'm not worried.

MEYER

You should be.

She doesn't say more after that. I wait a beat, phone in hand, but nothing comes. Perhaps she is right—it's dangerous to get my hopes up with her.

A couple hours pass as I settle into work, the dropped conversation with Meyer somewhat forgotten. Between paperwork and sorting through employee suggestions, I manage to *finally* order a new chair to replace the one I'm currently sitting in. I can already picture what Meyer is going to say, but that is one thing I'm unwilling to compromise on.

A knock on the door pulls me out of my head, and then Trystan sticks his head in. "Jackson," he says, "there's someone here to see you."

My brow arches. "Who?"

He shifts to the side, and in his wake, my best friend's form fills the doorway.

Wells looks no different than the last time I saw him, which was a couple months ago now. He, like me, is more often than not wearing a suit, but today he has opted for jeans and a t-shirt. It contrasts my button-up and slacks.

He grins. "Hey. Thought I'd finally come check the place out."

I stand from my chair and round the desk. He steps into the room and pulls me toward him, patting me on the back.

It's been a while since I've even talked to Wells, too. He has been texting me, but I haven't gotten around to replying. All of my focus has been on Meyer and the inn lately, which has left time for little else. I know he'll probably give me shit for it, and I deserve it. I've been a shitty friend. I have been since I collapsed in that conference room, if I'm honest.

But it's hard letting people, especially your family, see the parts of yourself that you're ashamed of.

"Hey," I say, then raise a brow. "You really drove up here just to see the place?"

He makes a show of looking around the office, inspecting it. "Is that so hard to believe?"

An out of the blue visit? "Yes."

Although my friend isn't a fan of much of the things his parents involve him in, he always sticks close to the city. Always shows up to this event and that party. While I may be beholden to my job, Wells is beholden to his family and the leash they've had attached to him since he was a kid. He's never strayed far because of it.

Wells doesn't have time to counter because Meyer bursts into the office then. She's wearing her signature jeans and t-shirt, but there's something about her that feels…different. It's in the way her gaze settles on me. Like maybe she is warming up to me after all.

"Vaughan, why the hell is there a fancy car parked out front?" she asks. "You have your own spot for a reason."

Wells clears his throat. "Sorry, that would be my fault."

Meyer whips around, taken off guard by my friend, who is now leaning against a filing cabinet beside the open door. He straightens, stretching out a hand.

"You must be the infamous Meyer Ellison. Jackson's told me *all* about you," he says. While I did mention Meyer and our rocky start when I first arrived, I haven't updated him on the progress I've made with her. But that doesn't matter—I don't miss the sly look he sends my way. "I'm Wells McKenna."

"That's me," she replies, shaking his offered hand. "Sorry, *someone* forgot to mention we needed to roll out the red carpet. It's at the cleaners from the last time a VIP stopped by."

It's often predictable how people will react when meeting Wells. They see his inviting grin, his good looks and his connection to his parents, and they think they can suddenly be his friend. As soon as the words leave Meyer's lips, I know that Wells is appreciative. Besides his job, one thing my friend does very well is poke fun at himself.

He grins. "Don't go to any trouble on my account. As long as I've got a solid gold toilet in my room, I'm good."

Meyer lets out a bark of laughter. "Wells, you have to tell me. How are *you* friends with *him*?" She jerks her thumb over her shoulder in my direction.

I scoff. "Now that's a little rude."

"My parents made me play with him when we were little," Wells explains. "He kind of grew on me after a while."

She hums. "Right. Like a fungus."

He chokes on a laugh, and then he turns to me. "I like her. Can she be my new best friend?"

"Sorry," she interjects, "but I'm partial to my Pippa."

His head cocks to the side. "Your Pippa?"

The door opens then, and Pippa herself sticks her head in.

"My Pippa," Meyer says, pointing to her.

"Hey, Meyer, we need—" Pippa's eyes widen as she takes notice of my friend. "*Oh.*"

An amused smile stretches across his face. "Is that a good *oh* or a bad *oh*?" Wells asks.

Pippa shakes her head. Her cheeks are already turning their usual shade of red. "Oh. Just...*oh.*"

Then her lips roll inward, and silence reigns. I can feel the awkwardness descending, and judging by the blush intensifying on Pippa's face, she can, too. She looks ready to bolt when Wells takes a step in her direction.

"I'm Wells," he says. "I'm a friend of Jackson's."

She nods, her chin tilting upwards to look at him. Pippa is on the taller side, but she's still shorter than him.

"You apparently already know my name," she replies. "I'm a friend of Meyer's."

Both Wells and Pippa stare at each other for a beat, silence descending over us yet again. All the while, Pippa's blush gets more and more prominent. I wonder if maybe I should save her.

Meyer's gaze meets mine, and her eyes widen pointedly. As if to ask, *Are you seeing this?* I shake my head in response. Whatever moment our two friends seem to be having, I'm not going to read into it.

Meyer clears her throat, drawing their attention away from each other. "So, Wells, what are you doing in Fraisier Creek?"

"Just wanted to check the place out." He shrugs. "Plus,

it's a little lonely in the city when your best friend decides he likes living in the country better."

I roll my eyes. That was a pointed dig if I've ever heard one. "Just admit you miss me, McKenna."

"Meyer," Pippa says again, "I'm really sorry to interrupt, but can I get your help out here? There's a table that wants to speak to the manager, but apparently I'm not good enough."

Meyer sobers at that. "Shit, yes. I'm coming!"

We both watch the two women leave, and though I'm certain Wells's focus is on Pippa, mine is on Meyer. When the door shuts behind them, he turns back to me.

"Show me around?" he asks.

Judging by his tone, however, I can tell he wants more than a tour. He wants to talk. I don't want any of the employees overhearing us, so outside it is.

I lead the way out of the office and start heading toward the front doors. He follows as we round the side of the building and come to a stop beside a small gazebo. It was in disrepair when I arrived, but now it looks brand new, with its fresh coat of paint and the flowers that have been planted around the outside.

I cross my arms over my chest. "What are you really doing here?"

Wells sighs. "You haven't been returning your mother's calls."

"Are you fucking serious? My mother sent you to check on me? I don't need a babysitter."

"It's not like that, Jackson. She's *worried* about you and how you're handling all of this."

My jaw clenches as I turn, fixing my gaze on the trees lining the other side of the property.

I know I've been bad at returning Wells's messages, and even worse at responding to my mother's. I could keep telling myself it's because I'm busy with the inn, but truthfully, I've been enjoying the quiet.

Not quiet in the literal sense, but the break from the prying eyes, worrying over me.

Something in the trees flashes, catching the sunlight. I shift, and it glints again. My gaze narrows. The patch of trees is small, but it's dense enough that I can't see beyond the branches of the evergreens from here.

Curiosity gets the best of me, so I set off across the grass.

"Where are you going?" Wells calls from behind me. "We were kind of in the middle of something here!"

I don't answer. I keep walking toward the trees, and Wells jogs to catch up.

"So what, you're just going to ignore me now?" he continues. "That's really mature, Jackson. Running from your problems won't get you anywhere in the long run."

"I'm not running," I snap. "I'm doing exactly what Cherie asked of me."

"Didn't realize she told you to ice your whole family out in the process. My bad, man."

I don't even dignify that with a response. When I make it to the line of trees, I push through the needles and branches. Wells is hot on my heels, ready to keep reprimanding me. We both stop short.

On the ground, a sleeping bag is rolled out. It looks a little dirty, like it's been there for a while. There are a few wrappers from chocolate bars scattered around the trunk of the tree.

"Whoa," Wells says when he sees the mess. "Has someone been camping out here?"

Camping or *watching*? None of the trash on the floor is what drew me over here in the first place. I look up, searching the branches.

There, wedged between the limbs of a tree, is a set of binoculars. And they're pointed in the direction of Meyer's cottage.

CHAPTER 19
JACKSON

Someone has been watching her.

Those five words reverberate inside my brain, over and over, as I stare at the binoculars.

Every morning, when she leaves her cottage to head to work, someone could be in this very spot, watching. Waiting. For what, I don't want to think about.

"What the fuck?"

The sound of Wells's voice pulls me from my daydreams of violence. He has taken note of the binoculars now, and I can almost see the realizations he's having as he takes in the evidence before him. From this very spot, someone has been spying on Meyer, right under our noses.

I think I'm going to be sick.

"Maybe someone left them here by mistake?" He says it like a question, but we both know the answer.

I shake my head, swallowing the sour feeling that is threatening to rise. "No," I say. "It's no coincidence."

Wells studies me. "I know you've been holding back lately. What haven't you told me?"

A lot.

"Meyer fired one of our employees a little while ago. He was caught stealing, so it had to be done." My fists clench at my sides, remembering the rage simmering in Reggie's eyes as I told him to get out. "Before he left, he called her a bitch. And then the next night, someone vandalized the inn."

Wells sucks in a breath. "Fuck. You think it was him?"

I nod. "I do. It has to be, given the threat left in spray paint. *You will regret this.* There are cameras outside the building, but they don't do a sufficient job covering the whole property. That side of the building was a blind spot."

"Shit, Jackson." He shakes his head. "Why didn't you say anything?"

In truth, it didn't occur to me. I truly have been so caught up in the inn and Meyer, it didn't even cross my mind. That, and I knew it would only make my family worry. They had been wary about me coming here by myself to begin with.

I clear my throat. "I'm saying something now." I look at the binoculars again, the mess on the ground. "I don't want to be the one to tell her."

I saw what the spray paint did to Meyer. How rattled she was after firing Reggie. Despite the unruffled façade she tries to cling to now, I see beyond it. And I don't want to be the one to ruin her day. To make her question her safety, when she deserves to feel more than safe in her own home.

"I know," Wells says, placing a hand on my shoulder, "but she needs to know."

I kick at the sleeping bag, and something small and white comes loose, fluttering to the ground. I pick it up and turn it over, and my blood runs cold.

I'm holding a picture of Meyer in my hands, taken the day I came back to Fraisier Creek. I can tell based on the teddy bear she's holding in her hands. The one she accused me of leaving for her.

I tear at the corner of the sleeping bag, upending it, and another handful of photos come flying out. They're all of Meyer.

While we stood on her porch having that conversation, someone was out here taking pictures of her.

"That is beyond fucked up," Wells says, looking over my shoulder. His words are coated in anger.

I take a deep breath, swallowing the bile that has risen in my throat. Whatever sick bastard is doing this is going to live to regret ever setting eyes on her. That's a promise.

I can't stand looking at the site anymore, so I push through the trees and start back toward the inn. Wells trails after me, but he's quiet this time. I have no doubt our conversation from earlier isn't finished, but I'm thankful he's leaving me be for now. I have more pressing matters to attend to. Like telling Meyer she's being stalked.

How do you even start a conversation like that? Fuck if I know. This isn't something life prepares you for.

Inside, I find Meyer in the middle of the restaurant. She's laughing with a family at one of the tables—the same table I was sitting at when I met her. This stops me in my tracks.

When she parts ways with the group, she heads for the exit, right toward me.

Wells pats me on the back as he makes a beeline for the bar, smiling in Pippa's direction. The redhead can't contain her blush at the attention.

"Everything okay?" I ask Meyer, jerking my chin toward the table at the back of the room.

She waves off my concern. "Oh, yeah. They just remembered me from last year and wanted to compliment me on how well their stay is going."

We walk back to the office in silence. I know I need to say something, but I can't get my mouth to form the words. She keeps looking at me, brow furrowed in confusion over my unusual demeanour.

Once the office door is shut behind us, Meyer starts rummaging through the filing cabinet, and I stand there like an idiot, staring at her. I knew this wouldn't be easy, but shit, it's harder than I thought. Her inevitable reaction sits heavily on my chest.

The last thing I want to do is hurt her. But I can't keep this to myself. Until the police are able to catch the person behind this, she needs to know to be on guard.

"Ellison, I need to talk to you about something," I eventually say.

"Can it wait?" she asks. "I need to—"

"No." The singular word comes out more forcefully than intended. I clear my throat. "Sorry, but no. It can't wait."

She abandons the file she was looking for and turns to face me. "What is it?"

I look down at the photos clutched in my hand. I probably shouldn't have taken them. When we tell the police about this, they're going to want them as evidence, I'm sure.

Now, my fingerprints are all over them. But I can't seem to let them go.

"When you and Pippa left, Wells and I went outside to talk. Something in the tree line caught my attention, so I went over." Meyer looks wary, like she has no idea where this is going but knows to tread lightly anyway. I swallow. "I found a set of binoculars nestled in the tree, pointed toward your cottage, and a few photos of you on the ground."

"What? I don't—" She shakes her head. "What are you saying?"

"I think someone has been watching you, Meyer."

With a shaking hand, she takes the photos I hold out to her. I watch her face as she flips through each one. She goes through a myriad of emotions in all of twenty seconds.

"Why?" Her voice comes out weak, but from the look in her eyes, I can tell she wants to rage. "Who would—?"

I shake my head. "I don't know."

Silence envelops us as she absorbs my words. I want to say more, to comfort her somehow, but I'm not sure how to do that. Her jaw works as she studies the photos, and then she shoves them back at me abruptly.

"Meyer, I—"

She holds up a hand. "Can we finish talking about this later? I just need to...*not* right now."

I nod. "Of course."

She smoothes a hand over her hair. I pretend not to notice the way it shakes. "I'm going to help Pippa in the restaurant," she says.

I've seen their schedule for today—they have plenty of

staff. But I can tell she needs a distraction, so for now, I let her walk out the door.

And I start to pace, thinking of all the ways I want to make this person pay.

———

While Meyer was preoccupied with the restaurant, I called the police constable that had been assigned to our vandalism case. He and his partner came over right away, and Wells and I showed them what we had found. Partway through our meeting, Wells got a call from work and was summoned back to the city.

He left with the promise that he would be back if I didn't start answering my damn phone.

Hours later, I find Meyer sitting on a crate in the storage room. I hadn't seen her in a while and that admittedly made me panic a little. But when I went looking for her, Pippa reassured me that she was fine. Logically, I knew she would be. Nothing would happen to her inside the inn. That didn't stop my mind from wandering, though.

She groans when she spots me. "How did you know where I am?" she asks. "I try to hide and everyone keeps finding me."

"I was worried about you, and Pippa told me to try here first," I say.

"Snitch," she mutters, but there's no malice behind her words.

I pull another crate from the wall and sit across from her. Then I hold out a hand for her bottle of wine. There's a glass sitting next to her, but it looks like it was abandoned rather quickly.

Her eyes shoot to mine, and I wiggle my outstretched fingers. "The least you can do is share."

She relinquishes the bottle with a sigh. "You and Declan both insist on stealing my wine."

I take a sip, letting the sweet taste settle on my tongue. For half a second, I let myself consider what it would be like to taste it on her.

"Is this what you were doing that night before you came to bang on my door?" I ask. She had the same glassy look in her eyes that she does now.

Meyer snatches her bottle back and takes her own sip. Then she lets out an adorable, irritated huff. "Maybe."

I let a grin settle on my lips. "So that's a yes."

"Fine, *yes*." She shakes the bottle a little. "I like to wash away my sorrows in a bottle of strawberry wine. Sue me."

She passes the bottle back without my having to ask. "It's very sweet," I say.

"Too sweet for someone so bitter?"

"Well, now you're just putting words in my mouth." I shake my head. "I don't think you're bitter."

"No, I'm just an ice cold bitch who now has a stalker and is afraid to be at work, even though it's been the only place where she has consistently felt safe her whole fucking life."

Then her eyes widen, like she didn't mean to say any of that out loud. But I'm glad she did. Not because I enjoy the thought of her feeling that way—because I want to help her. I want to know what she's thinking. I want to *know* her.

I certainly wasn't happy about coming here at first, but

now I enjoy the time I get to spend with her. I couldn't imagine my days without her, if I'm honest.

"Meyer." I place a hand on her knee, and her shining eyes meet mine. "We'll do whatever we need to do to make you feel safe here again. Just say the word."

"That's the problem." Her expression is pained, like she hates having to admit this. "The inn used to be my haven. My home. Now it just feels...tainted. I don't know *how* to fix it."

This look on her face... I know instantly that I would do anything to erase it. To take the pain away.

"We'll figure it out, and then we'll do it. He doesn't get to win."

She swallows thickly. "What if he already has?"

I shake my head sharply. "He hasn't. He won't. I talked to the police earlier."

Her eyes jump to mine then. "They didn't ask for a statement from me."

I offer her a small smile. "I convinced them to come back for that tomorrow. I didn't think you'd want to talk about it with them yet."

"Thank you," she whispers. She tips her head back against the wall and closes her eyes. A single tear slips down her cheek, but she swipes at it roughly. "Why are you so nice to me? I've been nothing but horrible to you this whole time."

"I'm just trying not to be your villain."

She opens her eyes, setting her attention on me. She's quiet for a moment, studying. "I think I've been so focused on making you out to be the bad guy, I've turned into someone I never wanted to be." She shakes her head. "I'm sorry. For all of it."

I stand from my seat, holding my hand out to her. "Hi, I'm Jackson Vaughan, your new business partner."

She eyes my hand and then her skeptical gaze meets mine. "What are you doing?"

I shrug. "I'm starting over. Care to join me?"

After a moment, she takes the bait and stands. Grabbing my hand, she shakes it firmly. "Meyer Ellison, your new business partner."

I smile as I give her hand a quick squeeze. I'm reluctant to let go, but I know that I have to. I *should*.

Then I clear my throat. "It's been a long day. We can sort everything out and talk to the police in the morning. For now, it's probably time for bed. Do you want me to walk you home?"

Even if she says no, I'll do it anyway. She can be mad about it if she likes, but I don't care. I'm not taking any chances with her.

Meyer shakes her head. "I'm just waiting for Pippa to be done and then I'm going to her place. She's making me stay with her and Declan tonight."

I don't say it, but an immense amount of relief sweeps through me, knowing that. That means I won't have to find an excuse not to leave her alone in that cottage of hers.

"I'm glad you have her," I say. I stick my hands in my pockets, unsure what to do with myself. "If you need anything, you know where to find me."

She chews on her bottom lip as she nods, and shit, the action makes it all the more enticing. I shouldn't be thinking about that right now. Or at all. She's made it abundantly clear how she feels about me, apology or not.

"I do," she replies.

I turn to head out into the hall to give Meyer her space. It feels strange, walking away from her after I watched some of her walls come down.

"Jackson?" she calls out. I stop and face her. "Thank you."

I tip my chin. "Anytime."

Instead of heading up to my room, I wait in the office until I hear Meyer and Pippa heading for the door. Then I make sure they both get into Pippa's car safely before I make the trek up the stairs.

As I'm getting ready for bed, my phone buzzes, and the text that greets me eases some of the worry still sitting on my chest.

MEYER

We made it to Pippa's place. Goodnight, Vaughan.

Goodnight, Ellison.

CHAPTER 20
MEYER

I haven't been alone in five days.

Ever since Jackson and Wells found those photos of me, I've always had someone around, whether it be Pippa, Declan or Jackson. I'm convinced the three of them have been colluding together, determined not to let me know a moment of peace.

I know they care, but I need to get back to my normal life at some point. I can't operate in this constant state of fear forever. The police have their evidence, so all I can do is be cautious as I try to live my life.

It's hard when my business partner is acting unusual, though.

"You're being exceptionally clingy today," I say as I shut the passenger door of Jackson's Audi.

He has the audacity to look confused. "I'm not being clingy."

I give him a flat look. "You all but got to your knees and begged to come with me to see my mom."

At this, he smirks. "If you want me on my knees, Ellison, all you have to do is ask."

I scoff. "It'll be a cold day in hell when I ask that of you."

"I'll pack layers."

I shake my head and pick up my pace. He matches my stride with ease, and he even holds the door to Mom's apartment building open for me.

We make it to the elevator in silence. As the car climbs to the seventh floor, my jaw clenches.

"Okay, seriously," I demand, whirling on Jackson, "what's going on? You're acting weird."

He narrows his eyes. "I want to put a better security system in place at the inn, including more cameras," he finally admits. "At your cottage, too."

Some of the fight leaves me. "Okay... Where is this suddenly coming from?"

He shrugs, feigning nonchalance. "I've been thinking about it since the whole spray paint incident. Especially since I found those pictures." His lips quirk as some mirth reenters his expression. "But someone has a tendency to jump down my throat when I suggest making a change, so excuse me for being a little nervous to bring it up."

I shove at his shoulder. "We both know you've never had an issue with getting under my skin."

"You do make it rather easy."

I roll my eyes.

"So the cameras," he says. "Are we agreed?"

I nod. "We're agreed."

A new system has been on my wish list, a dream for

sometime in the distant future, but with everything that's happened, waiting is a luxury I can't afford.

Jackson nudges my shoulder with his. "Look at us, making a joint decision. I think that's our first."

I fight my smile. "Don't bring attention to it. If I think about it too long, it'll make me nauseous."

Jackson chuckles, and the sound causes this weird fluttering feeling to emerge low in my stomach. The sensation is foreign—it's been a long time since someone has given me butterflies. It's a cruel twist of fate that this someone just so happens to be the business partner I love to hate.

As soon as those elevator doors slide open, I stride into the hall. I need to get as far away from him as possible. The close proximity is messing with my brain. Yeah, that's it. It's toxic being too close to him.

"Before we go in there, I just want to make something clear," I say, looking over my shoulder at Jackson. "Whatever you say, do *not* bring up the vandalism or the pictures."

His brows furrow. "You're not going to tell her?"

"Not if I can help it. She doesn't need that kind of stress." I raise a brow. "Understood?"

He nods, albeit reluctantly. I know he doesn't truly understand, but he doesn't have to. He just has to respect my decision.

My mother's apartment is the last one on this floor. I don't bother knocking, I just let myself in.

"Honey, I'm home!" I call.

Voices carry from the living room to the entryway as I toe off my shoes. Jackson does the same. Today, he's actually dressed in casual clothes. Flip flops included.

I almost fell over at the sight of those flip flops.

"Nice place," Jackson says with an approving nod.

"Yeah," I agree, turning over my shoulder as I walk toward the voices, "that's why it costs me an arm and a—"

"*His huge cock rams home. In and out, and in and out. My inner walls flutter as he stretches me to the max. The sound of skin slapping skin is erotic...*"

My jaw hits the floor. Sitting in my mother's living room is her book club. Here I was, thinking they individually read their books and then discussed their plots over tea. Little did I know they hold smut read-alouds.

"Meyer," Mom says when she sees me, "I wasn't expecting you."

I clear my throat. "I can see that," I reply. I gesture to my companion, who is shaking with restrained laughter. "We had a free afternoon, so I thought I'd bring Jackson by. But you're busy..."

My mother claps her hands. "Alright, ladies, pack it in. We can meet again tomorrow. Same time, same place."

At Mom's command, a group of old ladies rocking perms and near identical floral grandma sweaters begin to filter out of the room. Each woman holds a book in her hand, the cover showing off the naked chest of a kilted man.

"Meyer, good to see you, dear!" one of the women says.

I offer her an awkward smile. "Good to see you, too, Georgia."

Her gaze slides to the man standing beside me. "Is he your lover?" she whispers rather loudly, pointing at Jackson.

I shake my head with a scoff. "*No.* He owns Dog Days Inn with me."

"Oh." She frowns. Then her eyes drag down Jackson's body appreciatively. "He's *handsome*. You better get on that, dear, or someone else might just snap him up."

She fluffs her perm, and I grimace at the older woman. "Have a nice day."

She walks away, and I shiver. Jackson, however, seems to be all too amused.

"Georgia's a peach," he drawls.

I send him my best look of contempt, to which he simply laughs.

Once my mother's book club has exited the apartment, Jackson and I sit down in the living room. Mom's in her recliner, so I make sure to sit as far away from Jackson on the couch as possible.

"I hope my daughter isn't giving you too much grief, Jackson," she says.

My mouth pops open. "Hey!"

Jackson grins. "She certainly gives me a run for my money, but it's not totally unjustified," he tells her. "Sometimes I need reminding that not everything is a problem that needs to be fixed."

Oh.

Mom's smile is soft in return. "How are you liking Fraisier Creek?"

Jackson relaxes further into the couch. Making himself at home in my mother's presence. Something about that stirs a warmth inside me.

Indigestion. It's just indigestion.

"It's a huge change of pace from the city. I've lived in Toronto all my life, so it was jarring to move here, to say the least." His eyes flick in my direction briefly. "I think it agrees with me, though."

Mom has that look in her eyes that screams, *I'm about to meddle*. I know the look well. So I blurt out the only thing I can think of.

"So…huge cocks, huh?" Both my mother and Jackson look at me, blinking. My cheeks flame. "The book club," I croak. "You guys read smut. Out loud."

At this, Mom laughs. "Oh, *that*. We didn't for the longest time, but Doris suggested we try it one day and we found it's kind of fun. You should come sometime!"

Jackson coughs into his fist, but I know he's trying to cover up a laugh. I cast a dirty look in his direction before turning back to my mother.

Tugging at the collar of my shirt, I say, "I think I'm okay. Thanks, though."

Sitting in the same room as my mother while she and her friends read fictional sex scenes aloud is not what I would consider a good time. Mom and I are close, but not *that* close.

She shrugs. "Suit yourself."

"Anyway." I forcefully try to pivot the conversation. "I just wanted to come see how you're doing."

"She begged me to come with her," Jackson adds.

I throw him another dirty look. Mom glances between us, that same meddling glint in her eye, but then she settles on me.

"Oh, I'm perfectly fine. I'd like to hear about you, though. Why didn't you tell me about the vandalism?"

I should have known she would find out. She may not

live in Fraisier Creek anymore, but she has more connections than a politician's nepotism baby. There's hardly anything I can successfully hide from her.

I sigh, deflated. "Because I didn't want you to know."

She frowns. "Just because I'm not there to handle the day-to-day things doesn't mean I don't want to know what's going on. You can always talk to me. You know that."

My mother chastising me isn't anything new, but the guilt making a home inside me is. I don't keep things from her. But every time I tried to pick up the phone, I chickened out. Then I was in too deep and decided not telling her was the best option.

I eye Jackson. He seems to pick up on my silent cue, standing from the couch.

"I'm just going to step outside for a minute," he says. "I have a call to make."

Once the front door shuts behind him, I turn back to my mom. "I was scared you would be disappointed in me," I admit quietly.

Her brows furrow, which causes the lines on her forehead to deepen. "Disappointed in you? Why would I be disappointed in you?"

"As soon as I take control of the inn, something like *that* happens?" I scoff. "The inn means so much to you, and I let it get *vandalized*. I'd be disappointed in me."

Mom sits forward, turning fully to face me. "Meyer Ellison, you knock that off right now. I'm honestly a little offended that you think I'm that unreasonable."

I shake my head. "No, Mom, I just..." I look down at my hands in my lap. "I really want to make you proud."

"My girl," she says, "I've been proud of you since the moment I found you."

My mother has always given her love freely. She's never given me a reason to doubt her. But there has always been this part of me, this voice inside my head, that tells me I'm not good enough. That I need to be better if I want her to keep loving me. It's part of why I try so hard with the inn.

I stare at my hands in my lap. "I'm sorry I didn't tell you."

Guilt gnaws at me. Now is the perfect opportunity to tell her about what Jackson found, about the pictures. But I don't.

I gave the police my statement, and now I just want to move on. Forget it happened. Maybe that's not the smart thing to do, but the inn is my priority right now.

"I forgive you. Now, tell me," she says, raising a brow, "how are things really going with Jackson?"

"They're...good," I reply reluctantly.

Jackson was right the other day. I kind of hate admitting when I'm wrong, and maybe I was a little bit wrong about him. Although I still resist change, I can admit that some of his suggestions haven't been *terrible*.

Mom hums. "Glad to see your pride isn't getting in your way."

My nose scrunches. "My pride doesn't get in my way."

She pats my arm placatingly. "You forget I've known you for twenty-five years, my prickly pear. There isn't much you can get past me."

Rolling my eyes, I admit, "It was a little rough at first. I...

may have been a little stubborn. But things are going smoother now."

This makes her smile, and she reaches over to pat my knee. "Good. That's exactly what Cherie wanted."

"She truly wanted us to be partners?" I know I wasn't open to hearing this when Jackson first came to town, but I'll admit I am curious now.

Mom nods. "She did. She was worried about Jackson and all the time he was dedicating to his work in the city. She thought this would be a much more suitable position. For a couple reasons."

Now it's my turn to roll my eyes. "Not this again. Jackson and I are business partners, yes, but that is the only kind of partnership you'll be getting out of us."

Mom throws up her hands in surrender, the picture of innocence. "I didn't even say anything this time."

I go to say more—to tell her how ridiculous the idea is— but Jackson reenters the room. My lips snap shut, and I send my mother a look. One that tells her not to open her big mouth. I don't need Jackson getting any kind of silly ideas.

"So," he says when he sits down again. "I'm curious. Tell me more about this book club."

Mom grins, and I groan, wishing I could melt into the couch. Bringing Jackson here was a bad idea. Involving him in more aspects of my life beyond the inn will only end in disaster. But judging by the way he fits so effortlessly, I have a feeling it's too late.

I'm screwed.

CHAPTER 21
MEYER

> Have you seen Jackson today?

PIPPA

Not yet! I don't think he's been in.

Something feels off.

Not the same kind of strange as Jackson finding those pictures of me, but strange nonetheless. Usually Jackson is the first of us to arrive in the office, despite my efforts to come in early, and he always has a coffee waiting for me. This morning, there was no Jackson and no coffee.

I could text him myself. I've even thought about it, opening our message thread and staring at the screen. But this is everything I have been wanting since the day he set foot here—Jackson, out of my way.

Except...maybe that's not what I want anymore.

I stand from the desk abruptly, my chair rolling backwards. Stuffing my phone into my back pocket, I make my way into the hall and head for the stairs. I haven't been to Jackson's room at the inn since I went on my tipsy rampage. I told myself I wouldn't go back, for the sake of my dignity. But desperate times and all that.

After knocking on Jackson's door, I take a step back, feeling all sorts of awkward. *Why did I think this was a good idea again?*

Because I'm trying to be nice. Because, as loath as I am to admit it, I'm more than just curious about the reason he's missing work. I *care*.

When the door swings open, the sarcastic comment on the tip of my tongue promptly dies. "What's wrong?" I ask.

Jackson rubs a hand across his jaw. He is generally always clean shaven, but today, he's let the stubble take over. It isn't a bad look, though it is slightly concerning.

"Sorry, I meant to text you," he says. "I'm not coming in today."

Since he's been in town, Jackson hasn't missed a single day of work. Not once. I would be surprised if he has ever taken a day off in his whole adult life. He's definitely the type.

"You're not?" My eyes narrow. "Why?"

"Can't I take a day off without having some kind of ulterior motive?" he asks.

"This," I say, gesturing to his appearance, "is not like you." I try to gentle my voice. "What's going on, Jackson?"

He scoffs. "You don't know me. And you've made it perfectly clear you don't want to."

My brows jump in surprise. "Wow, this really isn't like you. You must be spending too much time with me."

He sighs, the weary look in his eyes growing stronger. "Fuck, I'm sorry. I shouldn't have snapped at you."

I lay a hand on his arm. The move shocks me almost as much as it shocks him. "Just tell me what's going on. Are you sick? I promise I'll leave you alone. I'm just...worried."

He shakes his head. "Nothing like that. It's Cherie's birthday today, and I thought I could handle it. Operate like normal. Evidently, that's not the case."

That stops me in my tracks. In all the years I had known Jackson's grandmother, I don't think I ever learned when her birthday was. I'm not sure my mother even knows. The last thing Cherie would have wanted is us making a fuss over it.

She wouldn't want Jackson to be alone today either.

"Alright," I say as an idea begins to form. "You have five minutes."

"Five minutes? For what?"

"To get ready." I gesture to his room behind him. "Come on, hurry up. I need your help with something."

He shakes his head. "I'm not really in the mood, Meyer."

"Well, tough." I cross my arms. "We can't let Cherie's birthday go by without making her favourite dessert. She'd find a reason to haunt us."

This earns me a small grin. "She would, wouldn't she?"

"She absolutely would. So get beautified, Hotshot, and then let's go."

―――――

Baking with Jackson was a mistake.

First, he doesn't know his teaspoons from his tablespoons, so he severely over-measured the salt for the pie crust. Then he almost choked me with the amount of flour that flew around my kitchen. After having to scrap everything for a third time, I finally relegated him to cleanup while I started over with the crust, then the filling.

As the shell bakes, Jackson leans against the island, watching while I slice the tops off a basket of strawberries. He reaches over and plucks one from the bowl, popping it in his mouth.

"Hey." I poke him in the side. "Those are not for eating."

"Pretty sure that's exactly what they're intended for," he replies.

I bite my tongue as I take a steadying breath. *Be nice, Meyer. He's having a hard day.* Though he seems to be in much better spirits now. I'd like to think I had a hand in that. I took a shot in the dark by forcing him from his room earlier.

Shaking my head, I say, "You sound like Atticus."

When I look over at him, I see a soft smile pulling at his lips. My heart does a little backflip. Ever since the day we were at the strawberry patch, Atticus has been obsessed with Jackson, even more than he was before. Atticus loves his uncle, but I think having another guy around has been good for him. Good for Jackson, too, it seems.

"He really likes you," I add.

"I really like him, too," he replies. "He's a good kid."

He was wrong earlier, when he said I didn't know him. Without my permission, I've become familiar with parts of Jackson I had no intention of knowing. When he's not being a gigantic pain in my ass, and I forget about the inn, he's actually...nice to be around. A fact I don't care to admit out loud, especially to him.

I've known he's attractive since I first set eyes on him back in April. But slowly, he's been challenging all of the preconceived notions I had about him.

Jackson reaches for another strawberry, but I pluck it from his grasp before he can eat it. My other hand presses against his chest, holding him back.

"This," I say, holding the berry between my thumb and forefinger, "is not for you."

I go to put the berry back in the bowl, but he grabs my wrist. When my eyes flit to meet his, something in them has changed. His gaze snares me, and I am held captive in the honey pools of his eyes. He pulls my hand toward him, and then he's taking a bite out of the strawberry.

Lips parted, I watch him swallow. The air in the room feels charged, like we're one second away from some kind of explosion. I'm not sure how I didn't notice the temperature shifting, but it's suddenly very hot in here.

I have no idea what's happening, but I am powerless to stop it.

Jackson drops my wrist, but he presses closer. My chest rises and falls with each strangled breath I take. Slowly, tentatively, he reaches out. I swear I'm not breathing as his brows lower, his attention then focused on his hand. Barely, at first, and then with more confidence, his thumb sweeps in an arch across my cheekbone.

"You had some flour there," he croaks, his throat tightening.

"*Oh*," I breathe, unable to hide the note of disappointment in my tone. I curse myself for what little restraint I seem to possess.

"What's wrong?"

"Nothing. It's just..." I swallow, and then words fall from my lips before I can stop them. "You looked a little like you were maybe going to kiss me."

"Oh." The silence stretches, threatening to consume me. "If I said that I was thinking about it, would you let me?"

My stomach bottoms out and my breathing shallows again. Would I let him?

Maybe it's the proximity or the sweetness of the pie filling, or maybe my oven is malfunctioning and filling the room with toxic fumes, but—

"*Yes.*"

He surges forward, taking my face in his hands. I expect roughness with his urgency, but he's gentle. Almost *too* gentle.

I close my eyes at the first brush of his lips. Then he's tilting my face up, angling it just so, before his mouth claims mine. I can taste the strawberry on him still, and it has my tongue sweeping out across his lower lip.

He groans in surprise, but he lets me in. It's a clash of teeth and tongue and lips, and I pull myself closer to him, wanting more. Wanting it all.

For a few minutes, I forget about where I am and who I'm with. I don't let myself consider the ramifications of my actions, I just feel. And it feels *wonderful*. For the first time in what seems like forever, my brain goes quiet. It's strange when something so loud finally shuts off.

Eventually, Jackson pulls away, and my body comes

crashing back into reality. His hands are still on my face, so I take a step back, letting them fall away.

My thoughts—all of them, every single one—roar inside my brain. *Oh, God. What did I just do?*

I clear my throat as I turn toward the oven, just in time for it to ding. The pie crust is, mercifully, ready. I take my time donning my oven mitts and pulling the tray from the oven, all so I can avoid looking at Jackson.

Maybe if I pretend the awkwardness isn't there, it will go away.

When I look up, he is staring at me. Trying to understand the shift. *Please*, my eyes plead. *Let me hide.*

A coward in every sense of the word. But me and Jackson, we no longer toe a line—we've crossed it. And now I'm trying desperately to scramble back to the place we once were, for going any further into the unknown will surely end in disaster.

A kiss. With my *business partner*, no less.

Shame threads through my veins like vines on a trellis. Mom had asked me to get along with Jackson, not do *this*. Despite the teasing way she talked about Cherie's hope for us and our partnership. And if anyone in town found out, they would question *everything*. My integrity.

The inn is more important—would *always* be more important—than a kiss. Even if that kiss sent a trail of blazing heat down my spine. Even if Jackson's lips slotted against my own like two puzzle pieces, joined at last.

Even if, goddamn it, I *liked* it.

"The filling needs more sugar," he says.

A beat of silence, then understanding. Out. He's giving

me an out. I grab hold of it with both hands, and I don't look back.

"Considering you can't tell your head from your ass when it comes to baking, I think you should let me handle it, Hotshot," I reply. "Recipes have specific measurements for a reason."

"If you say so."

I dip a spoon into the filling and then let it settle on my tongue. It tastes off.

"What the hell?"

He smirks. "Can't tell my head from my ass, huh?"

I glower at him, then frown at the bowl. "What happened?"

A distraction. Jackson Vaughan is nothing but a distraction, with his pretty words and his pretty face.

What usually takes me no time at all ends up becoming a large task as I remake the filling. Still, when the pie is done, chilling in the fridge, I smile. I like to bake a variety of strawberry pies, but this is one of my favourite recipes—the filling is mixed in a pot on the stove, then poured into the baked shell and set in the fridge. It's served cold with a dollop of whipped cream on top.

"We managed to spend the whole day together without any threats of death," I muse.

Jackson nods. "You should be proud of yourself. Impeccable restraint on your behalf."

I roll my eyes. "Don't act like you haven't thought about it."

"About what?"

"Killing me." When his brows jump, I amend my statement. "Not *actually*. Metaphorically."

He grins. "I know what you meant." He slides his hands into the pockets of his sweatpants, ever casual. "But I'm afraid I can't say that I have."

Now my brows jump in surprise. "I'm very stubborn, you know. I wouldn't blame you."

"That, Ellison, is precisely what I like most about you."

Not for the first time, Jackson has managed to render me speechless.

"The pie," he goes on, as if he hadn't just complimented me. My obstinacy. "When can we eat?" His eyes lock on mine, and I can almost swear something predatory—wolfish—flashes in them. "I'm hungry."

CHAPTER 22
MEYER

Today is *so not* my day.

We haven't had any updates from the police's investigation, even after Jackson gave them a not-so-gentle prodding. But we also haven't had any more creepy incidents, so I finally managed to convince my friends that I don't need a permanent bodyguard. Jackson has been accompanying me to see my mother every time I've been recently, but I went alone today.

My happiness was short-lived, though, because my air conditioning decided to crap out on my drive to Calderville, and then on my way back, one of my tires went flat.

Atticus's class is on a field trip to the strawberry fields today, and Pippa took the day off work to help supervise. Declan is at the lumber yard—I can't justify interrupting his shift to help myself out. And with that, I realize that my network is very small. I know lots of people in town, but none of them are close enough to warrant asking a favour.

The walk back to Fraisier Creek is long, albeit manageable, but in this heat, it's likely I'd keel over from heat stroke.

Which leaves me only two options: wait in the unforgiving sun for Kenny to come tow my car or call the last person I want to need something from.

Ten minutes later, a black sports car slows and then does a U-turn, pulling up on the shoulder behind me.

"I'm tired, hot and sweaty, so whatever teasing comment you're about to make—" I hold up a palm. "Just don't."

Jackson throws his hands up in surrender. "I was only going to offer to change your tire for you."

I raise a skeptical brow. "You know how to do that?"

He heads for my trunk. "Believe it or not, I'm very capable with my hands." After rooting around for a minute, he turns to me. "Ellison, where's your spare tire?"

I shrug. "I don't know, in there somewhere?"

He shakes his head. "There's nothing here."

"Son of a bitch." I kick at the flat tire, but I manage to hit the hubcap instead. My big toe throbs. "*Ow*. Fuck."

"Okay," he says, placing his hands on my shoulders and steering me away from my car. "Let's not start a fight you can't win, huh?"

I eye my old Ford Fiesta. "Should've gone with the Honda Civic."

Jackson laughs. "Come on, get in. We can call the tow truck on the way back."

Begrudgingly, I agree. In the blissful coolness of Jackson's air conditioning, I call Kenny and tell him where I left my stupid hunk of junk. But when we bypass the inn, I whirl on Jackson.

"Where are you going?" I ask. "The inn's back there."

He nods. "I'm aware."

My protests go unacknowledged until Jackson whips his car into the parking lot of Fraisier Creek High School. Class has already let out for the day, so the lot is empty except for the odd vehicle belonging to teachers and custodial staff.

"Taking me to relive my glory days?" I ask.

Jackson looks over at me, his eyes making a slow perusal of my body, and then he grins. "Come on, Ellison. We both know you didn't peak in high school."

Jackson unclicks his seatbelt and then he's pushing out of the car. I follow suit, more curious than I want to be. As it is, I'm not even sure why I'm going along with this. The air conditioning in Jackson's fancy car only did so much to brighten my mood—I'm still incredibly tired and dripping in boob sweat.

I meet Jackson at the hood of the car. "Are you going to tell me why we're here?"

"We're going to have some good old-fashioned, small-town fun," he replies, then begins to loosen his tie. "Think you can handle that?"

I glower. "What part of me being tired and sweaty made you think I would want to take part in whatever this is?"

He sighs. "I hate to play this card, but you owe me."

I scoff. "I'll give you two dollars for the gas you burned."

"Just humour me. Please?"

"Fine." Then I realize that both his tie and suit jacket are lying on the hood of his car. His fingers are now fiddling with his belt buckle. "Why the hell are you taking your clothes off in a school parking lot?"

"Because we're going to the creek."

"The creek?"

He shrugs. "I overheard Ashley talking to a friend about it. Seems as good a place as any to spend the afternoon."

While my initial instinct is to blow him off, I don't.

"Alright, Hotshot. But unless you want to choke on teen spirit, you'll follow me. I know a better spot."

Jackson nudges my arm. "You seem awfully familiar with this place."

I offer him a crooked grin. "Oh, I totally used to skip school to make out with boys here. Mostly Rudy."

"The pizza guy?"

"The one and only."

An odd expression crosses his face, but it disappears just as quickly as it arrived. We walk through the trees, away from the school and the local hangout spot, until we hit a secluded part of the creek farther down.

When I turn to Jackson, I stop short. The sight of him carefully unbuttoning his shirt has my mouth watering. But then I notice he has a small scar running down the middle of his chest, between his pecs.

I'm staring. I *know* I'm staring, but can I will my eyes away? Not a chance in hell. Which is exactly where I'll be headed for lusting after my business partner and eyeing his scars.

"You're doing that thing again."

My head snaps up. "What thing?"

He smirks. "That thing where you can't keep your eyes off me."

I scoff, crossing my arms. "Don't flatter yourself, pretty boy."

"Don't need to. You do such a good job of that already."

"You're ridiculous."

He takes a step closer. "It's alright, Ellison. Because I can't keep my eyes off you either."

My traitorous gaze blazes a downward trail once again, getting caught on that scar. It's most likely from surgery of some sort, but it's faded, like maybe it happened when he was a kid.

"Ask me."

Jackson's words pull my attention back to his face. "What?"

"Ask me about the scar, Meyer," he says. "Ask me because you're curious. Ask me because you care to know something about me."

He didn't put any particular emphasis on the word *care*, but it rings in my ears anyway. He's daring me to show my hand—to reveal that I do, begrudgingly, care in some way— and *damn him*, I want to.

I swallow. "The scar," I say, my voice unsteady. "How did you get it, Jackson?"

"Surgery when I was a baby." He runs his fingers along the scar at his front. "Coarctation of the aorta. That's the name of the congenital heart defect I had."

"And now?"

He huffs a laugh, running a hand through his hair. "That night you called me a workaholic," he says, "you were right. I, uh— Well, I've been known to throw myself into work, even if it means fucking up my blood pressure. Which is already too high, thanks to the whole shoddy heart thing."

"Why?"

Forget showing my hand. It seems I've just surrendered the whole deck to him.

"I don't know." Slowly, he shakes his head. "That's a lie. I do know. It's— Well, now that I'm trying to say it out loud, it sounds so fucking stupid. I spent time at the hospital and in doctors' offices when I was a kid, checking on my heart. I missed a lot of school. Overall, I feel like I wasted a lot of time, so in a roundabout way, I was trying to make up for it."

"Jackson..."

He shakes his head. "That doesn't really make sense, I know. And on top of all that, I think I was trying to prove to everyone that I was okay. Especially after Cherie's death. But I ended up making a fool of myself in the process."

I cock my head. "What do you mean?"

"Just after Cherie passed, there was a proposal I was supposed to present to my colleagues. I had been working on it for months. I wasn't sleeping much, was running on caffeine. Within a few minutes of my presentation starting, I knew something was wrong. I shouldn't have, but I tried to push through. I woke up in the hospital later that evening. Turns out, I had collapsed on the conference room floor from the stress I had put on my body."

I wrap my arms around my middle to stop myself from reaching for him. "Are you okay now?" I ask.

He smiles a little. "Getting there." Then he runs a hand through his hair again, mussing it up. "I didn't want to come here. To Fraisier Creek. When I found out about the inn, I thought of every way I could extricate myself. I didn't have time for this place."

A strange feeling washes over me. The knowledge that Jackson almost didn't come here is a little hard to swallow.

"What changed your mind?" I decide I need to know. Somehow, it feels important.

"Cherie left me a letter," he explains. "She asked me to give the inn six months. After my health issues, I was put on medical leave. Because I'm chronically under-slept and over-caffeinated, my doctor gave me six months." His lips quirk upwards. "Seemed kind of serendipitous at that point, so I figured I didn't have anything to lose."

"Isn't that cheating? You're still working."

He grins. "Thanks to your micromanaging, any work I've done for the inn is hardly detrimental to my health. Probably is to yours, though."

"I don't micromanage!"

"Really?" He arches a brow as he steps closer. "Is that why your fingers are fidgeting with the need to text Pippa and Trystan for updates?"

"Hey," I say, poking a finger into his chest. He's still advancing, and my breath hitches. "You don't have room to lecture me, Mr. High Blood Pressure."

"When I initially read my grandmother's letter, I didn't understand why she would send me here," he continues. "After I arrived, I decided the reason was because Cherie wanted me to help her beloved inn thrive."

"And what do you think now?"

"Now," Jackson says, "I think she saw that you and I

needed each other." I open my mouth to argue, but he holds up a hand. "I know, *Meyer Ellison doesn't need anybody.* Maybe that's the truth. In any case, I'm trying something new, and I implore you to do it with me."

"And what is it that you're *imploring* me to do?"

"Loosen up." His hands plant themselves on my hips, and my lips part in a silent gasp. "And live a little."

The next thing I know, I'm airborne. I shriek as I tuck my knees against my chest, just in time for my body to submerge in the creek.

The cool temperature of the water is a shock to the system, but it's undeniably refreshing after facing the unbearable summer heat wave. I breach the surface, sputtering as I brush sopping strands of blonde away from my face. Jackson stands on the shore, eyes alight in laughter as he takes in my drowned appearance.

I'm still fully clothed. I glance down at my chest, noting the way the fabric of my white t-shirt is clinging to my skin. I also don't miss the way Jackson's gaze traces the visible outline of my bra.

An idea—not a *good* one, but an idea nonetheless—infiltrates my brain. The rational part of me says to knock it off, but the rest of me tells it to get fucked. I wade closer to the bank of the creek.

Jackson follows my movements. He watches as I grip the hem of my shirt with both hands. Slowly, I begin to drag the material up. I lose sight of him as I tug the shirt over my head, but if his eyes were bugging at the sight of my midriff, I can only imagine what they'll look like at the sight of my tits covered in lace.

I toss my shirt to the ground at Jackson's feet. Then I let my gaze trail from his shoes up to his face. His jaw is clenched, his eyes roving over my chest. I mentally applaud past me for picking out a sexy bra today.

Edging closer, I cross my arms and rest them right on the bank. In this position, my folded arms push my bust upwards, giving Jackson an eyeful of cleavage.

"Alright, I'm loose," I say. "Now what?"

Jackson's eyes flash. I only meant to tease him a little, but now I think I may be in real danger.

He quickly tugs his shoes and pants off, and jumps into the water beside me. Then he advances, his gaze shining with predatory intent. I back away, but I'm not fast enough. His arm snags my waist, dragging me close to him.

Then his touch drifts to my hips, and I don't even think before my legs encircle his waist. I'm buoyed by the water, but he palms my ass anyway, holding me up.

His gaze flicks down to my lips, then back up to my eyes. His honey irises are flecked by fire, desire seeping through. My fingers twist into the hair at his nape, holding him steady. Then my heartbeat trips as I close the distance, my breasts smashing against his chest.

His hands tighten on my ass as my lips brush his, the kiss of a feather.

"You can do better than that," he goads.

I wait for my body to bristle at the taunt. To show some sign of defiance. Instead, my thighs squeeze around him, and I become acutely aware of the ache growing between my legs.

This time, I do kiss him properly. When I smash my lips

against his, he's waiting for me. He coaxes my mouth open, and then his tongue clashes with mine. I shudder.

I know, without any doubt, that I want more. Need more. So I pull back, breathing heavily.

"Jackson?"

He looks at me with hooded eyes. "Hm?" he murmurs.

"Take me home."

CHAPTER 23

MEYER

THE CAR IS STIFLING the whole drive back, but not from the late afternoon heat.

Normally, I would feel uncomfortable sitting here in damp clothes, but I can't seem to care about that. I can't seem to care about much of anything except this thrum of anticipation.

Jackson's knuckles are white as he grips the steering wheel in both hands. His jacket and tie are on the back seat, discarded. He looks good in just a button-down with the sleeves rolled up to his forearms.

Logically, I know this is a terrible idea. I can't seem to help myself from wanting it anyway. Maybe, with any luck, doing this will purge Jackson from my system entirely. If I flush all my attraction out in one evening, I can go back to simply surviving these next few months with him in town.

Jackson parks in his usual space in the parking lot, and I waste no time getting out. He follows close behind, and we make our way down the gravel path. Then I'm unlocking my front door, disarming the fancy alarm system Jackson insisted on having put in, and spinning to face him.

I frown when I see him standing on the edge of the porch, like he's about to leave. I lean against the doorframe. "Are you not coming in?"

His brows furrow. "Coming in? I thought—" He shakes his head as he comes closer. "Never mind."

I step into the entryway to let him by. "What did you think I meant by *take me home*?"

Jackson runs a hand through his hair. It's already a little dishevelled from my fingers back at the creek. He looks adorably nervous right now, which seems entirely out of character for him. Then again, this is new territory for us.

"I got in my head," he replies. "I guess I figured you changed your mind, and I would have to do a lot more than bring you coffee to get back into your good graces."

"Get back in my good graces?" I grin. "Who said you were ever in them?"

He shrugs as he takes another step toward me. "I don't know." He smiles. "I seem to be doing something right."

I'm not sure what happened, but something in me snapped back at the creek. I'm *tired* of fighting this pull between us. Now, I fully plan to give in.

I take hold of his shirtfront and tug him toward me, and I let my lips crash into his like an inevitable head-on collision. There will be broken glass and debris in our wake, but I can't bring myself to care. Not when he hooks his fingers into my belt loops and pulls me flush against him.

I begin to walk backwards, tugging him with me. He closes the door with his foot, and then I'm pushing his back up against it.

His hands gravitate toward my hips, anchoring there. Then he pivots us, and my back hits the door. His knee nudges my thighs apart.

"Just once," I say. "We're only doing this once."

I feel Jackson's smirk curve against my jaw. "I have a hard time believing you'll be able to keep your hands off me, Ellison. It's already difficult enough for your eyes."

In response, I reach out and pinch one of his nipples through his shirt. His answering nip of my earlobe sends a thrill down my spine. Jackson and I are evenly matched in this way—this push and pull. He gives and I take, and when I offer myself to him, his response is nothing but greed.

A glutton for punishment. A glutton for *me*.

"*One time*," I try again.

"Okay," he agrees. "Just this once."

Just once to purge this growing need from my body. Just once to sate the curious part of me that wonders what it would be like to have Jackson. All of him.

He takes my hand and starts tugging me toward the hallway. Toward my bedroom. But that sends a bolt of uneasiness through me. Because that makes things too real, letting him into my space, and that's not what this is. This is purely to scratch an itch.

"This way," I say, drawing him to the living room instead.

I push him onto the worn sofa, and he goes willingly. For a second, I just admire him like this, sitting against the back of the couch. His hair is slightly mussed, his lips are swollen, and his erection is visibly straining against his slacks.

A small part of me wants to savour this, but the longer this draws on, the harder it will be to keep myself detached. Quick and easy—that's what I need.

I unfasten the button on my shorts and slide them down my legs. Then I chuck them across the room before I slide onto Jackson's lap, straddling him. His hands slide up my thighs to rest on the curve of my ass. He rocks me against him, both of us groaning at the friction it creates.

I undo the buttons on his shirt, revealing his firm chest. I let my gaze wander as he slides it off his shoulders, then tosses it aside.

"Are you ogling me, Ellison?"

My eyes snap up, and I scoff. "Don't be ridiculous."

He simply leans back, giving me a better view. "Look all you like, baby," he says. "I love having your eyes on me."

Something twists inside my chest at the earnestness of his statement. Beneath the haze of lust, all I see is truth shining in his gaze, and it fractures a little piece of my soul. Too much—this is *too much*. He must sense the rising panic because he blinks, and that look he was giving me is gone.

"If I can only have you once," he says, eyes darkening, "then I'm not wasting any more time." He hooks a finger under my chin. "Come here."

I obey, letting my lips crash against his. And then Jackson is pulling back and helping me out of my t-shirt. He tosses it to the floor in the same direction my shorts landed.

I reach behind my back to unhook my bra. The straps slip off my shoulders with ease, and Jackson eagerly helps extricate the material from my body. His gaze heats at the sight of my bare skin. I've never experienced a man's eyes roving over me so reverently. Until Jackson, that is.

My fingers thread through his hair, tugging. I urge his mouth toward mine again and I'm rewarded with a kiss that has my thighs tightening around his hips. Jackson groans against my mouth, and then he begins to trail kisses down my neck. He blazes a path down my collarbone, the swell of one breast, and then finally to my nipple, which has gone rock hard under his attention.

His tongue swirls the peak. My head tips back as the sensation washes over me.

At the same time, one of his hands leaves my hip, and then I feel the brush of his fingers against my inner thigh. I ache in anticipation. He is *so close* to where I want him to be. But he doesn't go any farther.

I press my hips closer, asking for his touch. Before now, I've been too stubborn to admit it, but this is something I've been wanting for a while. Now that the possibility is so near, that fact is undeniable.

Jackson releases my nipple and grins. "Something you want to ask me, gorgeous?"

I shake my head.

He toys with the band of my underwear. "If I slide these to the side, what am I going to find?" he taunts. "Are you wet for me, Ellison?"

"No," I reply. My breath hitches when I feel the ghost of a touch on my clit, over my underwear.

Jackson sits back. "The truth. Give me one truth, and I'll think about playing with this pretty pussy of yours."

He removes his hand entirely, and I let out a whine of disappointment. "Come *on*."

"Answer me honestly, then you can have what you want."

Half of me wants to continue being contrary, but the other, stronger half is tired of games. I've already made it this far—I want my reward.

"Fine. *Yes*."

Amusement shines in his eyes. "Yes what?"

My teeth grind together. "Yes, Jackson. I'm wet for you. Happy?"

He grins. "Immensely."

I want to argue, but he kisses me before I can, and then his hand is back between my thighs. He pushes my underwear to the side and then eases two fingers inside me. My lips part on a silent gasp, feeling the stretch.

I grip his shoulders as I rock against his hand, chasing that pleasure. It feels good having someone else's hand on me, inside me. When I grind against his palm, I have to bite my lip to stop from crying out.

He pinches one of my nipples, and I almost lose control right then and there. I can feel my orgasm building, like the rise of a tidal wave.

"Jackson," I pant, "I'm going to—"

He withdraws from my breast, and he pulls his fingers out, leaving me feeling empty. He simply grins in response to my glare. I want to wipe that stupid proud look off his face.

"Patience, Ellison."

I frown. "You know I have very little."

This causes him to chuckle. "With this, you're just going to have to trust me. I promise to make it worth your while."

"What overwhelming confidence coming from someone with very little proof."

"Pull my cock out, baby. I'll show you proof."

Yes, please. I almost salivate at the thought. Finally, we're getting somewhere.

"Tell me you have a condom," I say. "Because we'll both be very disappointed if you don't."

I usually don't take my chances and have some on standby. But I ran out a little while ago, and I wasn't exactly expecting to fuck my business partner on my couch today. My bad.

Jackson nods. "In my wallet."

I rise up on my knees, giving him space to grab his wallet from his back pocket. Once he has the condom in hand, his wallet gets tossed aside.

I reach out, pulling on his zipper, and then he helps me tug his pants and boxers down, letting his cock free. Still annoyed about him not allowing me to finish, I snatch the condom from him and tear the packaging open. Then I roll it over his cock and grip his shaft.

I pump my hand a couple times, relishing his groan. He grips the back of my neck, trying to pull my mouth back to his, but I lean back as I notch the tip of his cock at my entrance.

"Be a good boy and sit still for me."

His gaze is full of fire, hearing my words. He leans back again, taking in the sight of me. "All yours, baby."

I sink onto his length slowly. Once I'm fully seated, my eyes close and my head tips back as I take in how deliciously full I feel. And then I start to rock.

"That's it, Meyer," he coaxes. "Use me. I want to watch you fuck yourself on my cock."

That's all the permission I need. I draw myself up until his cock is almost all the way out and then I drop down, slamming home. Jackson places his hands on my hips, helping me move.

"Oh, God."

"You're doing so good, baby. You're taking me so well."

The praise washes over me, and I bear down on him, hitting a spot inside that makes me cry out.

Jackson reaches between us, pressing a thumb to my clit, and I fall blissfully over the edge. Jackson follows shortly after, his release filling the condom as I clench around him.

My breathing comes in the form of ragged pants, and my legs feel like Jell-O.

His arms slip around my waist as I slump against his chest. We stay like that for a few moments, both trying to catch our breath. Then my mind starts whirring, thinking of all the implications of what just transpired.

I just slept with Jackson fucking Vaughan.

The regret tries to settle in, but I lock it away. *Later.* I can hate myself for being so goddamn weak later. Right now, I have to figure out how to politely tell my business partner he can pull out and go back to his room at the inn.

"So..." I draw back, putting some space between us. Our upper halves anyway. Our lower halves are still very much connected. "This was fun."

Jackson raises a brow. "Just fun?"

I slide off his lap, situating my underwear, and then I reach for my shirt, tugging it over my head. Jackson tucks himself back into his pants before he stands, and then we both pause, just staring at each other.

Fuck, this is awkward. Fuck, fuck, fuck.

This is, undoubtedly, why they tell you not to mix business with pleasure. If you do, you'll be forced into a staring contest with your business partner while you're half naked, both of you trying to will the other into breaking.

After another moment, I can't take it anymore. My eyes drop to the rug beneath my feet, watching my toes curl into the plush material as I force my mouth to form words.

"I have a...thing that I have to get ready for," I say. "So you should probably go."

I wince. I didn't intend to sound so dismissive, but panic is quickly creeping up my limbs. The only way out is to avoid thinking about what we just did, but the only way I can do that is if he gets out of my space. As it is, I'm sure I won't be able to fully lock the memories away. Not when his presence will still linger in the room, even after he's gone.

Fuck.

"Right." Jackson nods, shrugging on his shirt and buttoning it part of the way. The top half gapes open, leaving some of his chest exposed. "Good luck with your *thing*."

The expression on his face is one I can't quite puzzle out. He doesn't look upset, exactly. But he doesn't look happy either. Might as well officially add him to the long list of transgressions I've committed in my life.

We walk to the front door in stilted silence. And then I'm watching him leave, a nauseating whirl of emotions tearing through my insides.

He looks over his shoulder at me. "See you tomorrow, Ellison."

"This never happened!" I call after him. I don't know what possessed me to say it.

He turns now, walking backwards. "What never happened?"

And then he smirks.

Fuck.

CHAPTER 24
JACKSON

THIS NEVER HAPPENED.

That's what Meyer said last night. After everything that we did in her living room, I barely had time to zip up my fly before she was urging me out the door. Shutting me out. That part isn't new, but foolishly, I thought things might be a little different now.

She might want to forget, but I'm going to do everything in my power to make that impossible. Something this mind-blowing—this explosive—can't be wrong.

So I show up to work just like I always do, coffee in hand. This part of our morning has become so routine, Meyer doesn't even think twice about it. The muffin I place in front of her, however, gives her pause.

"What is that?" she asks.

"I'm fairly certain that is a muffin, if the bakery display at the café is to be believed."

She scrutinizes it and then me. "Why is it on my desk?"

"Because I know you didn't eat breakfast."

Her chin lifts. "And how would you know that?"

"Because you always help with the supply delivery on Tuesdays and you never give yourself enough time for food in the morning. Then you're starving by the time lunch rolls around." I gesture to the muffin. "So do me a favour and eat that."

Her suspicion mounts. "If this is about yesterday..."

I laugh. I laugh as if that's the most ridiculous thing I've ever heard. "Definitely not," I reply. "You're just easier to deal with when you're not hungry."

This is what she expects from me. She rolls her eyes, and I take that as acceptance. The slightest sign of caring on my end will have her running for the hills. Because I have come to care for her in the months we've been at this partnership. But that doesn't fit into her idea of who we are, and until I can convince her that maybe that's not the kind of guy I want to be, I have to play the game. Or I risk her pulling away even further.

There's a knock on the door, tugging me from my thoughts, and then Pippa pokes her head in. "Good morning," she says to me, a soft smile on her lips.

"Morning, Pippa," I reply. "I haven't seen Atticus in a while. How is he?"

Her smile brightens. It always does at the mention of her son. "He's great. Giving me a few grey hairs, as always."

"You're twenty-five, Pip. You do *not* have grey hairs," Meyer says.

"I plucked one this morning!" she insists. "Anyway, I was

just wondering if you could do inventory this morning, Meyer. I have tables I need to cover."

"I'll take care of it," I interject.

My business partner's eyes narrow on me. "You know how to take inventory?"

"I do know how to count, yes." I can tell she wants to bite out some snappy retort, a consequence of the vulnerable moment we shared last night still lingering. But I don't let her. Instead, I turn back to Pippa. "Don't worry about it. I've got it covered."

She looks a little apprehensive, glancing between me and Meyer, but then she nods. "Thank you, Jackson. I appreciate it."

Pippa heads back to the restaurant, and I gather the papers I need to take inventory. Meyer watches me, but she peels the wrapper from the muffin and begins to take small bites. She tears the top off first, her favourite part, and then finishes off the bottom.

I have to hide my satisfied smile as I step out of the room.

Once I'm shut inside the storage room, I slip my wireless earbuds in and decide to call my mother. It's a small miracle that I haven't heard from her yet today, but I count my blessings and press her contact. It's not that I don't love talking to my mother—I do. It's just that every call rolls back around to my heart and her asking if I'm truly alright.

I somehow manage to placate her and steer her toward other topics. And when the call eventually disconnects, I register how hot it feels in the storage room. I tug my suit jacket off and drape it over a stack of empty crates.

I keep working, but soon the air in the room starts to

grow thick, coating the inside of my throat. I begin to cough as warning bells start going off inside my brain. Something is wrong.

I abandon my clipboard and head toward the door. The smell of burnt plastic grows stronger the closer I get, and when I round a row of shelving, I see why. Fire.

A low wall of flames is blocking the way out, eating up every piece of cardboard and plastic in its path.

Panic flares in my chest, matching the growing flames. Not only because of the risk to the inn—the inn Meyer loves more than herself—but to all the people currently inside this building.

Shit.

I let myself panic for half a second, but then I force my brain to focus. I scan the wall until I find the fire alarm, and then I reach out and pull. Nothing happens. I try again, tugging hard on the switch. The little red box seems to mock me.

"Fuck," I curse aloud, followed by another cough.

Right about now, the sprinklers in the ceiling should be kicking in, detecting the smoke that continues to rise. But they don't. That thought worries me more, but I don't have time to examine why they aren't working.

I need to call 9-1-1, but I need to warn Meyer, too. If the fire alarm isn't working in here, who knows if it's working in the rest of the building.

I fumble with my phone, but I don't make it very far before I hear a voice calling my name.

"Jackson?" Meyer says from the opposite side of the door. "Are you still in there?"

"Meyer, don't—"

"Son of a bitch," she cries. "Why did the door handle *burn* me?"

"Don't panic," I call back, "but the storage room is kind of on fire."

I manage to hear her sharp intake of breath. "What do you mean, *kind of*?"

"There's a fire. The flames are in front of the door. And I don't—" I swallow thickly. "I'm not sure how I'm supposed to get out."

There are no windows to speak of in this room. The only way out is through the door. The door currently blocked by a wall of heat that only grows the more time it has to soak up all the oxygen in the space.

"Pippa!" If you didn't know Meyer well, you wouldn't be able to detect the tinge of panic in her voice. But I can. "I need your help with something!"

I can't hear what they're saying, but the next moment, the fire alarm starts to ring out in the hallway. The sound is shrill, but it's lessened by the crackling of the fire as it licks up more ground, and it's the sweetest thing I've ever heard. Some of the weight on my chest releases, knowing that the guests and employees at least now have the chance to evacuate.

"Meyer?"

"Yeah?"

I clench my fists. "You need to go. The fire department should be here soon, so I'll—"

"Shut *up*," she snaps. "Let me think!"

"I already told you that your safety isn't something I'm willing to argue about. Get *out*, Meyer."

"Fire extinguisher!" she yells instead, ignoring my requests. "There's a fire extinguisher in the back right corner!"

"I'll find it. Now *go*."

Covering my mouth and nose with the sleeve of my shirt, I pick my way through boxes and shelves, doing my best to avoid the source of heat. The smoke is thick, making the space hazy. Finally, I spot the corner Meyer was talking about.

When I make it back to the door with the fire extinguisher in hand, the flames have reached one of the shelving units in the middle of the room. For half a second, I watch the cardboard boxes curl in on themselves as the fire incinerates them. Then I force myself to move.

Pulling the pin, I aim the extinguisher at the base of the flames and press the trigger. A blanket of white coats everything, and my eyes water from the smoke still clinging to the room.

Eventually, I manage to get the fire down enough that I have a clear path to the door. Dropping the extinguisher on the floor, I then cover my hand with my sleeve and turn the door handle. It's still burning hot to the touch, but the buffer of the fabric helps. The door swings inward, and I stumble out of the room. I somehow manage to pull the door shut behind me, in an effort to keep the fire contained.

There isn't much I can do to save this place, but damn it, I'm going to try.

I place my hands on my knees, sucking in the cleaner air. Then Meyer's hands are on me, tugging me upright and pulling me down the hallway behind her. I should have known she wouldn't listen.

I can hear sirens approaching now. Some of my panic ebbs, knowing that the professionals are on their way. Hopefully, they'll be able to stop the fire before it spreads to the rest of the inn.

When Meyer and I burst outside, I fling myself down onto the grass, heaving. She drops to her knees beside me. Her hands find my face as her eyes rove over me, inspecting for injury.

Grabbing hold of her wrist, I squeeze once, but I keep her palm steady against my cheek. "*Never* do that again," I wheeze.

"What?" she asks. Her eyes are still wide with panic, her body thrumming with adrenaline. "Save your life?"

"Stay in a burning building longer than strictly necessary," I counter.

"It *was* strictly necessary. If you die, who else am I supposed to argue with?"

A laugh gets caught in my throat and turns into a cough. "Not. Funny. That was stupid, Meyer. You could have gotten hurt."

Her eyes flash. "And again, you could have *died*."

Any humour she tried to cling to has now washed away. Her defences are down, and she's *terrified*. I want to savour this moment for the simple fact that she's letting me see behind her walls for once, but I fucking hate that she's been put in this position.

"I'm okay," I say gently.

Her eyes shut and her forehead rests against mine, and

for a moment, nothing else exists apart from us. Her nearness settles the racing of my heart. She's okay. I'm okay. We both made it out of there alive.

"Meyer!"

We quickly pull apart, and Meyer drops her hand from my cheek.

Pippa is jogging our way, Wells hot on her heels. In the chaos of everything, I forgot he was coming back to town today. I've been trying to make more of an effort to keep him updated about my life.

"What the hell happened?" he asks when they reach us. "I pulled into the parking lot and there were fire trucks everywhere. I found Pippa outside panicking."

"The storage room somehow caught fire while I was inside it," I explain.

Pippa swipes at a tear that trickles down her cheek. "And I'm the one that asked you to go in there."

I shake my head. "Don't. Don't blame yourself for one second. I'm glad it was me and not you. Atticus needs his mom."

"Did everyone make it out alright?" Meyer asks.

Pippa nods as she releases a shaky breath. "It's just after check out, so a lot of guests already left. Thankfully, most with reservations for today haven't arrived yet either. Trystan made sure all others are accounted for, including staff."

"I should go help him," Meyer says, trying to get to her feet. "Talk to the fire captain."

I grab her wrist again, stopping her. Then I twist it so I can see her palm. "Baby, your hand," I say. "It's burnt. You should get it checked out."

She tugs herself out of my hold. "Only if you get some oxygen so you stop hacking up a lung."

"And just like that, they're back to normal," Wells says. He tugs Pippa to his side, his arm around her shoulders. "Told you they would be okay, Sunny."

Pippa doesn't acknowledge him. She wraps her arms around her waist, hugging herself. "Is it just me or do all these bad things seem like they're not a coincidence?"

Meyer and I share a look. They definitely don't feel like a coincidence. They feel like they're all connected.

"Rudy!"

Meyer waves to a passing firefighter. At her shout, the man changes course, heading for us. He removes his helmet and swipes a hand over his hair. It's the fucking pizza guy again. He seems to be everywhere in this town.

"Meyer," he says with a look of relief. "Make it out alright?"

She nods, waving away his concern as she stands. "I'm fine. What's—"

"Your hand." Without wasting a second, he grabs her palm and begins to inspect it. "What happened?"

"I grabbed a doorknob that was a little toastier than normal." She snatches her hand back. "I said I'm *fine*."

Rudy raises a brow as amusement tilts his lips. "I think *I'll* be the judge of that."

I push myself to my feet, and then I cross my arms as I watch their exchange. Behind me, I can hear Wells chuckling to himself. Laughing at me. But I don't give a shit.

Meyer scowls. "If you want to play nurse so bad, there's your patient." She points to me. "He inhaled a bunch of smoke and now sounds like he's never lived a day without a cigarette."

An ill-timed cough racks my lungs, proving Meyer right. Rudy abandons her hand and moves toward me.

"Don't you make pizzas?" I ask skeptically. "Are you qualified for this?"

Rudy chuckles. "Pizzas are my day job. I've been a volunteer firefighter since I was eighteen."

"He'll take good care of you," Meyer insists. "Please, Jackson?"

Fuck, I can't say no when she says *please* like that. So I nod, resigned. She leans over and places a quick kiss on my cheek, and then she takes off for the front of the building. Pippa follows after her.

"Alright, follow me to my rig and I'll get you set up with some oxygen," Rudy says.

I begrudgingly trail after him. Wells walks beside me. I can feel his looks of concern.

"Don't look at me like that. I'm alright," I say.

"You were just in a *fire*, Jackson. You don't have to be alright."

"Well, I am."

When Rudy hands me the oxygen mask, I take it and hold it to my face. Admittedly, it does help. Wells watches me approvingly, but my focus is on Meyer. She's standing across the parking lot with Trystan and Pippa.

"It could have been her," I say, pulling the mask away.

"What?" Wells asks.

I nod toward Meyer. "Pippa asked her to do inventory. It could have been her in that room."

I don't know what I would have done if she had been hurt. This was way too close of a call for my liking.

Wells shakes his head. "How would a fire even start in there? Faulty electrical?"

"I don't know," I reply.

And that is what worries me the most.

CHAPTER 25

JACKSON

By evening, the fire department had concluded that it was safe for people to return to the inn. Other than the damage to the storage room, there seemed to be no lasting impacts to the rest of the building, save for the smell of smoke that lingered in the air.

Meyer spent a great deal of time with Trystan, calling guests with reservations to keep them apprised of the situation and issuing cancellations where needed. I spent that time with Pippa, figuring out a solution to our new storage issue and deciding how best to replace our waterlogged inventory.

I also wasted a great many minutes on the phone with the insurance company. It was frustrating, but I wanted to save Meyer from having to do it. She was already stressed enough.

It's moments like these where I know we work perfectly together. Whether she wants to admit it or not, Meyer cares. A lot. Her strength is people. Talking to them, bonding with them, making sure their needs are met. My strengths lie behind the scenes.

After walking a still-jittery Pippa to her car and ensuring she is okay to drive, I enter the inn through the main entrance. Meyer is slumped against the front desk. She tries to fight it, but her eyes are drifting closed.

Seeing the bandage wrapped around her palm has my fists clenching as my anger surges anew. I know it's only a minor burn that will soon heal, but what if it wasn't? What if she was the one trapped inside that room? I'm not sure what I would have done.

"Meyer," I say gently, tucking a strand of hair behind her ear, "it's time to go home."

Her lashes flutter, and then she's blinking up at me. Her gorgeous blue eyes are tinged in fear, but they relax as they settle on me.

She shakes her head. "I can't leave."

"The night clerk is here, right?" She nods. "Then there's no need for you to be here, too."

She swallows as she weighs something in her mind. "I'm scared that if I close my eyes, I'll wake up and it will all be gone," she finally admits. "I can't lose this place, Jackson."

I round the front desk. Grabbing Meyer's hand, I tug her upright and into my chest. She stands frozen for a moment before her body sags against mine. She slides her arms around my middle. My touch settles on her back, one hand smoothing a circle against her t-shirt.

We've already had sex, arguably the most intimate you can get with a person, yet this feels more so somehow.

"You give good hugs, Mr. Vaughan," Meyer croaks.

I tighten my hold. "You can have one whenever you want, baby. All you have to do is ask."

"I'm not your baby," she protests.

I simply grin, my lips pressed to the crown of her head.

The walk to Meyer's cottage is silent. All that can be heard is chirping crickets and the soft whispering of the breeze. I keep my hand anchored in hers. To make sure she stays upright, but also to feel her. To reassure myself that she's okay.

I may have been the one trapped in that storage room, but all I seem to be able to focus on is Meyer and how easily that could've been her.

Once she has unlocked her front door and stepped inside, I take a step back, getting ready to leave. I wait until the door has closed before I start walking away.

But then I hear the creak of hinges, followed by—

"Jackson?"

I pause. Turning on my heel, I try not to let my hopefulness show. "Yeah?"

"Will you stay?" she asks. Her voice is small. "I, um, don't really want to be alone tonight."

I shouldn't feel victorious—not when Meyer is a shell of the woman that regularly enjoys busting my balls—but I do. Because for once, Meyer is admitting that she needs someone. That she needs *me*.

Maybe some would mistake this as weakness, but I know better. She has never been stronger than she is right now, asking for help.

"I don't want to be alone either," I confess. And I don't. Not after the day we've had.

I walk back up the porch and step over the threshold, into the house. Meyer rises on the tips of her toes as she takes my face in her hands. I drop my forehead to hers, and then my lips follow suit, brushing against her soft pink ones.

If someone were to ask me what I was doing with her, I wouldn't even know where to begin. All I know is being with Meyer—well, it feels right. More right than anything else I've ever experienced.

I knew from the moment I laid eyes on her that she would be the sweetest indulgence. Now that I've had a taste, I'm not sure I can let go. I don't *want* to let go.

But it's more than that, too. I care for her in a way that leaves me breathless sometimes. It snuck up on me, this feeling, but I want to lean into it.

"Lead the way," I say when we pull apart.

I close and lock the front door behind us, and then Meyer retakes my hand and guides me down the short hallway to her bedroom. If I wasn't so exhausted, I would take stock of the pictures lining the walls. Maybe I would get to see another gem from Meyer's childhood, like that photo hanging in Papa's Pizza Emporium.

Meyer's bedroom is just like her—a comforting kind of chaos. There's a basket overflowing with folded laundry that crowds the doorway. Meyer has to nudge it aside before we enter. The walls are painted white, but they can hardly be seen for all the photos tacked up in some nonsensical pattern. Her sheets, soft lilac in colour, are rumpled, the bed unmade. Her dresser is littered in perfumes and hair accessories. A second and third laundry basket sit at the end of the bed.

When I look at her, her cheeks are tinged in that embarrassed blush I love so much. It doesn't come out often, but fuck, it makes her look a million times more beautiful—a feat I hadn't thought possible.

"Ignore the mess," she says. "Turns out, having your place of work catch fire leaves little time for tidying your bedroom." Then she shakes her head. "That's a lie. It's always like this."

She tries to pull her hand out of mine, but I don't let her. I tug her closer as I tilt her chin upwards. I want her eyes on me—always, but especially right now.

"Hey. A little disarray never hurt anyone."

Her eyes narrow. "Says the man who rearranged my office because its former condition reportedly made his eye twitch."

I can't help the grin that stretches my lips. "What can I say? You're a bad influence, Ellison."

I bring the back of her hand to my lips and place a gentle kiss there. She softens.

"Can I have my hand back? I need to change."

I reluctantly let her go. As I watch her bustle around her room, collecting pieces of clothing, I sit on the edge of her bed and begin to loosen the knot of my tie.

"I think I have some extra hangers," Meyer says, gesturing toward a closet that is bursting at the seams, "if you need to hang your suit."

I shed my jacket. I'm not even sure why I put it back on when the firefighter handed it to me. It still smells heavily of smoke.

"It's fine. This suit will just be heading straight to the garbage." Maybe it could be salvaged, I don't know, but I don't want any reminders of this day. "Doesn't look like there'd be much room for it anyway."

Meyer rolls her eyes at my teasing. "Haha, *Meyer has a lot of clothes*," she says dryly. "I hate laundry, so the more clothes I have, the less often I have to put a load in."

"That logic is inherently flawed," I argue as I slip my arms out of my shirt. "More clothing leads to *more* laundry. Sure, you can get by longer, but then you have a mountain to contend with."

Meyer places her hands on her hips. "Tell me you did not just use the words *inherently flawed* in reference to my laundry philosophy."

I nod. "I believe I did."

Meyer grabs a pillow from beside her on the bed and chucks it at me. I catch it easily.

She huffs. "Suddenly, I don't need a bed buddy anymore."

I grin wolfishly. "Is that what the kids call it these days?"

She rolls her eyes. Then she holds up the clothes in her hands. "I'll be back."

I arch a brow. "You do remember that I've already seen all of you, right?"

"And we already established that was a one-time thing. You don't get a repeat performance just because we're having a sleepover."

She says it was a one-time thing, but the way she kissed me earlier begs to differ.

As if to prove my point, I stand from the bed and unzip my pants. Shucking them, I stand before Meyer wearing nothing but boxers. When I chance a look at her, her heated gaze has dropped to my crotch. In response to the attention, my cock twitches.

"You were saying?" I ask.

Her head snaps upwards. Then she turns on her heel and heads out into the hall, toward the bathroom.

With a grin, I make myself useful. I return the pillow that Meyer used as a weapon to its rightful place. Then I flip her bedside lamp on and shut the overhead light off, leaving the room bathed in a soft, warm glow.

When Meyer returns, she tosses an unopened toothbrush at me. Again, I catch it. In the bathroom, I make quick work of brushing my teeth. Before I leave, I drop the toothbrush into the holder on the counter. If I have any say in the matter, that toothbrush will be keeping Meyer's company for the foreseeable future.

Meyer is already in bed when I return, so I slip under the covers beside her and make myself comfortable. She ever so slightly inches closer, and I take that as an invitation to pull her against me.

"Bed buddies can do this," I say, slipping my hand under the hem of her shirt to rest on her bare back, "right?"

"I think so," she replies. "And this?"

Beneath the covers, her legs tangle with mine. I nod. "Seems legit to me."

We lie in silence for a few moments, letting our own thoughts consume us. If her brain is anything like mine, it's still trying to wrap itself around the events of the day. I know I was there, but I'm partially convinced it was all a nightmare.

"Jackson," Meyer says to the dark. The use of my first name, so rarely done by her, draws me out of my head. "Someone set the inn on fire."

I rear back, taken by surprise. "What?"

I won't lie and say that it hadn't crossed my mind, but she sounds sure, like she *knows*. Like maybe Pippa wasn't so far off base this morning when she said things seemed suspicious.

She sighs. "Rudy told me. I don't think he was supposed to, but he mentioned that they suspect foul play. They found some kind of accelerant."

Words die on my tongue. *Accelerant.* There's nothing I can say to make this better. In response, I draw her body impossibly closer.

"What are we going to do?"

"We're not going to let this stop us, that's for damn sure," I declare. "Whoever did this, that's what they want. We won't give them the satisfaction."

Slowly, Meyer nods, her hair tickling my arm as the strands move against it. "You're right."

"What's the date?" I ask.

"Um, July tenth, I think. Why?"

"Just marking this momentous occasion for future historians to study. The day Meyer Ellison finally admitted that Jackson Vaughan is *right*."

She begins to laugh. Her laugh—it's real, genuine, and it sends a shot of pleasure through my body.

And I mark this day for an entirely different reason.

CHAPTER 26

MEYER

IT TOOK a while for the investigation into the fire to conclude. With the vandalism and the photos we found, the police are beginning to suspect there's more to this—that we aren't seeing the full picture. At least they're taking things more seriously than they were in the beginning.

Once all the evidence had been gathered, we were given the go ahead to resume normal operations and fix up the storage room.

Luckily, there isn't any damage to the structure of the inn, but the room itself is not a pretty sight. The smell of burnt plastic still floats through the air, and there is a layer of ash over everything, even the parts of the room the fire miraculously didn't touch.

I stand in the middle of the destruction now, taking it all in. Every time I set foot in this space, I can't help but picture Jackson trapped between the flames. I try to push the image out of my mind, but it clings, almost as stubborn as me.

I don't know why I care this much. I'm grateful—

beyond grateful—that he made it out of this room that day. But I've lost sleep over this, and I don't know *why*. He's just a guy. Just a guy who owns the other half of the inn. Just a guy who I've slept with, innocently and...not-so-innocently.

With a sigh, I shake away my thoughts and then get to work. The first step is clearing out all the burnt inventory so we can get the walls and the shelving repaired. I spend about an hour sweeping up soot and ashes before I hear a knock on the door.

When I spin around, I see Declan standing there, a group of people at his back. I recognize a few of them as his coworkers from the lumber yard. We know each other enough to be friendly, but I don't think I've ever hung out with any of them before.

Declan steps into the room, and the group follows. They've got garbage bags and armfuls of supplies with them. I watch as they fan out, all taking a section of the room and starting to clear up the debris.

I whirl on my friend. "What are you doing here?" I ask.

Declan's eyes twinkle as he says, "We're here to help."

I eye him in suspicion. "Help with what?"

"With rebuilding the storage room." He pats the box he's carrying. "We've got all the tools. This way, you don't have to worry about hiring someone."

"What? No." I shake my head. "You guys don't have to do that. I can figure it out."

"We've all been talking, and we *want* to help you, Meyer. I know you don't like accepting it, but that's too damn bad."

I choke on a laugh. "I guess I can't say no, can I?"

He grins. "No, you can't."

The doorway fills again, and then Pippa and Jackson are entering the room. Jackson has ditched his suit again in favour of a t-shirt and jeans. I won't lie and say that I hate seeing him in his suits, but there's something about seeing him in casual clothes that makes my stomach dip. *What is happening to me?*

I pin Pippa with an accusatory look. "Did you know about this?"

She throws her hands up in surrender. "I swear I didn't. This whole thing was Declan's idea."

I glower. Until I feel the weight of someone's arm settle over my shoulders. Strangely, I don't have the urge to shrug him off, and that alone should worry me. It *does* worry me. I'm not supposed to like him being this close to me in a non-sexual setting.

"Let them help, Ellison. They want to be here for you," Jackson says.

"For both of you," Declan amends.

Jackson chuckles. "Of the two of us, I think Meyer has earned the goodwill of the townspeople more than I have."

"I think you've managed to work your way into their good graces, too," Pippa says. "Despite the rough start."

My brows furrow. "What do you mean?"

Jackson's jaw drops. "*What does she mean*? Basically the whole town had a vendetta against me when I first got here."

"I feel like that's a bit of an exaggeration."

Declan shakes his head. "It's not. Everyone kinda hated him."

"But people love you! It's beyond infuriating," I say.

"They don't love me when they know you hate me. I was

glared at for *weeks*," Jackson explains. "You underestimate your influence here."

I knew the people of Fraisier Creek could be protective, but I didn't realize my distaste for Jackson being here had spread so widely.

I offer him a sheepish grin. "Sorry."

He shake his head, but an amused smile sits on his lips. "No, you're not."

"You're right, I'm not." Then I clap my hands, stepping out from under Jackson's arm. "Alright, let's get to work. We've got a mess to clean up."

With the group of us, it still takes us all day to make any headway, but considering the fact that I was expecting to do all the cleanup by myself, I'm happy with the outcome. Hours fly, and by the time everyone is ready to call it quits, I'm a tired, sweaty mess.

But I've also never been more thankful in my life. I have my frustrations with living in a small town sometimes, but nothing beats this community and the way it shows up for people. It's easy to forget, when I get in my own head about my insecurities, but I've always had a place in this town.

I tie off my last garbage bag and then lean against the wall. My whole body aches from everything I put it through today.

I close my eyes for a minute, wishing I was already showered and in the comfort of my bed. When I open them again, Jackson is making his way toward me. His eyes are trained on his phone. When he looks up, I notice a streak of soot on his cheek, and the sight makes me smile. His expression turns quizzical, his head tilting.

"What?" he asks.

I laugh. "You just have a little something here," I reply, gesturing to my own cheek.

"Here?" He reaches up and swipes at his cheek, but it's the opposite one.

I shake my head, taking a step forward. "No, the other one. Here, let me." I reach for his face, swiping a thumb along his cheekbone, and I'm instantly transported back to that day we spent baking in my kitchen. My breath hitches, and I quickly pull away. "There, all better."

"My hero," he says with a smile.

I clear my throat and cross my arms. "You looked like you wanted to say something when you came over here." Changing the subject is for the best, lest I melt into a puddle of awkwardness.

"Right." His smile turns to one of pure excitement. "I have a new idea."

He looks like a kid on Christmas, bouncing on his toes in anticipation of opening his gifts. As much as I hate to admit it, it's adorable.

"Alright." I wave him on. "Let's hear it."

"I've been thinking about this for a while, how that green space beside the inn doesn't really have a use. But we could give it one. It would be easy enough to rent one of those large tents and host events out there. I even have our first client."

I arch a brow, admittedly a little impressed. "You've been busy today. Who's the client?"

"I overheard someone talking about this charity dinner that's happening soon, so I talked to the people who are running it."

This charity dinner for the local animal shelter gets thrown every year, and it's essentially an excuse for the Fraisier Creek elite to dress up and pretend they're New York City socialites attending some stuffy, highbrow art gala. It's a Big Deal. I'm not a huge fan of attending, but it does raise a lot of money when all is said and done, so I suck it up.

"And," Jackson adds, a glint of mischief in his eyes, "I'll even let you take me as your date."

"Yeah?" I ask, raising a brow. "Is that supposed to be a plus?"

"Oh, how you wound me, Ellison. What do you think?"

Of all the ideas I've had for the inn, something like this has never occurred to me. The side of me that is overrun by my own fears and insecurities wants to protest, to shut him down, simply because he was the one to come up with the idea. But I push that part of me aside.

We're supposed to be partners after all. I haven't been very good at the whole collaboration thing, but I want to try. I owe it to Cherie. I owe it to myself and Jackson.

"I like it," I reply. "Let's do it."

The way Jackson's face lights up with his smile sends butterflies swimming through my stomach.

The more I think about it, the more I recognize that maybe Mom was right. Sometimes, I do let my pride get in my way. But I'm trying to fix that.

"I think we make a good team, partner," Jackson says.

I offer him a tired smile. "I think we do, too."

His eyes soften on me. "It's late. Let me walk you home."

I push away from the wall as I nod. "I'd like that."

Walking this familiar path back to my cottage with

Jackson feels comfortable, and a warm feeling spreads over me. He doesn't touch me, just walks beside me, but it makes my heart race nevertheless.

After the fire, everything felt a little hopeless. But maybe things are starting to look up now. This plan of Jackson's has some merit, as long as we can pull it off.

And if we can continue working together like this, maybe our forced partnership will turn out to be a good thing after all.

CHAPTER 27
JACKSON

I THOUGHT that finishing the repairs after the fire would put Meyer more at ease, but with each passing day, she seems to grow more and more on edge. Every time I ask, she insists that she's fine, but I can't bring myself to believe her. I'm just waiting for the day she decides she wants to trust me with the truth. Her truth.

Since that day at the creek, we haven't slept together. Not for my lack of wanting to, but Meyer made it clear that she only wanted it once. So, although I think she's lying to herself more than she is to me, I've let it go.

As far as things with the inn, she has become a bit more willing to compromise. I'm not sure whether it's the fear of everything being taken away from her or if she's genuinely warming up to me and my ideas, but I'll take it.

I wave to Winona behind the front desk on my way by, and then I slip through the office door.

"Hey," I say to Meyer. "I bought us some lunch."

I learned rather quickly that although Meyer loves the restaurant at the inn, it gets old eating food from there every day. The deli downtown is her favourite alternative. They make the best reuben sandwich in the whole province, according to her.

Meyer is standing in the middle of the room, looking distracted. She shoves her phone into her back pocket as she nods. "Thanks," she says absentmindedly.

"Are you okay?" I notice the worry lining her expression. "Did something happen?"

Something else. Something new on top of all the shit we've had to deal with so far. I certainly hope that isn't the case, but the look on her face doesn't seem to bode well.

"Nothing like that. It's—" She sighs. "My mom found out about the fire and she's coming to town," she finally admits.

"Found out?" I ask. "You didn't tell her?"

She shakes her head. "No. Of course not!"

I set the bag from the deli on top of the nearest filing cabinet. "I think that's something she would have liked to hear from you. She just wants to make sure you're okay."

Meyer shakes her head again, and when she speaks, her voice is quiet. "I don't want to see the disappointment in her eyes."

I frown in confusion. "Why the hell would she be disappointed? She'll be worried. Probably mad that you didn't mention the fire before she heard it through the grapevine. But not disappointed. It's not like you set the fire. You didn't do anything wrong."

She doesn't seem to be listening to me. She's still caught in her spiralling thoughts, letting them strangle her. I want to comfort her, but I don't know how. I don't know if that would cross a boundary and send our progress backwards.

But fuck, I want to be the one she comes to for reassurance.

"Maybe this whole thing is a sign," she continues. "Maybe this means I don't belong here. It's only been a few months and I'm already a failure."

"Never fucking say that again."

My tone is harsher than intended, but her words piss me off. Not *at* her, but for her. That she can even think that about herself is maddening. In no way could Meyer ever be considered a failure. Not by me, and certainly not by her mother. Beatrice knew what she was doing when she let her daughter take the reins. There is no one more passionate about this place.

Meyer's eyes are wide in surprise when they shift to me. "What?"

I stalk toward her. Now she's leaning on the edge of the desk, arms braced on either side of her luscious hips. She's right where she belongs, and it frustrates me that she can't see that.

I take her chin in my hand, forcing her to meet my eyes. Her breath hitches from my closeness.

"*Never* say that you're a failure again. You hear me, Meyer? Because that is the farthest thing from what you are."

"What am I, then?"

Mine.

The word comes out of nowhere. So does the knowledge

that I want it to be true. From day one, Meyer has intrigued me. But getting to know her over these past months has been a privilege, and selfishly, I want more. I'm always going to want more when it comes to her.

I swallow thickly. "You're my partner," I say, instead of everything I want to tell her. "And I refuse to let anyone insult my partner, even you."

"Yeah?" Meyer fists the lapels of my jacket, a dare in her eyes. "What are you going to do about it?"

"Punish you, of course."

The next second, my lips descend on hers. She widens her stance and I step between her feet. Pressing into her, one hand winds around her back to hold her upright while the other braces my body weight on the desk.

Like with everything, Meyer gives as good as she gets. The kiss is bruising. We both try to get as close to each other as physically possible.

I'm not sure what this means. *If* it means anything. I'm too chicken to ask. Scaring Meyer away is the last thing I want to do, but I'm afraid that's where I'm headed if I try to get her to examine this too closely. So I won't. Instead, I just lean into the kiss.

My hands find the backs of her thighs, and I scoop her up. She clings to me, never breaking the kiss. A stapler and a handful of pens fall to the floor when I set her on top of the desk. From this position, I have easy access to what lies beneath her skirt, and I take full advantage.

My palm skates up her thigh until I reach her underwear. She grips my shoulders as she bites her lip in anticipation.

"Can I?" I ask.

She nods. "God, *yes*."

The desperation in her voice nearly does me in. I start rubbing circles over her clit through the material of her panties, and she tips her head back. Then I slide the material aside and begin to tease her entrance. She shifts forward on the desk, trying to get closer, but I grab her hip with my other hand, holding her in place.

"Not so fast, gorgeous. You're not in charge right now."

Meyer tries to protest, but it quickly turns into a gasp when I insert a finger. She feels so good like this, but she feels even better when she's wrapped around my cock.

I pump my finger a couple times, watching the way her eyes close and her lips part. She looks so pretty like this, preparing to let go and chase her release. I want to savour this moment. Instead, I pull away entirely, stepping out from between her legs.

Her eyes pop open. "Wait," she says, reaching for me, "where are you going?"

"Back to work."

Her jaw drops. "You're just going to leave? In the middle of that? I wasn't done."

I shrug. "I said I was going to punish you. Now be a good girl and eat the lunch I brought you."

I make sure she's watching when I slip my finger in my mouth, sucking off the taste of her. And then I grin to myself on my way out the door as she curses in frustration behind me.

———

"You're fucked."

I scowl. "And you're not helping."

Wells chuckles through the phone. He stayed for a couple days after the fire, but then he had to get back to the city. It was just as well, since I barely had any time to spend with him. I think he mostly hung out at the restaurant with Pippa.

"I'm just saying! I haven't seen you this gone over a girl in, well, ever. So again, you're fucked."

The back of my head thumps against my headboard as I shut my eyes. "I am, aren't I?"

That kiss with Meyer earlier today has solidified what I've been suspecting for a while, and that is the fact that I am so into her, it's not even funny. It's not just about the sex either. That is undoubtedly a plus, but everything about her draws me in.

"You are," Wells confirms. "Now the question is, what are you going to do about it?"

I sigh. "I don't know. She keeps pushing me away. I'm afraid if I try too hard, she'll run for good."

"Just be patient. Let her come to you, but be there when she does."

At this, I chuckle. "When did you become some kind of relationship expert?"

"Because I *listen*."

I know what he's saying is right. It took Meyer long enough to warm up to the idea of me being her business partner, let alone the idea of me being more. So I can be patient.

"How are things with the inn?" he asks, changing the subject. "Sorry I couldn't stick around to help."

"It's alright. Pippa's brother and some of his friends fixed up the storage room for us. It's almost like the fire never happened."

"But..."

"But it did happen, and I can't shake the feeling that things are only going to keep escalating." The hand resting on my knee clenches into a fist. "I just don't know what to do. It feels like we're always one step behind."

"The police don't have any leads?"

I shake my head, though he can't see me. "No. And short of never letting anyone I care about out of my sight, I don't know how to keep everyone safe."

"Jackson, that's not your responsibility. None of this is your fault."

Logically, I know that, but it's a hard feeling to shake when none of this danger arrived until I did.

A few months ago, I had no ties to Fraisier Creek or any of the people living here. Now, I care about this community and this inn, and the thought of any of it being harmed—of Meyer being harmed—guts me.

I don't say anything in response to Wells, and he sighs.

"You've got that charity dinner thing coming up, right? Try to focus on that and not everything that could go wrong."

"I'll try," I say.

"I mean it, Jackson. No stress."

I roll my eyes. "Have you been conspiring with my mother again?"

"Should I be?"

"*No.* I'm fine, Wells. Even with all of this going on."

"Alright." He doesn't sound like he entirely believes me. "I'll talk to you later. Keep me updated on the investigation."

When he hangs up, I set my phone on the nightstand, and then I let out a sigh.

I'm fucked.

CHAPTER 28

MEYER

"Pippa, that's my nipple!"

Tongue caught between her teeth, my best friend doesn't pay my protests any mind. When she's focused on a task, nothing can shake her—not even the fact that she caught my nipple with the tape she's using to keep my dress stuck to my boobs.

"If you're gonna see me topless, you should at least buy me dinner first," I mumble.

"*Please*," she says with a scoff. "I heard about that one homecoming dance. I highly doubt your date bought you dinner before that."

At this, I grin. "I wasn't the one who snuck a flask in my purse."

"Maybe I should rethink letting you babysit Atticus." She takes a step back, scrutinizing the neckline of my dress. "You're a bad influence."

"C'mon, Pip. You know you love me."

When she moves out of the way, I inspect myself in the

full-length mirror. It isn't often that I have the occasion to be fancy like this. My usual wardrobe is mostly made up of t-shirts and jeans. But it is nice to play dress-up every once in a while.

This annual charity dinner is the one and only time you'll catch me wearing stilettos, though.

Pippa is usually my date. Every year, she splurges on an evening babysitter, we get dolled up, and then we get drunk. This year, I've got a permanent shadow in the shape of my business partner.

"I'm still impressed that Jackson was able to convince them to host the dinner here," Pippa muses.

I roll my lips into my mouth to stop myself from readily agreeing. The truth is: it *is* impressive. Many others have tried before, but the organizers always insisted on renting the stuffy, run-down recreation centre. Somehow between charming smiles and smooth words, Jackson managed to sway them.

"Are you sure you don't want to come?"

Pippa nods. "I'm sure. I think Jackson will look better on your arm than I would."

It isn't the optics that I'm worried about. Not *our* optics anyway. Everyone loves Pippa, and everyone will love Jackson. They both have something about them that assures people. I feel like I have the opposite effect. Everyone likes me well enough, but I always feel like they're waiting for me to slip up.

A knock on my front door has my stomach tightening with nerves.

Pippa smiles and sets a hand on my arm. "I'll get the

door," she says. "You take a deep breath and then get ready to kill it tonight."

When she leaves me alone in my room, I fight the urge to take the dress off and crawl under the covers on my bed. It isn't the socializing that I have trouble with—that, I thrive on. The pressure of tonight and what it means is what's getting to me.

I know it's silly. This night is about raising money for an organization that needs it, but it's also a chance to show the town how the inn is doing without my mother at the helm. This dinner has no bearing on how successful the inn actually is and will continue to be. But it's the perception of having made it. Especially after everything that has been going wrong lately, I want the evening to run without a hitch.

As the finishing touch to my outfit, I take the strawberry earrings from the farmer's market out of my jewellery box and put them on. They don't exactly fit with the rest of my clothing, but they bring me some much-needed comfort.

I give myself another minute before forcing my feet to move. Each click of my heels on the floor is like the tick of a clock, counting down to my doom. Somewhere in the back of my brain, I realize I'm catastrophizing, but snapping myself out of it is easier said than done. I'm a worrier at heart.

Stepping into the living room, I take Jackson in. His back is to me as he chats with Pippa, allowing me a moment of unobstructed perusal. The suit he has on this evening is nicer than the others, which is saying something, considering how nice his usual suits are. Not that I've been paying attention or anything.

"There she is," Pippa says, drawing me out of my daydreams.

Jackson turns as I cross the room to them. His jaw works, and his honey eyes blaze with heat as they trail from my stilettos to my curled updo, stalling first on my hips and then my plunging neckline. He tries to speak, but a quick clearing of his throat gives him away. He's flustered.

The amount of satisfaction I feel from Jackson's reaction is somewhat troubling. Actually, it's *very* troubling.

"The way you're looking at me right now is very inappropriate, Mr. Vaughan," I tease.

His eyes jump to mine as a smile spreads across his lips. "Just returning the favour, Ms. Ellison."

I roll my eyes. "In your dreams."

At this, his grin turns wolfish. "Oh, I dream about a lot of things." He holds his arm out to me. "Shall we?"

I hesitate, but knowing that I'm liable to break an ankle walking the gravel path from my cottage over to the tent where the dinner is being held, I give in. Looping my arm through Jackson's, I inhale a fortifying breath. I can do this. I can spend one night pretending I have my shit together.

"Have fun!" Pippa calls after us. "I'll lock up for you."

I turn my upper body toward her and blow my friend a kiss. "Love you, Pip! Thank you."

When I face forward again, I inhale deeply and then release it, hoping some of the tension will bleed away with it. We walk for a moment in silence, which only gives me more time to stew in my thoughts.

"Are you nervous?" Jackson asks.

I purse my lips as I shake my head. "No," I lie. "Of course not."

"The bruises on my arm would beg to differ."

I internally curse when I realize just how tightly I've been gripping his arm. I could keep lying to myself and say it was purely for physical stability—these heels are a *bitch* to walk in —but really, I'm just clinging to anything that will keep me from spiralling.

"Okay, so maybe I'm nervous."

Jackson pauses, pulling me to a stop beside him. I look up at him quizzically.

"Alright," he says, "tell me why. Talk it out."

I shake my head. "You don't want to know what's going on inside my brain."

"On the contrary." His irises swirl with sincerity. "I want to know everything that goes on in that pretty head of yours."

I sigh. "I feel like no one in this town takes me seriously. I mean, you were there when Louis called me *little lady*, like I'm a kid playing pretend at this whole thing." I cast my gaze to the side, too chicken to look at Jackson. "Everyone loved and respected my mom in this role. And I guess I worry I'm...not enough."

Jackson reaches out and tips my chin up, forcing my gaze to his. The fire in his eyes makes my pulse jump.

"You, Meyer Ellison, are more than enough," he says. "I've never seen someone so well-suited for a job they also happen to love. That's rare. If this town is too small-minded to see that, then fuck 'em. Your success will be the only proof you need."

"But what if I fail?" I whisper.

He shakes his head. "You won't," he replies. He sounds so *confident*, and I wish, not for the first time, I could steal some of it and bottle it up for myself. "But if you did, you sure as hell wouldn't be the first. Or the last. And most importantly, you wouldn't be in it alone. Your name isn't the only one on that paperwork."

My lips quirk slightly. "The prospect of watching you go down with me does soften the blow a little."

Jackson grins. "Of course. Despite her best efforts, I have come to learn a thing or two about my business partner." He tucks a loose curl behind my ear. "There's no shame in giving something your all, Meyer. Even if it doesn't work out in the end."

His words twist around my heart, settling there. I have a feeling he isn't just talking about the inn. But right now, I don't have time to examine them and pick them apart, as I like to do. Right now, we have a dinner to host.

Inhaling deeply, I nod. "Alright, Vaughan. Let's go show them what we can do."

***

We somehow managed to pull it off. Our staff did us proud, working to ensure everything went smoothly, and the dinner organizers were pleased.

My nerves didn't entirely go away, but I was able to ease into things and relax partway through the evening. I was worried that someone would bring up the vandalism or the fire, and the dinner would derail from there, but no one brought any attention to our bad luck.

"This evening was lovely," Mayor Danby says as she walks up to me and Jackson. "This tent really suits the space out here. I've always had a soft spot for this place, and for Beatrice, but I'm excited to see where you take things, Meyer."

I smile, letting the utter relief flow through me. "Thank you. That truly means so much to me."

"Do you do weddings?" she asks. "My daughter is getting married in August and her venue just cancelled on her. She has been looking for a replacement, and this seems like it would be right up her alley."

I glances over my shoulder at Jackson, then back to the mayor. "We...don't."

"But we would love to," Jackson interjects, stepping up to take his place beside me. "We've been looking to expand, and that is an excellent idea. Have your daughter contact me and we can set up a time for a tour. Work out some details."

Mayor Danby grins. "Splendid!" She reaches out and shakes Jackson's hand, then does the same to me. "We'll be in touch. Have a good night, you two."

I watch her walk away. As soon as she's out of earshot, I whirl on my business partner. "What was that? Since when do we host weddings?"

He shrugs. "That's business."

"*That* came out of nowhere," I argue. "We haven't even had time to figure out if tonight was a success."

"In my experience, conducting business is a lot like performing improv," he says.

"Because when you do something stupid, people laugh at you?"

He chuckles. "No. It's the whole *yes, and* thing. You obviously have to take stock of the risks, but generally being open to opportunities that fall in your lap is smart."

"So now we host weddings," I say.

"So we do." He studies me. "Not that I'm complaining, but you don't seem to be protesting the idea."

"Lucky for you, I actually don't...hate it."

Admitting to liking any of the changes Jackson pushes for when it comes to the inn has become easier over time. And this one, in particular, seems promising.

Jackson grins. "That must have been really hard for you to say."

I nod, mock serious. "Oh, you have no idea."

He chuckles. "I'm flattered."

I glance over my shoulder, watching as our employees begin to break down the setup under the tent. Then I turn back to him. "We should probably help," I say.

He nods. "I'll get the chairs stacked up."

While Jackson is busy with that, I decide to help the catering staff clean up their stations. When everything has been packed up and the staff have finished clearing out, we find each other.

"Walk me back?" I ask.

Jackson nods. "Lead the way."

The walk to my cottage is quiet. Peaceful. It's a nice night, the sky clear enough to see all the stars.

"Bet you don't miss all that light pollution," I say,

breaking the silence. Because I was beginning to feel too comfortable, and that made me feel *un*comfortable.

He glances up at the sky and then over at me. "No," he says, "I can't say that I do. Can't say that I miss a lot about the city, to tell you the truth."

Stupid words roll to the tip of my tongue. Questions like, *does that mean you want to stay?* But I don't voice them.

We make it to my front door sooner than I would have liked. As surprising as it is, I actually enjoy Jackson's company. Not that I'd tell him that. His ego truly doesn't need the boost.

"Did you have a good night?" he asks.

"I did." My hands wring nervously in front of me. "Thank you for talking me off the ledge earlier."

He smiles, and those goddamn dimples appear again. "That's what I'm here for. Goodnight, Ellison. I'll see you tomorrow."

"Wait." I take a step closer, reaching for him. "I decided I'm taking your advice."

His eyes sparkle in the moonlight. "Yeah? What advice is that?"

"Taking stock of the risks," I reply as I fist his lapel, "and being open to opportunities that fall in my lap."

I wait for him to stop me. But when he doesn't, I waste no time dragging his mouth to mine.

CHAPTER 29

JACKSON

Kissing Meyer makes it easy to forget about everything that has gone wrong lately. The spray paint, those photos, the fire—everything else is just background noise when I lose myself in her.

I groan, wasting no time in wrapping an arm around her waist, tugging her impossibly closer. She comes willingly, which is more than I can say regarding most of our interactions. But in my arms, she's pliable. She lets go of her reservations and simply *feels*.

I knew that day after the creek wouldn't be enough for her. It certainly wasn't enough for me. I've just been waiting for her to admit it to herself. Even longer for her to admit it to me.

Meyer holds her pride like a shield, but beneath it all, she wants to be heard. Respected. And I want nothing more than to give that to her.

I also really want to fuck her again.

"This isn't exactly what I meant," I say, slightly out of breath. "Can't say I mind it, though."

Not when she's looking at me like that. Like I'm the answer to all her prayers. Fuck, I don't ever want her to stop looking at me like that.

Meyer shrugs. "You were talking about business opportunities. We're business partners, and this is an opportunity. I figured the same logic would apply."

I let out a surprised chuckle. "An opportunity, huh? And what is this opportunity?"

She takes a step back, and my arms fall away. Her eyes are fucking gorgeous, so full of heat. "For you to see me out of this dress."

I lean in, closing the space Meyer just created. "Are you trying to use me, Ellison? Feeling good and need someone to help you get off?"

Her chin tips up, defiant as always. "And if I am?"

"All I've ever wanted to do is help you, baby." I surge forward, cupping the back of her head and drawing her toward me. "Let me help you."

When our lips meet again, Meyer doesn't hesitate to open for me. It still awes me how free she is with her body, yet so reserved with her mind. I want to crack her open, lay bare all her thoughts. I want her to feel comfortable confiding everything in me.

For now, we have this.

"Inside?" I ask between kisses.

"Inside," she agrees.

She peels herself away from me and spins around. As she fiddles with her clutch to find her keys, I wrap an arm around her. With my palm on her lower belly, I pull her back into me. She moans as she feels just how much I want this—want *her*.

"Stop distracting me," she scolds.

"I had to watch you walk around all night looking like *this*," I reply, running a hand along her bare shoulder. "You don't get to say anything about distractions."

Meyer finally fits the key inside the lock, and then we're stumbling inside. As soon as the door shuts behind us, my mouth is back on hers. She's positively addicting, and I can't stop.

"This fucking dress," I murmur against her lips, "has got to go."

There are entirely too many layers between us and I want them all *gone*.

"You don't like it?" she teases, her voice breathy.

"In general? Love it. Looks like it was made just for you. At the moment? Not particularly." I meet her bright eyes. They're vivid blue, like the sky after the storm clouds have disappeared. "Right now, it's in my way."

"Do something about it, then."

Don't have to tell me twice.

I guide her back toward the kitchen island until she bumps against the edge of the countertop. Her back arches, her chest brushing against mine.

"One second."

She watches me intently as I reach up to her hair. It takes me a few seconds, but I manage to tug the clips and pins from the strands, allowing them to fall over her shoulders.

Meyer's eyes twinkle with amusement. "Happy now?"

"Almost. Just one more thing."

I really wasn't lying about the dress being in my way. As much as I love the way it accentuates my favourite parts of her body, right now, I need it gone. I tear at the fabric, working to free those tits that drive me absolutely wild. In the process, I hear the unmistakeable sound of material ripping. The front of her dress now gapes open, the seam torn.

Meyer gasps. "Jackson! This cost me two hundred dollars."

I shrug. "I'll buy you a new one."

I'd buy her a whole store full of dresses if that would make her happy.

She frowns. "That's just throwing money away."

"Worth every fucking penny." My eyes drink her in. Her lips are swollen, her hair cascades in waves over her shoulders, and her torn dress reveals her hardened nipples. And those blue eyes I adore are clouded in lust. "I love you like this, baby. Love knowing that I'm the one who makes you unravel."

Meyer grips the lapels of my suit. "You're awfully cocky this evening, Mr. Vaughan," she muses. She lets go of my jacket and runs her hands down my chest, my stomach. Stopping at the buckle of my belt, she looks up at me, a sly smile on her lips.

I pull her hands away from my belt. "No. You had your fun last time. Now it's my turn." I tug on the lobe of her ear with my teeth. Then I set my tone low as I murmur in her ear. "So you're going to be a good fucking girl and turn around for me."

I can see that spark of rebellion in her eyes—that part of her that likes saying no just for the hell of it. But it's gone just as fast, replaced by pure heat. Try as she might to deny it, this turns her on.

She spins, giving me her back. The smooth expanse of skin has been exposed all night, taunting me. Her blonde locks fall down her back now, just the way I like them. Her fancy hairdo was nice, but I much prefer this look.

"Did I tell you how pretty you looked tonight?" I ask. She shakes her head, and I *tsk*. "How rude of me. Because you, Meyer, are so fucking beautiful."

And she is. I've known it since I laid eyes on her that first day in the restaurant. She's always had my attention, but now that I've gotten to know her, she's beautiful to me for so many reasons beyond the physical.

Reaching around her front, I take one of her breasts in my hand, kneading the skin. Meyer's back arches as she moans.

"You like that, baby?" I ask. "You like when I play with your pretty tits?"

"*Yes*," she breathes.

I place kisses behind her ear, on her shoulder, and then at the top of her spine. My hands trail down her outer thighs and then slip under the hem of her dress. As I bunch the material up at her waist, I'm met with nothing but silky skin.

"You said you didn't want to do this again," I muse.

"I didn't," she insists.

"Then why aren't you wearing any panties, Ms. Ellison?"

Her breath hitches as I reach around her, my fingers dipping between her legs to brush against her clit. With my knee, I nudge her legs farther apart so I can fit into the space between them.

"You know what I think?"

"Hmm?" she hums, distracted.

"I think," I say, lips beside her ear, "that you're a liar."

She opens her mouth to protest, but a moan falls from her lips instead as my fingers enter her swiftly. She grapples for purchase on the island, gripping the edge with both hands.

"Not a liar." She shakes her head. "I just changed my mind."

My fingers pumps in and out, and Meyer's hips move with them, seeking friction.

"God, you're so wet, baby. Is that all for me?"

She writhes before me. "You know it is."

When her breathing changes, I can tell she's getting close, so I slip my fingers from her pussy. She whines in protest.

I pull out a condom, and then I slide my zipper down and free my cock from the confines of my pants. Meyer pushes her ass back into me, searching. I roll the condom on.

"Jackson," she breathes.

"Say my name, baby. Tell me how much you want me."

Lining my cock up with her entrance, I tease her slit with the tip, but I don't push inside yet.

She slaps the island. "If you aren't inside me in the next thirty seconds, I swear..." she says. But her threat holds no weight.

"Say please, baby. Ask nicely."

She growls. "*Please*, Jackson. Fuck me already."

Grinning, I say, "That's a good girl."

I thrust forward. Meyer's hips slam against the island as my cock gets buried in her pussy. We both moan, but I still, allowing her a moment to adjust.

"You good?"

"You're going to have to fuck me a lot harder than that to break me, Hotshot."

I grin. I lean forward, letting my lips brush the shell of her ear again. "Is that a challenge?"

"If that's what it takes to get you to *move.*"

I oblige. I draw back, only to thrust forward again. I brace my hands on her hips, giving myself leverage to bury myself inside her, over and over again.

"*Jackson.*"

I reach around again, finding Meyer's clit. Adding pressure, I keep thrusting. My other hand stays anchored to her hip, holding her in place.

"Let go, baby. Come for me."

With my words and the increased pressure, she does. Meyer slumps against the island, her orgasm overwhelming her. Her pussy pulses around my cock, and the feeling spurs on my own release. I pump into her a couple more times and then come with a groan.

"Holy shit," she breathes.

I place a gentle kiss on her shoulder, and then I pull out of her. I dispose of the condom and then tuck myself back into my pants as she spins around to face me. Her cheeks are beautifully flushed and her eyes are bright. I could look at her all goddamn night.

Meyer holds the ripped shreds of her dress against her

chest. "I'm going to shower," she says with a grin. "Want to join me?"

I'm already unbuttoning my shirt. "Right behind you, baby."

In the shower, we take our time getting clean, and then I fall asleep in Meyer's bed, my legs tangled with hers.

CHAPTER 30
MEYER

After the night of the charity dinner, things have been different between me and Jackson. I'm not entirely sure what to call it—what I *want* us to call it—but I do know that I don't want it to end.

Maybe starting up a sexual relationship with my business partner will still come around to bite me in the ass, but I'm willing to take that risk.

While things with Jackson seem to be going well, other things...not so much. I finally got the air conditioning fixed in my car, only for the vehicle to choose this moment to completely crap out on me.

"*Ugh.*"

After my tenth attempt, I give up on trying to get the engine to turn over.

I was supposed to be well on my way to Calderville by now. My mother finally wore me down and convinced me to join her and her bookclub for their meeting this week. I haven't managed to read the book, but something tells me that doesn't matter.

It really doesn't matter now that my car won't start.

With a sigh, I text Mom and tell her that I probably won't be making it after all, unless some vehicular guardian angel makes their appearance and helps me out. Then I drop my forehead to the steering wheel with a groan as I think about how much this car repair will cost me.

I make a decent salary, but I'm not exactly swimming in piles of money, especially considering how much I spend to keep my mom in her apartment. Unexpected expenses like this usually hurt a little.

When I lift my head up, I spot Jackson across the parking lot. He's speaking to our maintenance guy, but when he glances my way and notices my car sitting here, he claps Hank on the back and then makes his way toward me.

"You're still here," he says, bracing his forearms on the car and leaning through my open window.

My glare is withering. "You're really observant, Hotshot."

He chuckles, earning him another glare. "And why are you still here? What's up?"

"My stupid car won't start!" When he opens his mouth to speak, I hold up a hand. "Yes, I've tried whatever you're about to suggest, and just about everything else, and now I'm over it."

"I was going to suggest you take my car."

My brows shoot up. "You're letting me drive your car?" I ask. But I'm already unbuckling my seatbelt, ready to exit this hunk of junk.

Jackson steps back and opens the door for me. From his pocket, he produces his key fob, dangling it in front of me like tempting forbidden fruit.

When I grasp it, he doesn't let go. Instead, he sets his free hand on my hip and guides me backwards until I hit the driver's side of his car, conveniently parked next to mine. The black metal is warm at my back.

"I'm letting you drive my car," he says, "on one condition."

"Yeah? What's that?"

With the press of his body against mine, I prepare to agree to any number of sexual favours so I can spend the afternoon in the sleek Audi. But, as he often does, Jackson surprises me.

"Take the rest of the day off."

My lips part. "But—"

He shakes his head. "No buts. Go enjoy the day with your mom and her eccentric friends. We've got everything covered here." He smirks. "If you're a good girl, I might even take you to dinner later."

"At Papa's Pizza Emporium?" I ask, fluttering my lashes. "You really do know how to treat a woman."

He pinches my hip. "Meyer."

"*Fine*. I promise to take the day off."

"Thank you."

With a quick kiss on my lips, Jackson relinquishes the keys. I grin as I unlock the car.

"You should be careful what strange woman you lend your car to, Hotshot. She might not give it back," I tease.

He laughs. "It would hardly be the first thing she's

stolen," he replies. That makes my breath hitch, but Jackson doesn't notice. He gives my ass a light tap, urging me into the driver's seat. "I'll see you tonight."

"Tonight."

"Text me when you get there," he adds, his expression shifting to one of concern.

After everything, concern has become our default. But there's been no movement in our case, so I'm all for putting things behind us. Jackson isn't as quick to forget.

"I will, I promise."

I wave as I pull out of his parking spot, and then I leave the inn feeling lighter than I have in a while. Despite everything bad that's happened in the last few months, the good far outweighs it. Jackson outweighs it.

As I cruise along the highway, I fiddle with the controls on the dash. Jackson's car has a slew of features my Fiesta could only dream of, and I want to try them all. Blessedly, the air conditioning is on full blast, cooling me down despite the sticky humidity outside.

Up ahead, a line of cars slows. A pickup truck at the front is holding them up, waiting to make a left turn onto a dirt backroad. I take my foot off the accelerator and press on the brake.

When the car doesn't slow, I press a little harder. Still nothing.

My hands tighten on the steering wheel as I try the brake again. I grit my teeth, my gaze switching from the pedals at my feet to the windshield, where I can clearly see the vehicle I'm running the risk of rear-ending. Panic tries to take hold, but I shove it down.

Abandoning the pedal, I try the emergency brake. This is, after all, quickly becoming an emergency. Sweat begins to bead on my temple when that, too, doesn't want to function.

Everything feels like it's happening in slow motion, dragging on for endless minutes, but I know it's only been a matter of seconds. The bumper in front of me is getting closer and closer, and the emergency brake still *won't fucking work*.

With a muffled scream, I turn the wheel, steering the car away from the vehicles in front of me. I hit the dirt shoulder roughly, but the car keeps going. Tears slip down my cheeks unbidden as I desperately try the brakes again.

Finally, the car rolls down into the ditch, and a scream works its way loose when I crash into the trunk of a tree. My body slams forward on impact, but my seatbelt keeps me locked in place as the airbag inflates.

Shock descends as everything that just happened threatens to sweep me under. A numbness slides over my skin, dulling any pain I'm supposed to be feeling right now.

I don't think I'm hurt, but I can't tell for sure.

A frantic knock at my window has me turning my head, but I can't even fully see who stands on the other side.

"Miss?" someone calls. "Are you alright?"

I think I nod. My fingers fumble with the latch, trying to unhook my seatbelt. My whole being shakes. I feel like I'm floating; like I don't know where my body is.

All I do know is that those brakes should have worked.

———

I refused the ambulance that was offered to me, but one of the police constables that responded to the scene, a regular at the restaurant with his wife and kids, insisted that I go to the hospital. He didn't take no for an answer, so here I am, sitting in the waiting room.

I spoke to a doctor not that long ago, and she said she wanted an x-ray of my chest to check if my ribs are broken or simply bruised. Although there's nothing simple about the discomfort I feel right now.

When I pull out my phone, I see a text from Jackson waiting, asking if I made it to Calderville. I wince as I begin to type a reply.

> So exactly how attached are you to your car?

His reply comes instantly.

HOTSHOT

> What happened?

> I may have gotten into a bit of an accident.

I try to start typing another message, but my phone begins to ring. I grimace as I pick up the call, preparing for his inevitable anger. I wrecked his car, after all. I'd be pissed at me.

"I'm so sorry," I say immediately. "I—"

"Where are you?" he demands.

"I'm at the hospital. Jackson, I—"

"In Fraisier Creek?"

"Yes?" It comes out more like a question than a statement.

"I'll be there in five."

I don't have a chance to say anything more before the line clicks. But true to his word, five minutes later, the sliding doors of the emergency department open. He scans the waiting area until he spots me, and then he's crossing the room in quick strides.

Jackson drops to a crouch in front of my chair. "Are you okay?" he asks. "What happened?"

"How did you get here so fast?" I ask instead.

"Pippa dropped me off. Tell me where you're hurt."

I frown. "Sorry about your car."

He tucks a strand of hair behind my ear, then rests his hands on either armrest of my chair, caging me in. "Baby, I don't give a shit about the car."

I shake my head. "I tried to stop, but it just wouldn't. I promise I didn't—"

"Hey," he says gently. "I mean it, Meyer. I could not care less about the fucking car. All that matters is you. So *are you okay*?"

There's a restless edge to his words. When I take a second to study him, I can see the panic thrumming beneath his outwardly calm façade. *I* did that. I affected him like that.

There's a burning in my chest. Whether from my potentially broken ribs or Jackson's words, I'm not sure. But the need to reassure him wins out.

I nod. "I'm okay," I say. "Mostly."

His gaze hardens. "Define *mostly*."

"My chest hurts a little. I'm waiting to be called back to radiology for an x-ray." In this moment, it's easier to be upfront. "And I'm probably going to have a gnarly bruise on my jaw from the airbag... But you should see the other guy."

My stupid joke falls flat as Jackson's own jaw works, clenched to the point of grinding his teeth. His hand reaches up, fingers brushing the column of my throat. I'm sure he can feel it when I swallow thickly, my breath shallowing. Again, from the chest pain or from his touch, I'm not sure. He tilts my head to the side, inspecting my jaw.

"Fuck," he curses.

"That bad?" I ask. "I guess my usual tinted moisturizer isn't going to cut it while it heals. I'll have to cover it with foundation so I don't scare the guests away. It's—"

"Meyer," Jackson says, cutting me off again. "Make no mistake, you're fucking beautiful, bruised or not. I just hate that you're hurt."

I nod as I chew on the inside of my cheek. "Sorry. This is how I cope with things. Or avoid them, I guess."

His gaze softens as he continues to take me in. "You have nothing to apologize for, baby."

Everything—the fear, the exhaustion, the pain—stacks up and takes my breath away. And then tears begin to prick my eyes. I blink furiously. Crying in public is a line I won't let myself cross.

My chin wobbles as I stifle the sob working its way up my throat, begging to be set free.

I hardly notice at first, but Jackson's arms slide under me, and then I'm being settled on his lap. I curl around him, hiding my face against his shoulder. I pay no mind to the burning in my chest when I shift. I need the comfort more than I care about the pain.

We stay like that for what feels like forever, but I eventually manage to calm myself enough to lift my head. "Jackson," I say. "Something was wrong with the brakes in your car."

His arm tightens around me. His kiss ghosts my temple. "We can talk about it later. Right now, let's just focus on getting you out of here."

I want to argue, but I've already been at the hospital for what must be hours, and I'm exhausted. I don't have it in me.

"Meyer?" a nurse calls. "You can head on back to radiology now. Just make a right at the end of the hall and follow the signage."

Jackson pulls his arms back, allowing me the space to stand. I do so on shaky legs. Now that the adrenaline has seeped from my body, I feel wrung out, like a used sponge. I want nothing more than to go home and crawl into bed.

When he starts following me, I turn to him. "You don't need to come with me," I say. "It's okay."

He takes my hand. "And you don't need to be alone."

Alone.

I'm often alone—with my thoughts, with my hurts. Not for lack of trying on Mom's and Pippa's parts. But it's much easier to keep this cage around my heart intact if I don't give anyone the tools to dismantle it.

But Jackson Vaughan has thoroughly wormed his way in. He came prepared with instructions and snuck past my defences, in such an effortless way I had no choice but to let it happen.

Alone used to be a comfort. Now comfort comes in the form of a pair of honey-coloured eyes.

"Thank you," I say.

"Always, baby." He squeezes my hand. "Always."

CHAPTER 31

JACKSON

AFTER A FEW MORE HOURS AT the hospital, we finally push through the door of Meyer's cottage. She leans heavily into me, ready to fall asleep at any moment.

"I'm beyond ready for bed," she says, pulling away from me. "I'm gonna go brush my teeth."

"You okay on your own?"

She gives me her signature eye roll, and fuck, if that doesn't ease some of my worries. "I've been brushing my own teeth for twenty years, Hotshot. I think I've got it covered."

I hold my hands up in surrender. But I still watch her walk down the hall, just in case. Once the bathroom door shuts behind her, I take my time locking up the cottage. Then I head for Meyer's bedroom.

Just as I flick on the bedside lamp, my phone vibrates with a text.

PIPPA

How's our girl?

> Tired but okay. We're finally home.

PIPPA

Thank you, Jackson.

> For what?

PIPPA

For being good to her. I had a feeling you
would be.

My throat tightens with emotion. I was so scared earlier. When Meyer said she had been in an accident, I got tunnel vision. The only thing I knew was that I had to get to her— to see with my own eyes that she was alive and breathing.

Pippa had been with me in the office. She was off today, but she happened to stop by to drop something off. One look at my face and she had led me to her car, no questions asked. We got to the hospital in record time. She would have come inside if she hadn't needed to go home to her son.

> Thanks for the ride. You're surprisingly
> fast. Ever thought about joining F1?

PIPPA

Haha. Just because I'm a mom doesn't
mean I drive like a grandma.

Now get some sleep!! Tell Meyer I'll come
see her in the morning.

I set my phone on the dresser and then cross to the bed, pulling back the corner of the comforter on Meyer's preferred side of the mattress. Just as I finish, I hear soft footsteps pad into the room, and then she enters.

"Pippa says to expect a visit from her tomorrow," I say, as I work on unbuttoning the sleeves of my shirt. If she thinks I'm leaving her alone tonight, she's mistaken.

When Meyer doesn't respond, I look up. She stands in the centre of the room, arms wrapped around her middle. The stricken expression on her face makes my stomach drop to my feet. She looks seconds away from breaking down.

I carefully approach. "What's wrong?"

A stupid question after the day she's had. What *isn't* wrong right now? She's hurt, and it never should have happened.

"The brakes didn't work," she croaks. "Why didn't they work?"

I've been asking myself the same question since she mentioned it at the hospital. I wasn't sure where my car had been towed at first, but I managed to find out that it was taken to an auto body shop in Calderville. My insurance company—and the police, since Meyer had to give them a statement at the accident site—also wants to know why the brakes failed, so my car will remain at the shop until they can assess all the damage.

I take good care of my car, though. I'm always on time with my oil changes, and I have it inspected regularly. It was last serviced two months ago. The brakes were perfectly fine then.

I swallow the lump in my throat. I'm not sure what to say. I don't want to scare her when I can tell she's already spiralling. But I can't lie either.

"I don't know, baby."

I open my arms to her, and she steps into them. All I can

offer right now is to hold her, so that's what I do. Her body sags against mine, grateful that I'm bearing the weight of the day. I'd take it gladly.

She inhales a shaky breath and then pulls back. "Do you think it's all connected?"

I know what she's implying, but I'm wary to voice it. "Is what all connected?"

"All the fucked up shit that's been happening," she replies. "First the spray paint, the pictures, and then the fire in the storage room. Now your brakes. What if they were tampered with? It's like someone's out to get us. Or me."

"You think Reggie could be capable of all this?"

Our former employee, as far as we know, is still in the wind. He was suspect number one when the spray paint occurred, but if that wasn't an isolated incident, I'm not sure. Surely someone would have seen him if he's been lurking around, causing trouble. It isn't exactly easy to hide when everyone knows everyone in this town.

She shrugs. "I don't know. Maybe? I didn't think he was capable of stealing from the register, yet he did."

"Theft and vandalism are a far cry from arson and tampering with brakes."

The consequences of the latter are a lot more severe. Meyer could have *died* today. The fire in the storage room could have trapped numerous guests if they hadn't all been evacuated in time. If that fire extinguisher hadn't been there, who knows what would have happened to me.

If someone is behind all of this, they are playing a dangerous game with other people's lives.

"Whoever this is, they don't seem like they're going to

stop," Meyer says. Her voice cracks. "I don't know how much more of this I can take."

I frame her face in my hands. My thumb brushes her cheekbone as I meet her gaze.

"We'll get through this," I assure her. "Everything will be okay."

I try desperately to keep the uncertainty from my voice. The truth is, I don't know what's going to happen. If, like Meyer said, whoever this is doesn't stop, someone is going to get hurt. It's only a matter of time, especially if they escalate.

She nods at my words, but I know the reassurance is temporary. We're both aware that I can't promise anything, not really.

"Alright," I say, "time for bed. Do you need anything? Water?"

With a small wince, she sits on the edge of the mattress and then leans back against the headboard. "Water would be nice. Thank you."

Her gratitude shines in her eyes, but it's the least I can do for her. So I head out to the kitchen and pour her a glass. When I return, I find Meyer watching me. The expression on her face is hard to read. I settle on the bed beside her and then turn in her direction. She's chewing on her bottom lip so hard, I'm surprised she hasn't drawn blood.

"Please tell me this isn't a guilt thing," she says.

My brows furrow. "Is what a guilt thing?"

"This." She waves her hands around. "This fussing all over me, getting me water."

While some part of me would always wonder what would have happened if I hadn't let her borrow my car—if I had driven her myself instead—that isn't why I'm here right now. In truth, there is nowhere I would rather be, whether Meyer was hurt or not.

Fussing over her, in a situation where I feel almost no sense of control, helps me stay calm.

"This," I say, handing her the glass, "is an *I want to take care of you because you've had a long day* thing. Is that acceptable?"

Her head cocks to the side as she thinks. "Yeah, I think that's acceptable. As long as you don't go off the deep end and start offering up your organs or something."

I laugh. "I think I can agree to that."

While she drinks her water, I get myself ready for bed, and then I slide beneath the sheets right beside her. I'm hesitant to touch her, but she makes the decision by shifting closer to me.

"I don't want to hurt you," I say as I tense.

She shakes her head. "You won't."

I take her hand and intertwine our fingers. "Not taking any chances."

She rolls her eyes, but a soft smile slips onto her lips. "Thank you," she whispers.

I tighten my hand in hers. "What are you thanking me for?"

Her shoulder lifts in a half shrug. "I know I don't make caring about me all that easy," she replies sheepishly. "Thanks for doing it anyway."

I'm already shaking my head. "I don't know who let you believe that you're difficult to care about, but I'd like to have a word with them. Because let me tell you, Meyer, it's the easiest thing I've ever done."

Tears pool in her eyes. The stopper she put on her emotions after the crash has fully come free now. I resent the pain in her gaze, but it's much better than the robotic numbness that took over instead.

One tear falls and then another. Soon, a cascade of them is trailing down her cheeks. She presses her face against my chest and finally, *finally* lets go. Lets go of everything she's been holding in these past weeks, months—hell, maybe years.

Her catharsis is a living, breathing thing between us. It eats at my resolve, the need to dry her tears. But she needs this release more than I wish I didn't have to see her cry. So I hold tight to her hand, never wanting to let it go.

Eventually, the tears cease, and then her breathing slows as she slips into sleep. My own eyes feel heavy with exhaustion, but I don't let myself close them. Not yet. I need to drink her in for a while.

When I first came to Fraisier Creek, I never imagined that I would be here. My feelings for Meyer have shifted so abruptly, I'm not sure when the change even happened. But I do know that hearing her say she was in the hospital had never made me feel so panicked.

And I know, without a doubt, that there's nothing I wouldn't do to keep her safe. I just worry that won't be enough.

CHAPTER 32

MEYER

In the morning, I wake up alone.

It isn't out of the ordinary. Before, I would have said I preferred it that way. It was less complicated. But now I feel nothing but complications, and I thought, foolishly, that things were different now. That we were different.

Tears burn my eyes, still puffy from crying the night before. I push the heels of my hands into them, stifling them. It doesn't work as well as I want it to.

I let out a frustrated huff. "Enough," I scold myself. "I refuse to cry over that man."

That infuriating, thoughtful man. Who left me to wake up alone.

More than anything, over the aches and pains from the accident, my mind hurts from the emotional whiplash. From cleaving my heart open and laying it bare for Jackson to see the inner workings. I thought he could handle it. That he could help stitch me back together.

But maybe I misjudged. Maybe this is too much—*I* am too much—for him. Wouldn't be the first time.

What I said to him last night was true. Caring about me *isn't* easy because I don't let people. Because anything is better than feeling vulnerable like this.

Finally, I muster up the strength to leave my bedroom. I can already tell my hair is a mess, but I'm alone anyway, so what does it matter? I trudge into the bathroom, still not entirely awake, and fumble through my morning routine.

Seeing that stupid toothbrush I lent Jackson the night of the fire, just sitting there beside my own, rips the wound open anew. I don't even feel a little bit bad when I throw it in the trash.

When I exit the bathroom, Fish darts past with an excited trill. I stand there, confused, until I hear movement in the kitchen. Pippa must be here already. Of anyone, Fish seems to tolerate her the most.

I hope she brought food. Because no way am I cooking this morning.

Rounding the corner from the hallway, I expect to find my best friend, ready to patch up my emotional wounds. What I don't expect to find is Jackson Vaughan, feeding my cat.

Fish swishes between Jackson's legs, purring, as he opens the can of cat food. Gone is the feline who hated his guts and in his place is a cat so enamoured by the thought of being fed, he throws away his principles.

Like mother, like son.

Jackson smiles when he spots me. "Morning," he says. "How did you sleep? Are you in any pain?"

I don't respond as I cross the room. I shove at his shoulder, showing my frustration, and then I wrap my arms around his middle and burrow my face into his chest. It takes him a moment, but he cautiously slides his arms around my back, holding me to him.

I breathe in his familiar scent. "You left me," I accuse, voice muffled.

"I did," he says. "I'm sorry. I wanted to have breakfast ready for when you woke up."

I tighten my grip on him, fisting the back of his shirt. "Don't do that again."

One of his hands trails up my spine and cups the back of my head. The way he holds me, like I'm strong and delicate all at once, is nearly my undoing.

"I won't," he promises.

He knows. He knows without my saying how hard all of this is for me. It's not like I expect him to never wake up before me. I'm not that unreasonable. But after pouring my feelings out until I have nothing left inside me, I don't want to be alone. I refuse to be alone.

After another moment, I pull back, pull myself together. "It looks like you managed to get into Fish's good graces."

"It's a wonder what a little food can do." He studies me for another moment, looking for signs of distress, maybe, but then he relaxes. "Come eat, it's getting cold."

Sitting on the island is more food than both of us will be able to eat. Pancakes, eggs, bacon, sausages, and home fries sit on plates. Beside them, a bowl of fruit salad.

I eye the spread as my stomach grumbles. "Did you make all this?"

His smile is embarrassed. "I left a very generous tip for the employees at the diner."

I grin. "That's okay. I still like you, even if you are just a pretty face."

I feel him near my back, crowding me against the island. I spin in the cage of his arms to face him.

"Are you calling me pretty, Ellison?" he taunts.

"Maybe," I reply. I pat his chest. "Don't let it get to your head, Hotshot."

"Any compliment from you is a straight shot to my ego."

"Duly noted. We can't let that get too inflated."

"I recall you offering to stroke that ego a couple months ago."

I roll my eyes, and he laughs. Then he leans in, and my eyes flutter shut. But his lips never meet mine. Instead, they brush against the crown of my head, and then Jackson is urging me toward the food again.

Warmth, unfamiliar but not unpleasant, rolls through me. This feeling is entirely new, but I already don't want it to leave.

Now that the worry of Jackson being gone has subsided, the soreness starts to make itself known. My whole body aches, a low thrum that reminds me of what happened yesterday. Not that I could easily forget.

I grimace as I take a seat at the island. But before I can say anything, a glass of water and a pain pill are set in front of me.

I look up at Jackson, words getting caught in my throat. "Thank you for breakfast," I say. "For taking care of me."

His gaze is soft. Possibly even adoring. "Of course. Anything for you, baby."

———

"How much longer?"

Jackson chuckles. "We've been in the car for two minutes."

"I don't like being unable to see!" He doesn't respond. "I'm going to open my eyes," I threaten.

"Baby, I promise we're almost there. Keep them closed for a little while longer."

I sigh as I settle against the back of the passenger seat in Jackson's rental. The car was delivered from Calderville this morning. It isn't as nice as his Audi, but it's better than my piece of junk.

I heed Jackson's plea and keep my eyes closed. True to his words, a few minutes later, I can feel the car come to a stop, and then the engine is being shut off. Jackson already told me to stay put until he could help me out, so I unbuckle my seatbelt and wait impatiently for him to round the hood.

"Here," he says, "take my hand."

I place my palm in his and let him guide me to wherever it is we're going. We haven't left Fraisier Creek, at least. Beyond that, I have no idea where we are.

I hear a door creak open, and then a familiar voice shouts, "Auntie M&M!"

My eyes pop open just in time to brace myself as Atticus comes barrelling toward me. Jackson reaches out, trying to slow him down so he doesn't hurt me, but Atticus dodges him easily. I suck in a breath as he knocks into my legs, wrapping his little arms around me. I return the hug as I look, surprised, at Pippa and Declan standing in the doorway of their house.

Once Atticus lets me out of his embrace, he takes my hand—the one Jackson was forced to drop—and drags me inside. Jackson trails after us.

Pippa waits for me in the entryway.

"You said Attie was sick," I say. Her text came in just as Jackson and I were finishing up breakfast, saying she couldn't make it this morning.

She shrugs, a small smile on her lips. "I lied." She gingerly wraps her arms around me, cautious of my sore ribs. "I'm so glad you're okay," she whispers.

I squeeze her tighter, uncaring that it hurts. "Me, too."

When Pippa eventually lets me go, Declan swoops in for his own hug. "Good to see you, kid," he says.

I laugh. "Hey, you're the kid, not me."

He releases me and grins.

A knock at the door has me spinning on my heels. Declan reaches over and opens it, revealing Wells standing on the porch.

I shake my head. "You did not come all the way here for this."

Whatever *this* is. I still don't really know what's going on, but it feels good to have all my people in one place.

He grins. "Oh, I definitely did."

I look at all of them, my friends, my family, in disbelief. "You guys really didn't have to do this."

"We did," Pippa says firmly. "In case you haven't noticed, we kind of love you."

Declan throws an arm over my shoulder, tugging me against his side. "Had to make sure our Meyer was okay. We all deserve a sick day anyway." He reaches out and ruffles Atticus's hair. "Gotta teach him the art of playing hooky."

"I wanna play!" Atticus says. "Show me!"

With a laugh, Declan leads his nephew away, explaining what he meant.

"Come sit," Pippa urges me. "You shouldn't be on your feet."

"My ribs are bruised, Pip. I don't have one foot in the grave."

She crosses her arms. "*Sit*."

I'm tempted to roll my eyes at the babying, but I know she's just showing that she cares in the only way she can. A lot of this situation is out of her control—out of my control—so if doting on me makes her feel better, then I'll let her.

Pippa follows me over to the couch while the guys all crowd around the kitchen. I'm not sure what they're doing, but if Jackson is involved, I don't think I want to know.

"Hey, Sunny," Wells calls. "Where are your mixing bowls?"

"They're in the bottom cupboard beside the stove," she says.

Wells smiles and returns to his task, and I don't miss Pippa's blush. When her attention falls back to me, I raise a brow.

"What?"

"You know what." I poke her arm as I lower my voice.

"Someone has a crush," I tease. "And a new nickname, *Sunny*."

She scoffs. "I do not!" she hisses. "Besides, I'm with Shawn."

"Barely," I mutter.

Her sorry excuse for a boyfriend barely comes around, let alone talks to her. I truly don't know if there's anything going on with Wells, but it would be much better for her than how she's being treated now.

Pippa gives me a flat look. "Meyer."

I throw my arms up in surrender. "Fine, I'll keep my observations to myself."

"Thank you." Pippa takes a strawberry from the bowl on the coffee table and pops it in her mouth. "Speaking of relationships, though, something you want to tell me about you and Jackson?"

Now it's my turn to look across the room at the other man standing in Pippa's kitchen. Jackson laughs at something Wells says, and then he picks Atticus up when he begs to help. Watching him with my pseudo nephew sends warmth flowing through me.

My gaze returns to my friend. "So you're allowed to voice your observations, but I can't?"

"Mine actually has the potential to go somewhere, so yes."

Does it have potential?

I've spent so long being wary of relationships. The only semblance of a real one I've had was with Rudy, and even that was almost a decade ago. I'm out of practice. But suddenly, the reasons I had for keeping my distance don't make much sense anymore.

Jackson has already seen parts of me I've never shown anyone else. Has already broken in and staked his claim, whether he knows it or not.

Now it's up to me whether I can be brave enough to take that leap, not knowing if he'll fall with me. But I have a feeling he's already there. I was just too scared to see that.

"It might break your brother's heart."

She rolls her eyes. "Please. He knows he never had a real chance with you. He's just a shameless flirt."

I grin. "As of right now, I have nothing official to report," I say. "But I'll let you know if anything changes."

She points a finger at me. "You better."

"And you have to do the same." When she goes to protest, I hold up a hand. "I know, I know. You're with Shawn. I'm just saying."

"Uncle Dec, you're burning it!" Atticus shouts, followed shortly by the sound of the smoke detector.

"I'm pretty sure pie crusts aren't supposed to smoke like that," Wells muses.

"Don't look at me," Jackson says. "Meyer has already banned me from baking in her kitchen."

Declan groans. "I swear I followed the stupid recipe!"

With a sigh, Pippa pushes off the couch. "I better go help them."

Laughing, I nod. "Good idea. We don't need another fire."

The half-burnt pie shell gets thrown in the garbage, and we settle for eating strawberries and ice cream instead. But the fact that they tried to make a pie for me heals some part of me I didn't know needed mending.

I spend the rest of the day with my friends, not thinking about the car accident or what happens next. For once, I set my worries aside and focus on the people I love.

Every so often, I catch Jackson's eye, and the overwhelming warmth in his gaze solidifies something in me. These feelings I have aren't going anywhere. They're here to stay.

Now I just have to figure out what I want to do with them.

CHAPTER 33
JACKSON

"Your father and I were thinking of coming to visit you," my mother says. "Maybe this weekend?"

I unlock the door to my room and swing inside, my cell wedged between my ear and shoulder. I toss the keycard on the dresser and begin to unfasten my shirt. What had started as me trying to help in the restaurant had ended in disaster and a promise to never return. Provided they agreed not to tell Meyer. I knew I would never live it down if they did.

"Ah," I say, stalling. It's not that I don't want to see my parents, but if they come here, they'll quickly become privy to everything that has been going on, including this situation with Meyer. I'm not ready for that. "Now's not really a good time."

I chuck my shirt toward the pile of laundry teetering on the chair in the corner. I normally wouldn't be caught dead doing something so disorganized, but in the absence of a hamper, I'm making do.

"You *always* say that."

"I know, Mom. There's just a lot to do when it comes to taking over a business."

"We could *help* you! And Meyer. We..."

My mother's words fade to the background as I turn toward the wardrobe that houses the rest of my clothing. A wedge heel that definitely does not belong to me rests at the base. My gaze moves upward, scanning the rest of the room.

A perfect match to the heel sits beside the bed. And beside that, a silky blouse. A familiar pencil skirt points toward the bathroom like a compass guiding me due north. And there, sitting outside the ajar bathroom door, is a pair of panties and a lacy black bra.

"Jackson Vaughan, are you listening to me?"

My mouth feels dry, my tongue leaden. "Sorry. It's— Well, there's something I have to...take care of. I'll call you later."

She huffs. "You better. Or I might just have to show up and force you to have a conversation with me."

"I'll call," I promise, though I'm surprised I can get the words out now that my brain and body are preoccupied. "Bye, Mom."

"Bye, sweetie. Love you!"

As soon as I hang up, I toss my phone toward the laundry chair, not at all concerned at this precise moment about where it lands.

I push open the bathroom door and then lean against the frame, simply admiring. Meyer rests in the clawfoot tub, bubbles surrounding her. Her hair is fastened in a knot on top of her head. She holds a glass of wine in her hand. And when her gorgeous eyes land on me, I feel like I've been set aflame.

"I've always wanted to take a bath in one of these," she says, running dexterous fingers along the lip of the tub.

"Is it living up to expectations?" I ask. My voice has gained a husky edge.

"Almost." Her fingers brush along the exposed, glistening skin of her clavicle. Then her hand dips below the surface of the water, obscured by the foamy bubbles, but I can imagine what it's doing. The small and sharp intake of her breath confirms that her hand has found a home between her legs. "I just can't quite seem to relax."

In two quick strides, I cross to her. I pluck the half-full glass of wine from her hand, set it aside, and then I slide my palm along the curve of her jaw. Her skin is soft and her lips plump, begging me to savour them.

My thumb caresses her lower lip. "Would you like some help?"

An answering nip to my thumb is all the confirmation I need. I tilt her chin upwards. She sits straighter, hands braced on either side of the tub, the swells of her breasts now visible amongst the bubbles. I groan low in my throat as I bend to her will, my lips descending on hers.

I can taste the strawberry wine on her tongue. It's intoxicating, a heady mix of her and her favourite drink.

I lower myself to the floor beside the tub, knees biting into the tile. Meyer watches me with a satisfied smile. Fuck, the things I would do to have her look at me like that all the time.

"What happened to your shirt?" she asks.

I shake my head. "Not important right now. Right now, I need to touch you."

She leans back again, head resting on the edge behind her. "What are you waiting for, Hotshot?"

Grinning, I don't waste another second. My arm plunges into the bath water. Settling first on her knee, my hand makes a slow exploration of her silky skin. Meyer's eyes flash as my fingers trail along the inner side of her thigh, and she lets them fall farther apart the closer I get to her centre.

Just before I arrive, I pause. Her eyes flash again, this time with frustration. I only smile as I stroke her inner thigh, so close to being where she wants me. Needs me.

"Abusing your access to guest rooms?" I *tsk*.

"Oh, so you're a *guest* now? Remind me to call someone to escort you out the next time I find you in my"—she gasps as my thumb brushes her clit—"office."

With my free hand, I grasp the back of her neck, tugging her face to mine. I can't resist tasting her again, so I do. She gasps into the kiss when one of my fingers enters her pussy, and I take the opportunity to sweep my tongue into her mouth again.

Everything about Meyer is like a dream come true.

"More," Meyer demands, out of breath.

"Only if you say please."

She arches a brow as her gaze meets mine. "I have no trouble finishing this myself."

And I have no doubt she would, too.

But I shake my head. "Not a fucking chance. If anyone is going to make you come right now, it'll be me."

A second digit fills her, and she lets out a curse. Hand on

my shoulder, her nails dig into the skin, leaving half-moon indentations. That's good. I want her to leave her mark on me.

"Still think you could have done better on your own?" I taunt.

She shrugs. "The jury's still out."

With a grin, I accept the challenge. Although our working relationship has shifted, this push and pull when we come together like this is just as explosive as the first time.

Water sloshes over the edge of the tub as she involuntarily rocks her hips, meeting the thrusts of my fingers. I keep my eyes on her face, studying the way her lips part. The way her head tips back, exposing the column of her neck. The way her eyes close, like she can't possibly keep them open a second longer.

"Jackson," she gasps, and my name on her lips like that is music to my fucking ears.

My thumb presses down on her clit.

And then she explodes. Her inner walls pulse around my fingers, and I take pleasure in watching her ride out her high.

When her head lolls to the side, her gaze, coated in lust, meets mine. She looks so fucking pretty. Sometimes, I have to stop myself from simply staring at her.

She walked into my life at the perfect time, and I don't ever want to look back.

Pulling my fingers from her pussy, I hold them up for her. Her eyes flit to meet mine, a question in them. Hunger, too. My dick throbs at the carnal want in her gaze.

"Suck," I demand, and she does. I watch with rapt attention as her tongue swirls around my fingers, tasting the remnants of herself. I don't mistake the rising heat in her eyes. "What a greedy fucking girl you are."

She drags my fingers from her mouth with a *pop*, and then her lips stretch into a sly grin. She shrugs. "I know what I like."

I love that about her. She isn't afraid to demand what she wants, inside and outside the bedroom.

Pushing herself up, she stands from the tub, and I shamelessly watch the water trail down her naked body. Droplets cling to her breasts, the softness of her stomach, those tempting thighs.

Beautiful. So goddamn beautiful.

My head fills with visions of my mouth on her skin, kissing her chest, between her legs. I want that. I've been craving it since that day on her couch.

I rise from the floor, holding my hand out. Meyer takes it, carefully stepping over the lip of the tub. Then she places a hand on my chest and lets it trail down my stomach, her fingers snagging on the waistband of my pants, then my belt.

Words escape me as I watch her drop to her knees in front of me. Head tilted back, she looks up, a faux innocent smile curving her lips. Then she reaches up and tugs the elastic from her bun, letting her hair fall down around her shoulders.

"My turn," she says.

"As a self-proclaimed gentleman, I feel I should protest a little," I reply. "For integrity's sake."

She shakes her head with a laugh as she reaches for the button on my pants. "I don't want you to be a gentleman."

"Oh, *thank fuck.*"

Between the two of us, we make quick work of the rest of my clothes, and then she's wrapping a hand around my cock and applying the perfect amount of pressure to make me groan.

One of my hands grips the counter behind me while the other buries itself in Meyer's hair, fisting the strands. I tug a little, and her grip on me tightens in response.

Her tongue darts out, catching the drop of moisture on my tip, and then she licks a line up my shaft that has me sucking in a sharp breath.

Holy fuck.

"Good?" she asks.

"Great," I croak. I'm surprised I even managed that one word.

She sits back on her heels, looking up at me. "You can tell me what you like. Don't be shy now, Vaughan."

"Gonna be completely honest with you, baby. Anything you're willing to do to me right now is what I like."

She considers this, considers me, for a moment, and then she leans forward again. Her grip on my cock tightens as she lets the tip rest on her tongue.

When she takes me a little deeper, I place a hand on the back of her head. My fingers tangle in her hair as I coax her to keep going, and they tighten when she swirls her tongue.

A low moan vibrates her vocal chords, and the sound makes my hips jerk.

"Shit," I curse. I pull back, drawing out of her mouth. "Did I hurt you?"

She shakes her head. "No, keep going."

After a moment, I relent and ease back into her mouth.

She looks fucking exquisite, kneeling there with my cock in her mouth. I'm tempted to let her keep going, but I can feel my release threatening to build and I have other plans. So, reluctantly, I withdraw.

Meyer's lips dip into a confused frown. "You didn't finish," she says.

I grab her hands and help her to her feet, grinning. "Not yet. I have something I want to do first."

CHAPTER 34

MEYER

Jackson takes my hand, leading me out of the bathroom. I follow willingly as my heart gallops in anticipation. He may have just gotten me off, but I still crave him. Still want more.

Beside the bed, Jackson pulls me against him, and then he's drawing my mouth to his. The kiss is quick, but it curls my toes and sends a lick of heat through my core. The orgasm in the tub was nice, but that need is building again, and I need him.

He pulls away, and I look up at him in confusion. He sits on the bed, leaning back against the pillows, and then he beckons me toward him.

"Come here," he says.

My limbs are moving before my brain even has time to catch up. I climb onto the bed and settle myself on his lap. My fingers thread through the hair at his nape while his hands anchor to my hips.

Desire hums in my veins. Jackson Vaughan has very

quickly become an addiction, one I can't see myself tiring of anytime soon.

When he kisses me, I lose myself in him. My hips bear down, grinding against his cock. He moans low in his throat as his tongue volleys with mine.

We're both breathless when we pull away. Still, Jackson trails a line of kisses along my neck, and I tip my head, allowing him better access. I shiver when his teeth scrape against my collarbone.

"You're really taking your sweet time," I say.

The smile he gives me is crooked. "I'm trying to savour this. Unless you have a better suggestion?"

I nod. "I do. Fuck now, savour later."

Jackson laughs. "A compelling argument."

My thighs squeeze his hips as I grind against him again. I'm not sure how he's able to hold this much restraint after he stopped himself from coming when I was on my knees in the bathroom.

"Hands on the headboard, baby."

A thrill travels my body at the order. Still, I can't make it *too* easy for him. It would be against my nature.

"And if I refuse?"

He shrugs. "You're sitting on my face either way. I just figured you'd appreciate having something to hold on to."

My surprise hardly has time to register before Jackson slides down the bed, maneuvering until I hover, straddled over his face. I quickly take hold of the headboard, heeding his advice. But then he grabs my hips and pulls me down further, and I let out a squeak of surprise.

The first sweep of his tongue sends a jolt through me. If I

wasn't already on my knees, it would have sent them buckling. My fingers dig into the headboard.

The feel of his tongue on me, inside me, is the most overwhelming sensation. My knees crowd his ears as I try not to put all my weight on him, but *fuck*, he makes it hard. Especially when he adds his fingers into the mix, inserting one inside me as he sucks on my clit.

"*Jackson*," I moan.

"Yes, baby?"

I'm getting close, but I don't want to finish this way. Right now, I want him. This yearning won't be sated until I have him inside me.

"Jackson, *please*."

"Please what?" he taunts.

"I want you inside me," I reply, not caring about his smug tone. "I need you."

Something in my voice must convince him because he removes his finger from inside me, and then he slides up against the headboard, half sitting.

I rest back on his thighs as I reach between us, taking his cock in hand. His fingers dig into my hips as I stroke him. He is impossibly hard in my grasp, and when wetness beads at the tip, I swipe it away with my thumb. Then I bring my thumb to my mouth, and Jackson watches, enraptured, as I lick the wetness away.

"Sometimes, I can't believe you're real," he says in awe. The words slip out under his breath, almost like he didn't mean to utter them.

My lips part as I struggle for a reply. Jackson shakes his

head, and then with purpose, he takes hold of my chin, tugging me into him so he can claim my mouth.

Our lips part with a groan. His or mine, I'm not sure. Maybe both. And then he eases me onto my back, my head resting at the foot of the bed.

Leaning over, he grabs a condom from the bedside table and rolls it on before he settles himself between my thighs.

My eyes lock on his, and I'm drowning. But if this is sinking, then I never want to float. Something has changed between us. Some kind of gravitational shift that leaves me breathless for an entirely different reason than the weight of his body on mine.

"You are so fucking beautiful, Meyer," he says. The look of devotion in his gaze makes me want to weep.

I have never had someone look at me this way. Like I am both the beginning and the end of their deepest desire. My first instinct is to push him away, but I'm tired of enforcing that wall. Fucking *tired*.

So I let it fall.

Trailing a finger down his chest, relishing his answering shiver, I say, "You are the most beautiful man I've ever met."

"You're so good at stroking my ego."

I arch a brow. "Just your ego?"

My finger has trailed all the way down his stomach now, so I reach down, taking hold of his cock and positioning it at my entrance. I think I've waited long enough.

"No, baby," he replies. My lips part on a gasp as he thrusts forward, pushing himself partially inside. "I love the way it feels when you're wrapped around my cock."

Then he thrusts again, filling me completely. The slide of

his hips is slow and sensual. Unlike the other times we've slept together, this isn't rushed. And I don't want it to be.

Warmth spreads through me. With one arm braced on the mattress beside my head, he reaches between us with his other hand, finding my clit.

"*Jackson.*"

My orgasm rocks through me, and I clench around him. My thighs quiver, but he keeps up his pace, drawing out the aftershocks of my pleasure. And then with one final thrust, he's tumbling after me.

His head falls to the crook of my neck, where he places a light kiss. We stay like that, his body over mine, his dick inside me, for a few moments. I find myself running my fingers through his hair as I work to catch my breath.

Jackson heads to the bathroom to dispose of the condom, and when he comes back, he has a cloth in hand. I sigh as the warmth hits my skin where he cleans up our mess. I know I should get up to use the bathroom, but my limbs don't want to move.

I've never been one to cuddle after sex. Yet one round in a bed with Jackson has me burrowing under the covers, resting my cheek against his naked chest as he draws patterns on my back with his fingers.

I think that's why I've avoided having sex in a bedroom with him—I knew once I did, it wouldn't just be fast and dirty fucking to scratch an itch anymore. I knew it would be something real.

I've never truly had real before. It's as scary as it is exciting.

I want to say something. I *should* say something. I owe it

to myself to address these feelings, even if he doesn't feel the same. But he *does*. I know it. I can't be alone in this.

It takes me a good few minutes, but I eventually work up the courage to speak.

"This doesn't seem very casual anymore," I whisper.

His quiet sigh ruffles my hair. "Baby, I don't think it ever was," he replies.

I shift in his arms so I can face him. Half lying on my stomach, I regard him with something akin to hope.

"We've both been pretty damn good at lying to ourselves," he continues. "This isn't just sex. If you say it is, then you just haven't been paying attention."

Jackson lazily trails a hand down my bare back. The contact makes me shiver.

"Oh, yeah?" I challenge. "What should I have been paying attention to?"

His hand retraces its trail up my spine until it rests at the back of my head, fingers tangling in the strands of hair at my nape. Strangely, I again feel like weeping at the tender way he caresses me.

"The way I admire your uncanny ability to connect with everyone you meet. Even when you don't want to." He sends me a pointed look. "And I love the way your pretty blue eyes look when you first wake up. The way your cheeks flush when you're mad, but even more so when you're shy about something. Your smart mouth, even though half the time it's used against me."

"If I didn't know any better..." My heart hammers so hard, I can feel it in my throat. *Be brave.* "It sounds like you're trying to be my boyfriend, Vaughan."

"If the fact that I can't fucking get enough of you hasn't clued you in, let me be clear," he says. "I want you, Meyer Ellison. However you'll have me."

My lips part. "What?"

"Let me date you."

"You want to...date me?"

"Is that so hard to believe?"

It used to be. But I realize now that every moment I've spent with Jackson has culminated into this.

"No," I reply, biting at my lower lip. "You're sure?"

He laughs, pinching my waist. I swat his hand. "Yes, Meyer, I'm sure."

Slowly, I nod. "Okay. I just—" I suck in a deep breath. "Please don't break my heart."

My whispered plea settles between us, and Jackson's gaze turns even softer.

"Never," he vows.

I believe him. It's strange, feeling this secure. I haven't felt that in a long time, if ever. But everything feels settled when I'm with him. Like I can fully be myself and he won't leave.

He's seen a lot of ugly parts of me and he's still here. It's a powerful thing to see the worst sides of someone and still stick around to inspire them to be their best.

"My turn to say nice things about you," I declare.

He mocks me with a gasp. "Meyer Ellison, being nice to me? Never thought I'd live to see the day."

"You might not still," I warn, but I can't help my laugh.

His answering grin is blinding. It makes him look so handsome, I can't resist leaning over and kissing him once more.

"You are so incredibly nerdy when it comes to data. I roll my eyes, but I think it's hot. So are your suits. I love your rational brain, the way it competes with my hotheadedness," I admit. "I love the way you challenge me to step outside my comfort zone and try different things with the inn. You match my sense of humour." I pause as I draw in a deep breath. "Mostly, I just love the way you didn't give up on me."

I know I'm difficult. I'm not easy to crack open. Letting someone in enough to trust them isn't a quick task. But, as always, Jackson has been patient.

He shakes his head. "Once I got here, that never even crossed my mind." His gaze roves mine, searching. "So we're doing this?" he asks.

I nod. "I think so."

I let out a gasp when I'm rolled onto my back, and Jackson hovers over me. I throw my arms over his shoulders and tug him closer. Our lips collide.

There's a lot of uncertainty in the future, not knowing if the person that has been terrorizing us will leave us alone, but with Jackson by my side, I feel like I can conquer anything.

CHAPTER 35

JACKSON

WE'RE GOING to be late.

A quick glance at my watch proves we're *already* late. It typically wouldn't matter all that much, given how many extra hours we both spend at the inn, but we're supposed to be having a staff meeting this morning.

"Ellison, we've gotta go."

"Almost done," Meyer says. She tries to pull a muffin out of the hot tin and accidentally touches the metal around the edge. "Ow, fuck."

She tries again, getting the same result. I frown. "Are you sure you don't want help?"

She raises a brow as she looks at me. "You do remember what happened when we made Cherie's pie, don't you? You and baking don't mix, Hotshot. You and *kitchens* don't mix."

When I caved and told her about the kitchen staff banishing me from the restaurant a couple weeks ago, she couldn't stop laughing. So then I had to find a creative way to shut her up. She didn't complain.

I shrug. "We had a chef when I was growing up. I never had to learn."

She finishes packing the muffins for transport and then rounds the island. She pats my cheek affectionately. "Oh, you poor little rich boy."

I take the muffin container from her before she can protest. Then she locks up her cottage and we walk down the gravel path toward the inn.

I can tell by the way Meyer keeps wringing her hands in front of her that she's nervous. It was her idea to tell the staff today, but it's clearly weighing on her.

"We don't have to do this if you're not ready," I offer. "It can wait."

She shakes her head. "No. I don't want to keep secrets. I'm only a little nervous."

I stop, taking hold of her hand in mine. "What are you nervous about?"

She frowns. "That people are going to judge me. That they're going to think I'm only with you to get what I want with the inn."

"If they think that, then they don't know you at all."

Chewing on her lower lip, she shrugs. "I don't know."

"I do," I say. "If they were really paying attention, they would know you get your way with the inn whether we're sleeping together or not."

She rolls her eyes. "Like you haven't made changes."

"That you agreed to. Eventually." I squeeze her hand. "In case I haven't made it abundantly clear, I understand and respect how much Dog Days means to you, Meyer. I only have your and the inn's best interests at heart."

Her gaze softens. "You have made that clear. I just didn't really want to listen before."

"And now?"

Her nose wrinkles. "Now I can be persuaded to hear you out."

With an amused shake of my head, I tug on her hand, and then we're heading for the front door of the inn. When we make it there, I turn to Meyer.

"Ready, baby?"

Slowly, she nods. "Ready."

She goes to take another step, but I wrap an arm around her waist, tugging her against me. Her hand lands on my chest as she steadies herself.

I lower my mouth to hers, and she meets me halfway, melting into the kiss.

"What was that for?" she asks when we pull apart.

I grin. "Just because."

Her answering smile is breathtaking. There was a time, not all that long ago, that she refused to smile at me, and now she gives them away freely. The thought makes something expand inside my chest.

Everyone packs into the restaurant before opening, just as they do every time we hold a staff meeting. I walk the muffins around the room. Since that first meeting I attended, I haven't brought any of my own competing baked goods.

Once everyone has had their fill, we get down to business.

"Thank you for coming," I say. "We appreciate it."

"Did we have a choice?" Marsaili jokes.

"No," I reply, "but I like to give you the illusion that you do."

That earns me a laugh, from everyone except for Meyer. She's standing blank-faced beside me, trying not to let her worry show. I touch a hand to the small of her back, encouraging her.

"The reason we called you here today is because we have something we wanted to tell you," she says. She inhales deeply, steeling herself, before she continues. "Because of the nature of our partnership, it didn't feel right to keep this from you. We want to be transparent. That said, I want you all to know that Jackson and I are...in a relationship."

There is a moment of stretched silence, and then a collective cheer rises through the room. I spot Pippa grinning amidst the crowd, which mirrors the expressions on everyone else's faces.

I can practically feel the relief that sweeps through Meyer. She was truly worried for nothing. These people love her.

"About damn time," someone says.

"I knew it!"

"Dibs on planning the wedding!" Ashley calls.

Meyer's cheeks flame as she glances shyly at me and then back to Ashley. She laughs awkwardly. "We're a little far off from a wedding, Ash," she says.

"That's okay," Ashley replies. "I can be patient."

Meyer covers her face with her hands, embarrassed, but I just grin. I could see it one day. We only just got together, so Meyer might get sick of me before then, but I can't deny I like the idea of it.

"Was that all?" Marsaili asks. "You two had us scared half to death, thinkin' you were sellin' the place or something."

Meyer laughs. "Sorry we scared you. I promise that selling is not in the cards."

The older woman nods. "Better not be."

We still have a while before the restaurant officially opens, so we all spend some time chatting and catching up. Now that we're in the thick of summer, our days are plenty busy, so it's hard to talk about anything not strictly related to the job.

When my phone buzzes, I take a step away from the group and pull it out of my pocket. A notification from the security cameras I had installed at Meyer's cottage lights up my screen. Worry settles low in my gut as I click on the tab.

When the camera feed comes up, my spine stiffens. There's someone walking around the outside of the cottage. I can't see their face, but I have a bad feeling. With everything stacking up these last few months, this can't be a coincidence.

"Hey, Hotshot," Meyer calls. My eyes stay glued to the camera feed as she comes up beside me. "Jackson?"

She touches my shoulder to get my attention, but she soon gets distracted by my phone screen. I barely hear her gasp. Her hand wraps around my arm, clinging to me as we watch. We should probably do something—call the police. But I feel frozen in place.

Then a new notification pops up, telling us the motion-sensor security alarm was triggered.

"Oh my God," Meyer says. She sounds like she's on the verge of tears.

My jaw clenches. No need to call the police now—they should already be on their way thanks to the security company.

"Fish," she gasps.

"Meyer, wait—"

But she's already gone, racing out of the restaurant.

I curse as I follow after her, through the inn and out the front door. She flies down the gravel path leading to her cottage, and cold dread slithers through me at what she might find. *Who* she might find.

I manage to catch up with her just before her feet hit the front porch. Looping an arm around her waist, I draw her to a halt.

"Let me go," she demands as she struggles. "Jackson, let go!"

I shake my head. "I'm sorry, I can't do that, baby. I'm not letting you go in there until the police have cleared it."

She fights me, trying to force me to release her. "What about Fish? What if he gets hurt?" she cries.

My heart cracks open. I know how much the cat means to her, but she means everything to me. I'm not risking it. Whoever tripped the alarm could still be prowling around outside. Worse, they could be inside, just waiting for Meyer to come home.

"Fish is probably hiding like he always does. We'll get him as soon as everything is safe, I promise," I reply, gentle pulling her back toward the inn.

I can hear sirens in the distance and the chatter of our staff. They're spilling out of the inn now, no doubt curious why Meyer and I ran off without an explanation. Pippa pushes through the crowd, meeting us halfway down the path.

"What happened?" she asks.

I look down at Meyer. Her lip trembles as she sucks in a steadying breath. I tuck her closer against my side, and she hides her face against my chest.

"Someone was lurking around the cottage, and then they tripped the alarm," I explain. "We watched it happen on the cameras."

There's pure fear in Pippa's eyes, but she quickly blinks it away and lays a comforting hand on Meyer's arm. And then we wait.

The police arrive shortly after, and they head straight for the cottage. They instruct us to wait inside the inn, so I guide Meyer to one of the chairs in the lobby. She clings to my hand, not allowing me to let go. Not that I would. I'm not going anywhere.

It seems like hours pass before one of the constables comes to retrieve us. I keep holding Meyer's hand as we follow him back outside.

"I know this isn't easy to think about," Constable Reyes says, "but we need to go over this. Can you tell me what happened?"

I relay what I saw on the cameras, and I pull out the footage to show him what I'm talking about.

Constable Reyes grimaces. "It looks like a rock was thrown through the side window into the living room," he explains. Meyer's grip tightens on my hand. "There was a note attached."

He holds a piece of paper toward us.

I warned you, it says.

"It's a reminder," Meyer says. "Of the spray paint on the wall. Now this."

"Reggie?" I ask.

Constable Reyes shakes his head. "We finally tracked him down. He's been sleeping on his cousin's couch down in Scarborough. He wasn't in Fraisier Creek when any of the incidences occurred, including the vandalism."

My heart stops, and Meyer stiffens beside me. If Reggie wasn't involved in any of it...then who was?

"We'll have to hold this scene for a while to gather any evidence they left behind," the constable continues.

"Can I go inside?" Meyer asks. "I won't touch anything, I just need to find my cat." Her voice cracks, threatening tears. "Please."

He hesitates, but the desperation in her eyes wins out, and he nods. "Just the cat. If you need anything else, make a list and one of the other constables will get it to you."

With a quick nod, Meyer is up the porch steps and through the open front door. I follow close behind. Like hell am I letting her out of my sight right now.

After a cursory glance through the living room and kitchen, we decide Fish isn't there. With all the commotion, he's likely at the back of the house. We head for Meyer's bedroom next.

We check the laundry baskets first, his preferred place to sleep, but they're empty. Then Meyer lowers herself to the floor and peers under the bed.

With a relieved cry, Meyer reaches underneath and pulls Fish out from his hiding spot. The cat lets out a perturbed meow, but he doesn't struggle in her arms. He lets her crush him against her chest, almost like he senses that Meyer needs this right now.

I can feel Meyer shaking. "Hey, you're safe," I say, placing a hand on her back. "I won't let anything happen to you."

She shakes her head. "I'm not scared right now, I'm fucking *angry*." When she looks up at me, her blue eyes are blazing. "This has to stop."

"I know, baby." With my arm around her, we exit her bedroom. "We'll figure it out."

I'm not sure how, but we will. Because Meyer is right. We can't keep living like this, wondering when this sick person will strike next. Constantly looking over our shoulders.

Not to mention, this could be detrimental to the inn. If word gets out to tourists about the shit that's been happening, they aren't going to want to stay here, and I wouldn't blame them.

This has to end.

CHAPTER 36

JACKSON

"For the third time today, I'm *fine*."

Meyer's voice rings out through the speakers of my car, and hearing it eases something in my chest. Leaving her this morning was the last thing I wanted to do, but one of us needed to stay back to help at the inn while the other picked up supplies in Calderville. Having Meyer surrounded by a group of people that love her seemed like the safest option to me.

"Just checking," I say.

She laughs. "I know you're *just checking*. I'm safe and sound, right where you left me."

"Good, let's keep it that way. I just left Calderville, so I'll be back soon."

"I'll be waiting for you. Bye, Jackson."

"Bye, baby."

The calls disconnects, and I let out a sigh.

Driving back from the city, setting aside the stressors that come with an anonymous stalker, it occurs to me how relaxed

I feel. Even the most stressful days at the inn leave me feeling a sense of peace when I climb into bed at night. The same couldn't be said for the life I lived back home.

My leave from my job in Toronto is quickly nearing its end. I thought I would feel grateful, but instead, all I can feel is an impending sense of dread. And with that thought is the realization that I don't want to go back. I'd trade in my condo for Meyer's cottage in a heartbeat.

Fraisier Creek feels like home in a way the city never has.

Sure, I would miss my parents and my friends, but I've found a new group of people to rally around me here.

"This is what you wanted, isn't it?" I mutter aloud. "You always had to have the last word."

My grandmother was a lot of things, but in this instance, she was right. About me, the inn. Meyer. She knew exactly what she was doing when she left me that letter, and honestly, I couldn't be more grateful. She gave me more than I ever could've thought to ask for.

All the pressure that comes with the inn doesn't feel like pressure when I have someone to share it with. When I have Meyer. My only wish is that Cherie could have been here to see this—to see what Meyer and I have created together, despite all the things trying to set us back.

Instead of driving straight to the inn, I decide to make a detour into town. I manage to snag a parking space right on Main, a great feat these days. I cut the engine, but I don't get out of the car yet. Pulling my phone from the cupholder, I begin to type out a text.

> Know anyone in the market for a condo?

It doesn't take long for a response to roll in.

WELLS

Have I officially lost my best friend to the
country?

I may be in the market for a good realtor.

WELLS

Happy for you, man. Even if it does mean
you'll be ditching me.

You could always move here.

WELLS

Maybe. If I had the right reasons.

Wells has never liked the city, not really. He tolerates it, at best. But I have a feeling that if I move to Fraisier Creek permanently, he won't be long to follow.

Stepping out into the August sunshine, I lock my car. I only have a quick walk before I reach my destination.

The bell above the door chimes when I enter Little Treasure Flower Shop. Ilsa, the woman Meyer and I spoke with at the farmer's market, stands behind the counter wearing a welcoming smile.

"Hi, Jackson," she says. "What brings you in today?"

My eyes scan the displays. "I was hoping to find something Meyer might like," I reply. Redness creeps up my neck at the admission.

Besides my mother and Cherie, I've never bought flowers for a woman before. But Meyer has me wanting to do all kinds of things I've never done. She makes it easy, though.

One flash of that soft smile she pulls out just for me and I'm a goner, plain and simple.

Ilsa's grin turns knowing. "Are you looking for cut flowers? Or a plant?"

Considering I'm not sure my girl has a green thumb to speak of, cut flowers are probably safest. At least their inevitable death will be through no fault of ours.

"Cut, please." I eye the array of different coloured blooms. "Whatever you think will look the best together."

As Ilsa turns toward the fridge, I wander around the store. On top of all things flowers, Ilsa also stocks a variety of trinkets from local small businesses. Along one wall, there are shelves filled with handmade soaps and artisanal crafts. I recognize a few products from the farmer's market.

When the bell above the door jingles, I don't bother looking up from the candle I'm inspecting. It seems like something Meyer might like.

"Hi!" Ilsa calls out. "I'll be with you in a—"

The sound of glass shattering causes my head to whip up. I abandon the candle and head back toward the front counter. Ilsa now stands with her back against the fridge. Her face has gone worryingly pale and her eyes are blown wide. A vase sits in pieces at her feet.

I take a step closer. "Ilsa, are you alright?"

She looks like she has seen a ghost. I thought I understood the expression before, but seeing her now tells me I hadn't.

She holds a hand out in front of her, as if to ward someone off. "You need to leave," she says, her voice shaking.

But she isn't talking to me.

My head swings to the right, finally taking notice of the man standing just inside the shop. He looks to be in his early forties, roughly Ilsa's age. Nothing about his outward appearance—jeans and a plain black t-shirt, hair going a little grey at the sides—raises any red flags, except for the wired look in his eyes.

Something about him seems familiar, but I can't quite put my finger on it.

His head cocks to the side. "You don't recognize me?" he asks. "It's me, Ilsa. You remember."

She nods. "I remember, Felix. And that's why you need to leave."

To her credit, her voice doesn't waver this time. But I can see her hands begin to shake. I inch closer to her as I keep an eye on the man.

"I'm not going anywhere," he replies. He means it, too.

"Hey, man," I interject, stepping forward, "I think it's best if you head out. Ilsa asked you to leave."

He flat-out ignores me, his eyes never straying from their target. "*I'm not leaving,*" he grinds out.

"You have to. You're— You're trespassing." Despite the small stumble in Ilsa's words, her voice remains strong. Her eyes flick to me quickly. "Jackson, call the police."

I have no idea what is going on, but a sinking feeling has begun to grow in my gut. I don't question Ilsa—I reach for my phone, but that simple action sends Felix into a rage. With a yell, he sweeps an entire table of flower arrangements to the floor. Glass and soil and broken blooms litter the concrete at his feet.

"*No.*" His voice has sharpened. "Don't fucking move."

Then he lifts his other arm, producing a gun. It was concealed at his side before, hidden by his leg and the table he stands behind, but now I've made him angry enough to brandish it.

"Felix." Ilsa's voice is little more than a whisper now. Tears have gathered in her eyes, but she doesn't let them fall. "*Please*. What are you doing?"

His hard glare lands on me. "Taking back what's mine."

My brain spins as I try to connect the dots, but I have no idea what he means. I don't have time to mull it over before he's gesturing with the gun, telling me to stand beside Ilsa.

I keep my eyes on him, my hands in plain sight, as I move. He watches me, too. When he's satisfied that I'm corralled, he walks back toward the front door and flicks the lock. Then he shuts off the fluorescent Open sign in the window.

"Who the hell is he?" I whisper.

Ilsa seems to shrink in on herself, looking both scared and ashamed. "My high school boyfriend," she replies.

Her thumb rubs absentmindedly over a scar on her wrist. My eyes flit to Felix, who is looking through the window to the sidewalk out front. When I'm sure he's still far enough away to not overhear, I turn back to Ilsa.

"Did he hurt you?"

Her eyes snap to mine. "What?"

"You're rubbing your wrist while you talk about him." I grab it gently, eyeing the scar. It's faded now, but it's still visible. "Did he hurt you? Is that why you're so scared?"

"Yes," she says on an exhale. "I haven't seen him in so long. His family moved while we were still in school. I thought I was rid of him for good."

I nod. "You will be. We're going to get out of this," I vow. "Everything is going to be okay."

Somehow. I have to believe this won't end in tragedy. I have too much to live for. I'm not dying before I get the chance to tell Meyer that I love her.

Tears fill her eyes once more. "I am so sorry, Jackson. This is the last thing I wanted to happen. You don't deserve to be caught up in this."

Shaking my head, I say, "Neither do you."

Felix stalks across the shop, back toward us. He makes a move in Ilsa's direction, but I step in his path. He sneers. Gun or not, I'm not letting him get anywhere near her. He's already hurt her enough.

Before I have time to react, he swings the butt of the gun up and into the side of my head. I stumble back a step, the force throwing my centre of gravity off, and knock into another table. More planters crash to the floor, but I can hardly hear the sound over the ringing in my ear.

My temple throbs, and when I reach up to touch it, I hiss at the sharp pain. My hand comes away covered in blood. I can feel it trailing down the side of my face and soaking into the collar of my shirt.

Ilsa gasps. "Jackson!"

"I'm fine," I say quickly. She places a hand on my arm, turning me to face her. "Ilsa, it's okay."

Her chin dips. "It's not." Lower, she whispers, "I'm sorry. I'm so sorry. I'll fix this."

I shake my head. This isn't hers to fix, and I don't want her doing something rash because of her misplaced guilt.

Whatever happens next, we have to be strategic. Felix doesn't seem to be operating within reason.

Felix pulls something off the front counter and shoves it at Ilsa. Her phone, I realize.

"Text her," he demands.

"Please, Felix," she begs. "Don't do this."

His stare is unrelenting. The anger in his eyes never falters. "Text. Her. I want our daughter here. *Now.*"

Ilsa fumbles to take the phone. The threat of the gun in his hands feels heavy as he watches her. Ensures she does as she was told. He would know—if we tried to run, tried to call for help. We wouldn't stand a chance, and then the town would be left unsuspecting of the danger that lurks in its midst.

"Who?" My gaze swings from Felix and then back to Ilsa. "Who is he talking about?"

Her watery gaze meets mine, and even before she speaks, ice is filling my veins. Because I know what she's about to say.

"Meyer."

CHAPTER 37

MEYER

TODAY IS a busy day at the inn.

I look forward to kicking up my feet and watching a movie tonight, curled into Jackson's side. If the Meyer from April could see me now, she'd be laughing. But a lot has changed since then. *I've* changed since then. Or more accurately, I've given myself permission to let my guard down. To fall.

Pippa drops into the chair opposite me with a sigh. "My feet hurt," she whines. "I love you, but I'm kind of excited to not see you for the next two days."

I laugh. "What are you and Attie getting up to on your days off?" I ask.

"Atticus has decided he wants to learn how to fish, so Declan and I are gonna take him out to the lake. They can play with the fish while I read."

"Not a fan of scales?" I tease.

She shudders. "Not in the slightest. Besides, my dad

wouldn't have taught me to fish, even if I had wanted to. So Declan is the only one that knows how."

Not for the first time, my blood begins to boil at the mention of Pippa and Declan's father.

I wave a hand, letting go of my anger. "Let the boys play. You relax."

My phone buzzes in my pocket. When I pull it out, I find a text on the screen.

ILSA

Hi Meyer. Can you come to the shop? I have some questions about some flowers and I need your opinion.

"Will you be okay if I run to Ilsa's?" I ask. "She wants me to come by to discuss the flowers for the mayor's daughter's wedding."

The flowers for the ceremony itself were chosen by the bride, but some of the wedding guests have chosen to stay at the inn while they're in town, so we wanted to match some of our floral pieces to the theme.

Pippa waves me off. "Go. We'll be fine. I think the rush has mostly died down now."

I push out of my chair. "Text me if you need me and I'll come right back. Jackson should be around, too. He's on his way home now."

Home. Does he consider this place home? Or is he itching to get back to the city, to his life?

An uneasy feeling—like maybe letting myself get attached was a mistake—settles in my gut, but I push it away.

Jackson and I have to talk, yes, but that doesn't automatically mean the outcome is going to be bad. Right?

Pippa nods, closing her eyes. "And if you need me, I'll be right here, taking a nap."

That uneasy feeling spreads, and I find myself bending to envelop Pippa in a hug.

"Oof." She hugs me back. "What's this for?"

I pull away. "You know you're my best gal, right?"

Slowly, she nods. "And you're mine." A look of suspicion takes over her face. "Are you okay?"

Nodding, I paste on a smile. "Yeah, I'm okay. Just a little off today, I guess, but I wanted you to know how much I appreciate you."

She smiles back. "I appreciate you, too. Now go before Ilsa thinks you've gotten lost!"

Heading over now! See you soon.

I send a quick text to Jackson, letting him know where I'm going. I don't want him to freak out when he gets back and can't immediately find me. We've all been on edge since the rock was thrown through my window. Or, more accurately, for the past few months.

Fifteen minutes later, I walk down the sidewalk on Main Street. It took me forever to find a parking spot—all the ones nearest the florist were taken, but that's par for the course in Fraisier Creek during the summer. When I make it to Little Treasure, I stop short. The sign in the window says it's closed, and when I peer through the glass, it seems like all the lights are off.

Pulling out my phone, I check my text from Ilsa, thinking maybe I misread it. But I didn't. She asked me to meet her at the shop. This causes a strange feeling to settle in my gut. I'm not sure exactly what it is, but something is up.

I round the side of the building and head for the back entrance. I know it's usually used for deliveries, but this is also where Ilsa parks her car. The sedan is still sitting in its spot, so she must be inside.

I tug on the back door, expecting some resistance, but it opens for me easily. Trepidation slithers through my veins. Still, I keep going.

Poking my head in, I look around. "Ilsa?" I call.

I don't hear anything in response. Stepping inside, I let the door close behind me. Back here, the lights are still switched on, but the eerie stillness of the shop has goose-bumps rising on my flesh.

Something is *wrong*.

"Are you here?" I try again.

"Meyer, don't—"

Ilsa's voice, coming from somewhere farther inside the shop, is abruptly cut off.

Dread coalesces in my gut. I steel myself, unsure of what I might find. Whatever it is, I know it's not good. I can feel it.

When I come around the corner, I spot them immediately. Jackson and Ilsa are standing together by the flower fridges, Ilsa with a hand on Jackson's arm. His arm that is covered in blood. Panicked, my eyes search his body, looking for the source. A wound on the side of his head seems to be the culprit.

"Jackson," I breathe, taking a step forward. "What—?"

Ilsa's irises flare in warning, but she doesn't have time to speak. Another figure enters my line of vision, stepping between us. I was so focused on Jackson, I didn't even notice there was anyone else in the room. Or the fact that he has a gun.

I freeze in place, and then a million thoughts flit through my brain.

"*You.*"

I recognize this man. The day Jackson and I got pizza and ate it at the park—he was there. He commented on the weather. Ever since, he's been around town. At the restaurant, the grocery store, the strawberry patch. I bumped into him inside the market.

I thought he was simply a tourist spending the summer here. How wrong I apparently was.

"Hello, Meyer," he says.

"Who are you?" I ask. My brain is telling me to run, to get the hell out of here. But I can't. I won't leave Jackson and Ilsa behind. "How do you know my name?"

He smiles, and it sends an icicle of fear down my spine. That smile spells danger. "I'm your father."

My face pales as my breath catches. "What?"

He nods. "Don't you worry, I'm going to put our family back together. I promise. Soon, everything will be the way it should have always been."

He's not looking at me when he says this. He's looking at Ilsa. When I turn to face her, I see the apology in her eyes. Regret, but...no shock.

"Ilsa," I whisper, "what's going on?"

Her eyes glisten with unshed tears. "I'm sorry," she says. "I didn't mean for any of this to happen."

"What are you talking about?" I can hear my voice creeping higher—in anger, in panic. "Did you *help* him?" It's a stupid accusation, but my brain can't make sense of anything that is happening right now. "Are *you* behind all the—?"

"Do *not* speak to your mother that way," the man snaps, interrupting me.

Bile threatens to creep up my throat. "My...mother?"

The world swims as the words sink in. Ilsa, the woman I've known my whole life. Ilsa, with her comforting smiles and warm laughter. Ilsa, who...looks exactly like me.

I'm not sure how I missed it. Maybe because I wasn't looking. I have always been somewhat curious, of course I have, but I've never had the desire to seek out my birth parents. I didn't want Mom to feel like she wasn't enough for me.

"I didn't know this would happen, I swear. I'm sorry," she says again. Then she turns back to the man. "Felix, please. Let Meyer and Jackson go. I'll do anything you want."

He frowns. "What I *want* is my family."

Ilsa swallows. "I know. And you can have that—you can have me. But you have to let them go."

Felix shakes his head sharply. "I'm not letting anyone go. I'm going to get rid of *him*," he promises, pointing toward Jackson, "and then we're going to live like the family we should've been from the start."

Ice cold fear shoots down my spine, like someone has dumped a bucket of glacial water over me. The reality of the situation has finally set in. Everything Felix is saying, he means. And I don't know where to go from here, but I do know that we need to get *out*.

"Why are you doing this?" I ask. "Why keep Jackson here?"

Why *hurt* him?

Felix turns to me, his gaze softening. I feel sick. I don't want his affection.

"I did it for you, Meyer. Everything I've done these past few months has been for you. Did you like my gift? I had a bear just like it when I was a boy."

Everything I've done.

It hits me then, what he means. He's behind the vandalism, the stalking, the fire, Jackson's brakes. My cottage. It was him. And the teddy bear on my front porch...

I shake my head. "I didn't ask you to do any of that."

His gaze hardens. "He is a threat to the inn, which is a threat to you. I heard you complaining about having to work with him. So I tried to take care of it. For you."

I am seconds away from throwing up. All of this is because of *me*?

"He's not a threat," I say desperately, head shaking. "I didn't want him here at first, I agree, but now I do." My eye flit to Jackson, apology written in them. "He has helped me so much."

Felix's grip tightens on the gun. "You're just saying that. He *tricked* you."

"He didn't trick me." I hold my hands out in front of me in a placating gesture. "Please, can we talk about this? Without the gun."

Felix's jaw tightens. "No. You're not going to convince me of anything. It's all *lies*. He has to go."

Tears spring to my eyes. I hate appearing so vulnerable in front of this man, but my terror is quickly taking hold.

"Please don't hurt him," I beg. I turn to Jackson. I fucking *hate* that I'm saying this for the first time while being held at literal gunpoint. "I love him." My gaze lands back on Felix. "I *love* him. If you care about me and my happiness at all, you'll let him go."

Felix shakes his head. "*No*. You don't know what you're talking about. I'm helping you!"

"Please," I sob. "*Please*. I don't want this."

"I said *no*!"

My cheek begins to sting before I've even registered what happened. I have no doubt that if I looked in a mirror right now, I would see a bright red handprint marring my skin.

Felix takes a step back, stunned. "Meyer...I'm sorry. I didn't mean to! You were crying and you wouldn't stop and you made me so *angry*. You were being ungrateful..."

He keeps murmuring to himself, apologizing, though I tune him out when I spot movement from behind his shoulder. But I keep my attention focused on him, trying to buy Ilsa some time.

While I had him distracted, she managed to sneak up behind him. Now, she aims a large flower pot at Felix's head and swings. The move disorients him enough to loosen his hold on the gun. Jackson takes this opportunity to swoop in, trying to disarm him.

Time almost stands still. My heartbeat hammers so loud,

I can hear it inside my head. Like with my car accident, everything happens in slow motion.

Thump, thump, thump.

Jackson struggles against Felix, and my breath catches in my lungs. Distantly, I register the pot falling from Ilsa's hands and crashing to the floor.

Thump, thump, thump.

The gun goes off, and I let out a strangled scream.

In the next second, all I can picture is blood and a world without Jackson in it. I hear nothing but silence and the ringing in my ears. My heart stops as tears stream down my face.

But then I hear him groan, and I've never loved a sound more.

"I'm okay," Jackson says through gritted teeth. "It hit the wall."

"You fucking better be okay." I cross to him and press my hand against his arm where the bullet must have grazed him. Blood leaks from the wound, staining his shirt. "Don't do that again!"

His wild eyes settle on me. "Don't do *what*?"

"Don't almost get yourself killed!" The tears won't stop flowing. "You idiot. I can't lose you. You're not allowed to die!"

Jackson tucks me against his side and guides me across the room, near where Ilsa is standing. Felix sits against the far wall, head in his hands. He rocks as he mutters to himself. He's bleeding, too, but I'm finding it hard to feel sorry about that.

Sirens sound outside, and I breathe a small sigh of relief.

"Is it over?" I whisper.

Jackson presses a kiss to the top of my head. "I think so, baby."

The next few minutes feel like they last an eternity, but as soon as Jackson hands over the gun and Felix is led out the door in handcuffs, I turn in Jackson's arms. And then I fall apart.

CHAPTER 38

MEYER

CHAOS REIGNS in the aftermath of Felix's arrest. Jackson's blood is all over my hands, and I want nothing more than to wash it off. Wash this whole day away. Sink into that clawfoot tub in his room at the inn and forget about *everything*.

I take a few steps back from the ambulance, sucking in a deep breath. After forcing Jackson to get assessed by the paramedics that just arrived on the scene, I need a little space.

My head is spinning. In the span of an hour, I not only found out who my birth parents are, but I also had to talk my father down from shooting the man that I love.

Talk about daddy issues.

For now, I try to stuff those thoughts in a box and store it in the back of my mind. I don't want to think about *him*.

Leaning against the outer wall of the flower shop, I close my eyes and pretend my hands don't feel tacky from the blood. I really should find a way to get that off.

When my eyes open, I spot Ilsa wrapping up her conversation with a uniformed police constable. When they part ways, she turns and locks gazes with me, and then she tentatively makes her way toward me. She has a water bottle and a towel in hand, and she offers them both to me.

"Hi," she says quietly.

I take the items gratefully and begin to clean my palms as best as I can. A scalding shower is in my future, one where I can scrub at my skin until it's left raw, but this is better than nothing right now.

"Hi," I reply.

Once I've done what I can, I rub a hand against my arm, goosebumps trailing my flesh even though the summer heat is still bearing down. This is *awkward*, and I don't want it to be.

"I am so sorry, Meyer. I didn't know Felix was in town until just yesterday. If I had known, I..." She looks down at her feet. "I would have done things a lot differently."

I place a hand on her arm, the need to comfort instinctual. "It's not your fault, what he did." I swallow thickly as my next words lodge in my throat. Maybe it's not the time, but I can't help myself. "What he said... Is it true? Are you my mother?"

Ilsa shakes her head. "Beatrice is your mother," she corrects. "But I did give birth to you. When I was sixteen."

"I don't think there's such a thing as having too many mothers," I argue. "Besides, she's all the way in Calderville, so right now, I think I could maybe use a hug from my other mom. If you wouldn't mind."

We have a lot to discuss, there's no denying that, but I *do* really need a hug. I can't pick apart all of my feelings on the matter right now, but I'm feeling unmoored and I need a steady presence to keep me grounded.

Ilsa's resolve crumples. She winds her arms around me and holds me tight. Smoothing my hair back from my face, she begins to sway, and I imagine this is what it would have felt like for her to hold me as a child. At that thought, I let the tears fall freely, for all that we missed out on together.

"Schatzi," she whispers.

I pull my head back. "Excuse me?"

She places her hands on my upper arms. The smile she offers me is watery. "Schatzi," she says, clearer. "It's German. It means my little treasure."

"Little treasure..." I trail off as my thoughts try to organize themselves. "That's the name of your flower shop."

She nods, a soft smile gracing her lips. "It's because of you that little Ilsa's dream became a reality. Even though you would never know it, I wanted to make you proud, Meyer. I wanted to show you that you could have whatever you set your mind to."

Too much. This day has been entirely too much. Both good and bad, a dizzying combination that leaves me spinning. It feels like it will take years to process everything properly.

"Gah," I exclaim, "is this normal?"

"Is what normal?"

"For my heart to feel like it's being squeezed inside my chest."

She laughs. "I don't know about normal, but I can tell you that I feel the same way." Her eyes turn somber, and my heart begins to ache. "I'm so relieved you're okay. I don't know what I would do if you weren't. You and Jackson."

"I'm relieved *you're* okay. I—" I break off, my mind running a thousand kilometres an hour. There's so many things I want to say, to fit into these fleeting moments we have. "I'm just relieved."

"You probably have a lot of questions. We—"

"Meyer?" one of the paramedics says.

I look over my shoulder, then turn back to Ilsa, conflicted. I want to keep talking, to learn everything there is to know about her, but this other part of me is tugging in Jackson's direction.

"Go," she urges. She pulls her hands back and clasps them in front of her. "Please tell Jackson I'm sorry he was hurt because of me. This never should have happened."

"It shouldn't have, but it's not your fault." I go to walk away, but then I think better of it. Quickly, I step forward and wrap my arms around her again. "Sorry. I decided I wasn't ready to let go just yet."

Ilsa presses her temple to mine. "You never have to be sorry about that."

"Okay, I'm really going now! I'll come see you in a couple days. We can talk."

This time, her smile is familiar. Warm. "I'd like that."

I offer her a parting wave, and then I walk over to the ambulance. Jackson is sitting on the back, an ice pack held to his head. He looks a little worse for wear, but he's whole. That's the only thing that matters to me in this moment.

"What's the verdict?" I ask. "Did the blow to the head manage to knock all the smugness out or what?"

Jackson glowers, but Gina, a woman I went to high school with, laughs. "All in all, your boyfriend is pretty lucky," she says.

Lucky because he was *this close* to getting more than just a flesh wound. That sick feeling from earlier comes back.

"His arm has been bandaged up. That wound is superficial. And there doesn't seem to be signs of a concussion, but I'd like you to keep an eye on him tonight just in case. Extreme headache or dizziness, that sort of thing, you should head to the hospital."

I take Jackson's face in my hands and inspect the bandage plastered to his hairline. "Will this scar?" I ask Gina. "His face is his most redeeming quality."

The hand resting on my lower back skates down and pinches my ass. "And here I thought you loved me for my personality," he says with a pout.

I roll my eyes, but the relief that sweeps through me nearly knocks me over. The fact that he's teasing right now means that he's alright. That Felix didn't succeed in taking him from me.

Turning back to the paramedic, I say, "He has a wonky heart, too. Did you check that?"

Jackson sighs from beside me. "She did, and it's *fine.*"

"I think I'd like to hear it from the medical professional, thanks."

Gina tries to hide her laugh. "I listened to his heart and it sounds perfectly fine, all things considered."

I nod. "Thank you. I promise I'll take good care of him tonight."

She smiles. "Good to see you, Meyer, though I wish it was under better circumstances."

Jackson stands from the ambulance's bumper, and we let Gina and her partner pack up their rig.

I take Jackson's face in my hands again. I search his eyes, checking for the millionth time that he's alright.

"How are you not freaking out right now?" I ask. "Because I'm kind of freaking out."

He shrugs. "Must be the head injury."

I frown, not finding it all that funny anymore. "That was really fucked up," I say quietly. "He could've really hurt you or Ilsa. He could've—"

"But he didn't." Jackson tucks me against him, his chin resting on top of my head. "You and Ilsa did good. I'm okay."

I press my ear to his chest, listening to the steady pumping of his heart. To double check. For a guy who was held hostage earlier today, his heart is beating at a relatively normal pace.

"You're okay."

I take a few moments to soak him in, his comforting presence, and then I pull back. Now, he reaches out and cups my cheek, his thumb brushing against my skin.

"Meyer?"

"Yeah?" I whisper.

When he smiles, the sight nearly takes my breath away. "I love you, too," he says.

"You promise?"

The weight of the day is heavy, but having Jackson here to lessen the load makes even the bleakest moments feel surmountable.

He nods. "Cross my heart. Now let's go home, baby."
I take his hand. "Alright, Hotshot, let's go home."

CHAPTER 39
MEYER

"MEYER, I promise everything is going to be great."

I smooth a hand over my outfit again, inspecting it in the mirror. I debated wearing a dress today, mainly because I like the way Jackson looks at me when I do, but I knew I would feel more confident in pants. And I need all the confidence I can get right now.

Today, the mayor's daughter is getting married. I wonder if she's half as nervous as I am, because I am on the verge of freaking out.

Those fears of disappointing my mom and ruining the inn have faded over the last couple months, but it would be a lie to say that they've completely gone away. I'm not sure if they ever will, truthfully. But I've learned to take that scary next step anyway, even if I'm convinced I will fail. Because chances are, things will work out just fine.

My eyes flit from my clothing to Jackson, who stands over my shoulder. "You're right," I say. "And if it's not, I'll place the blame on you."

He steps closer, his chest pressed to my back, and snakes his arms around my waist. He grins as he places a kiss on top of my head. "Ah, so that's why you've been keeping me around. Insurance in case things go wrong."

I tip my head back, looking up at him. "Precisely. I'm glad you know where you stand."

I turn in his arms, and then I reach for his face, turning it to the side. The bruising on his head from that day in the flower shop has faded considerably, but the faint traces still make anger coat my veins.

Felix was arrested, but I can't help feeling like that wasn't enough. Like there isn't a punishment fit enough for hurting Jackson. Is this what it means to love someone like this? Because it kind of sucks, this constant worry over his health and happiness. I wouldn't change it for the world, though.

"Hey," Jackson says, drawing me out of my thoughts, "not today. Don't let him ruin today."

I nod. "You're right."

Dramatically, he places a hand on his chest. "Twice in the span of one conversation? Who are you and what have you done with my Meyer?"

I roll my eyes, but a smile stretches my lips. "*Your* Meyer has gone soft. Something about being in love or whatever. Gross."

Jackson traces my cheekbone with his thumb, hands caressing my face. "No, you've been like that all along. You just allow me the privilege of seeing it now. Seeing you. And that is the greatest gift you could ever give me."

Letting Jackson in wasn't a conscious decision, but it was the best I've ever made. Not only is the inn thriving, but I feel more like myself than I ever have before. That eighteen-year-old girl who felt like her world was being torn apart had no idea what was in store for her.

I swallow my emotions. "Stop being sweet, you'll make me ruin my makeup."

He leans down and kisses me, and I'm tempted to stay like this forever.

"I love you," I say when we part.

His irises almost sparkle. "I love you, too," he replies. "Now let's go to a wedding."

The green space off the side of the inn has been transformed in a matter of hours. Chairs and tables have been set up beneath the large tent to shade everyone from the sun, and flowers from Ilsa's shop have been placed all around.

"Meyer!"

Turning in her direction, I watch Ilsa pick her way through the crowd of people still setting up. Her hair is thrown into a messy bun, and bits of flower stems are caught in it.

"Hey," I say. "You have something in your hair."

She laughs as I pick out the pieces for her. "This morning has been a little chaotic."

After the shock of the revelations wore off, I went to see Ilsa armed with a list of questions. It was hard to even know where to begin, but I needed answers. I think Ilsa needed to give them to me, too. She had been holding on to them for so long.

Felix hadn't known she was pregnant. She had managed to keep it a secret until his family moved him away, and by then, she was too afraid to tell anyone. When she had finally given birth to me as a terrified sixteen-year-old, she hadn't known what to do. She ended up leaving me at the fire station, and that's when Mom found me.

I came away from that conversation with a lot of mixed emotions. Jackson stayed up with me all night as I talked everything through, and he held me when I couldn't fight the urge to cry anymore. The tears were for me, for Ilsa, for growing up with her so near, yet never having the chance to truly know her.

But it wasn't long before I decided that I want her in my life. She's always been there, really, but now things feel different. The truth makes everything feel different.

"Thank you for doing all this," I say. "The flowers look beautiful."

A bright smile lights up her face. "Thank you for recommending me to the bride and groom. I'm glad I was able to help make their day special."

I glance at my phone, noting the time. "Speaking of, I should probably go check on the food. I'll see you later!"

"Meyer, wait."

I spin around, facing her again. "Yeah?"

Ilsa wrings her hands together. "For what it's worth, I am...immensely proud of the woman you've come to be. Watching you grow, even from afar, has been a joy and a privilege."

I blink back the tears threatening to fall. Between her and Jackson, I'm surprised my makeup has survived at all today.

"That means more to me than you'll ever know."

I close the space between us and throw my arms around her, sinking into her embrace. She holds me just as fiercely, and the remaining nerves I have about today simply melt away.

———

At the end of the night, Jackson and I both practically collapse on my bed.

Since everything that happened with Felix, we've been tiptoeing around talking about us. Our future. I know Jackson loves me, and I love him, but I need to know what that *means*. Now that the wedding is out of the way, I can't hold myself back from asking.

"Jackson," I say into the quiet.

My bedroom is dark, save for the moonlight filtering through the curtains we forgot to close. We'll probably regret it in the morning, but I know neither one of us is willing to get out of bed to fix it.

"Yeah, baby?"

I turn on my side to face him. "When do you go back to the city?" I ask, tentative.

"My leave is up at the end of September," he replies.

My heart sinks. "Oh."

That doesn't give us much time at all. A couple weeks, at best, since he'll likely want to return early to get settled back into his condo. The thought of it makes me sad. Toronto is only a few hours away, so it isn't as if we can't make it work, but not having him *here* feels wrong.

He doesn't say anything for a moment, and then, "Ask me to stay."

My breath catches. "What?"

"Ask me to stay, Meyer, and I will. I'll quit my job and sell my condo, and I won't look back." He cups my cheek. "But you have to ask. I have to know you want this as much as I do."

I don't hesitate.

"*Yes*. Stay. Please, stay."

I don't even care that my words come out like a plea. Don't care if that makes me seem desperate. Because I am. For Jackson, I am. I want him close—need him.

"*Thank God.*" He releases an overly dramatic breath of relief. "I thought you'd never ask."

Jackson guides me onto my back, and then he's hovering over me, smiling. I grin back, looping my hands around the back of his neck. And when he kisses me, I *feel* it—that thing I've been quietly searching for since I was a lonely teenager, drunk in a field. It fills my heart up until it overflows, and I sink further into Jackson's embrace.

"I love you," I whisper when we pull apart.

"I don't think I'll ever get used to that. But fuck, Meyer, I love you, too."

He kisses me again, and I get lost in the feel of him.

"I think we should start renting the cottage out," he muses. "Guests would love the secluded feel."

"That's a great idea," I say, "except I kind of live here."

"Not for long." His eyes gleam with hope and mischief. "I have big plans for us, Ellison."

The person I was six months ago would have picked a fight. Wouldn't have wanted to hear him out because she was afraid of change. But this new version of me takes comfort in the fact that whatever lies ahead, she doesn't have to handle it alone.

"I can't wait."

EPILOGUE
MEYER

"Honey, I'm home!"

At the sound of my voice, I hear a small mew, and then the ten-week-old kitten we found the other day, in almost exactly the same spot I found Fish, comes running across the room.

I bend down and scoop her up, cooing to her like I did to Atticus when he was a baby.

The kitten starts to purr as I hold her, kneading her paws against my arm. She's much more affectionate than Fish. I run my fingers over her soft, light-coloured fur while I walk deeper into the house.

"Hi, baby," Jackson says when I enter the kitchen. He's standing by the counter, stuffing something in his pocket.

I lower Honey from near my face. "Jackson," I say, "I didn't know you were home."

"You called out to me when you walked in the door."

I laugh. "No, I called out to her." I brandish the small kitten in my arms. "Meet Honey."

The poor kitten has been nameless since we found her, but I didn't want to settle for just anything. Then this morning while I was driving to Calderville, the perfect name hit me.

He raises a brow. "You named her Honey?"

I nod. "I did."

"And why did you do that?"

"Because she reminds me of the colour of your eyes." With the hand that's not holding on to the kitten, I loop around the back of his neck and tug his face down to mine. "Hi, honey."

"That's going to get confusing," he argues as his hands find their home on my hips.

I brush my lips against his. "Don't care."

He pulls me in closer, deepening the kiss. It's been a year, but kissing him still feels like the first time, and I don't ever want that to stop.

Honey mewls in protest to our attention being elsewhere. We draw apart, and then I hold the kitten up to Jackson's face. She playfully bats his nose with the pads of her paw.

"Isn't she so freaking *cute*?"

"Adorable," he affirms, stroking between Honey's ears. "Though I'm not sure Fish would agree."

The only being not content with the newest member of our family is the orange tabby with a propensity for stealing underwear. We introduced him to Honey last night, and he regarded her with a wary expression, followed by a lot of hissing. Baby steps.

"He'll get used to her. He got used to you, and Honey is *much* cuter."

Jackson slides his hand from the small of my back and gives my ass a light smack. "How are Beatrice and Ilsa today?" he asks. "Did you have a nice morning?"

"We did," I say, and then I grin. "I think Mom has finally convinced Ilsa to join her book club."

It took me a while to tell Mom what I had discovered about my birth mother. I wanted to let it all sink in for myself first, but I was also scared. For the same reason I never went looking for answers, I was worried about telling her who Ilsa is to me. I didn't have to worry, though.

As it turns out, Mom had suspected over the years, so the news didn't come as a shock. Mostly, she was happy that we didn't have that unknown looming over us anymore, and then she started including Ilsa in everything. They had already been friends, but folding Ilsa into our little family came even easier.

"Those ladies are going to give Ilsa a run for her money," he says, amused. "Are you ready to go?"

"Depends." My eyes narrow playfully. "Are you ready to tell me where we're going?"

He chuckles. "Nice try, baby. That didn't work the first ten times you asked, and it's not going to work now."

"Fine." I let out a huff as I head toward the bathroom and close Honey inside. She's still too small to have full run of the house while we're gone for extended periods. When I return, I put on my sweetest expression. "I'm ready. But can I check one thing first?"

Jackson shakes his head, though he smiles. "The inn will be alright without us."

"I know," I say. "I just want to double check before we're off the clock for the rest of the day."

While Jackson and I would never truly be off the clock as business owners, we had made a concerted effort over the last year to cut down on the amount of time we spent hovering at the inn. Okay, the amount of time *I* spent hovering. It's a... work in progress.

"Okay," he agrees. He grabs my hand and starts leading me out the front door. "But after that, I get you all to myself until tomorrow. Deal?"

I watch him fit his key into the lock on the door. Not the door to my old cottage, but the door to our house. Our home. It needs a lot of work, but it's ours.

The first step in Jackson's master plan was finding a house for us to buy. It couldn't just be any old house, though. It needed to be *perfect*, according to him. I wasn't all that concerned—I simply wanted to be wherever he was—but he made lists. *Lots* of lists, full of pros and cons.

It was an extremely convoluted operation, but I left him to his precious data, and finally, two months ago, we closed on this house just up the highway from the inn. It has aspects we both like, but it's enough of a blank slate that we can really make it our own.

I smile. "Deal."

———

Once we get in the car after checking in with Pippa and Trystan, Jackson makes me close my eyes. I'm tempted to peek, but I hold back. Nervous anticipation fizzles in my belly as I think about all the possibilities.

After driving for a few minutes, we come to a stop.

"Where are we?" I can't help but ask.

Jackson laughs. "Meyer, we've been over this. It's a *surprise* for a reason."

I huff, but I let him help me out of the car and lead me to our destination. I can tell that we're outside—the summer afternoon sunshine is bearing down on us, warming my exposed skin.

"Alright, you can look now."

My eyes fly open, and I blink as my vision adjusts. "The creek?" I glance back at Jackson and then to the spread before me. "What are we doing here?"

It's been a full, busy summer, and we haven't been back since that day last year. The creek would always feel special, though. It was the start of something new for us.

Today, a blanket has been set out on the grass on the bank of the creek. On top of the blanket is a small picnic basket and a bottle of strawberry wine. My heart hammers in my chest.

"Oh my God, are you proposing?" I spin around, meeting Jackson's wide-eyed stare. "Shit, I messed up your whole spiel, didn't I?"

His lips twitch in amusement. "I was going to wait until later, but I suppose it isn't a surprise anymore."

"Wait, let me turn around. We'll start over." I spin again, giving him my back. He laughs, but I can hear him coming closer. I resist the urge to bounce on my toes in excitement. "Ready?"

"Ready," he says.

This time when I turn, I find Jackson holding something between his thumb and forefinger. The ring glints in the summer sunshine. The oval stone is a gleaming sapphire that sits on a thin gold band, small clusters of diamonds on either side of it.

And it looks familiar.

"Is that—?" I point toward the ring as my eyes shine. "That's Cherie's."

Jackson nods. His throat bobs as he swallows his emotion. "It is. Along with the inn, she also left me her ring." He shakes his head, though a wistful smile stretches his lips. "She was always scheming."

My mother had said as much, but I didn't truly believe it until this moment.

He looks down at the ring for a moment, then back up at me. "She knew what it took me a while to see. She sent me to Dog Days knowing that I would find you. Hoping that I would be smart enough to understand."

"Understand what?" I whisper.

"That you and me belong together. That our strengths are complimentary. That slowing down was exactly what I needed."

Logically, I know what's about to happen, but I still feel a wave of shock when Jackson lowers himself to one knee on the blanket. My heart pounds harder now.

"When I came to Fraisier Creek last April, I had no idea what I would be getting myself into. How tangled up in you and this town I would become. But I wouldn't have it any other way. I love you, Meyer, and I want to spend the rest of my life proving that to you. It would be an honour to be your husband."

My heart stutters as tears well in my eyes. "Jackson…"

"Marry me, baby," he says. "Let's make a life together."

I nod, a couple tears now sliding down my face. "Yeah, okay," I say through a sniffle. "I'll marry you."

I grip Jackson by the shirtfront and haul him to his feet. Then I drag his mouth to mine, sealing our agreement. This time last year, I never would have dreamed this would be my reality. That Jackson Vaughan, my *fiancé*, would be holding me in his arms. That everything would feel so right.

We eventually pull apart, and Jackson dries the tears on my cheeks. Then he takes my hand, and I suck in a breath. The ring slides over my knuckle with ease, resting at the base of my finger, the perfect fit.

"I'm not changing my name," I warn. Ellison means too much to me to give up.

He laughs. "Of course. I wouldn't expect anything less."

I grin, letting the giddiness I tried to curb finally break free. With a small squeal, I launch myself at my fiancé, my arms snaking around his waist. His arms fold around me in turn, his chin resting on top of my head.

"I love you," I say.

"I love you, too, baby," he replies. "Do you want some wine?"

I shake my head, pulling back from his embrace. "There's something else I want first."

"Yeah?" His brows raise, a sly smile spreading across his face. "What's that?"

Planting my hands on his chest, I start backing him closer to the creek. Now, he looks down at me in confusion. Once we're close enough, I shove him with all my strength. He lands in the water, ass first and fully clothed.

When he comes up for air, shaking out his wet hair, I grin.

"Payback, honey," I say.

And then I peel off my clothes and jump into the water after him.

ACKNOWLEDGMENTS

Finishing *Middle Ground* turned out to be a lot harder than I had anticipated, but seeing my second(!) book fully come to fruition has been incredibly rewarding. But without the community I have surrounding me, none of this would have been possible.

To my family, thank you for being my most hardworking marketers. Even though you embarrass me in the process, I appreciate your unwavering support as I try to make a go of this whole author thing, and your understanding when I hole away for hours to write. And since I apparently can't stop you from reading this, I hope you enjoyed the book.

To Karley, my best friend, it feels like I've known you for a lifetime and it's only been a year. A year full of thousands of minutes-long voice memos and somewhat confusing plot ideas. I am so incredibly thankful for you and your friendship. Without you, this book truly would not exist. Thanks for holding my hand and reminding me that my ideas aren't stupid every time I wanted to quit. I'll never forgive the universe for putting an international border between us!

To my Baddies, my Fantasy Sluts and my Menaci, thank you for adopting me. You push me out of my comfort zone when I need a little nudge, and for that, I'm not letting you go.

To Cole, thank you for listening to me talk about my book stuff, even though you don't always understand it. And thanks for believing in me, too.

To my beta readers: Tiffany, Rebeca, Tana, Jess, Kahra, Kayla, Marina, Malani, Katie and Jenn. I'm forever grateful for your help in moulding *Middle Ground* into the best version of itself. This book was made infinitely better by your feedback and enthusiasm. Reading your comments about how swoony Jackson is made my day when I was slogging through edits.

Lastly, to my readers, thank you for picking up Meyer and Jackson's story. Sharing my characters with you is such a joy, and I hope you love them as much as I do. I look forward to many more books in our futures!

ABOUT THE AUTHOR

Bobbi Maclaren is an indie author from a small town in Ontario, Canada. When she isn't writing, she can be found reading, wrangling her mischievous black cat or booking her next trip to a new country. She also loves fall, dresses with pockets, and her emotional support water bottle.

Find her @bmaclarenwrites on social media.